Fantasy

CW01468622

The Department of Certainty

Jessica must not die today

S. C. Paterson

Stairwell Books //

Published by Stairwell Books
161 Lowther Street
York, YO31 7LZ

www.stairwellbooks.co.uk
@stairwellbooks

The Department of Certainty © 2024 S. C. Paterson and Stairwell
Books

All rights reserved. No part of this publication may be reproduced,
stored in or introduced into a retrieval system, or transmitted, in any
form, or by any means (electronic, mechanical, photocopying,
recording, e-book or otherwise) without the prior written permission
of the author.

The moral rights of the author have been asserted.

This is a work of fiction. Names, characters, businesses, places,
events, locales, and incidents are either the products of the author's
imagination or used in a fictitious manner. Any resemblance to
actual persons, living or dead, or actual events is purely
coincidental.

Cover art: Oliver Hurst

Paperback ISBN: 978-1-913432-97-3
eBook ISBN: 978-1-917334-01-3
p7

For social workers, everywhere.

"I've discovered that I'm not the centre of my own brain. I'm just one of the many things that my brain does. There's a whole lot of things going on in there that I'm not aware of."

Ken Campbell, *Brainspotting*, 1996

PART ONE

MORNING

1

The thing about pain is the noise it makes.

The worst sorts of pain are the ones that go on and on. Toothache is a car alarm, piercing the air with an incessant whine. And then there's period pain; when Jessica feels like her lower insides are being fed into a shredder, that's a deep, resonant thmp, thmp, thmp. It's like it is four in the morning, there's a party in the flat upstairs, and somebody has just turned up the bass.

Pain is broadcast on the Real Time Monitor so everyone hears it; the lab technician in Liver, the signal officer in Bladder, even the valve engineer in the vast pumping station of Heart. No-one who works in Jessica's body can avoid the noise of pain.

Her depression had a sound all of its own; a sort of white noise like static in the system. Some days it was louder than others and it had been going on for so long that we were all used to it, like the constant drone of air-conditioning or the distant rumble of a dual carriageway. One of those sounds that you notice when it stops, then you breathe out and say: 'Ah, *that's* better.'

When I arrived at work that morning it was dark and Jessica was still asleep. The large Real Time Monitor, or RTM as we call it, was a blank screen. That meant that Jessica was in a dream-less sleep and that the night shift, operating throughout the Body, would be finishing up their duties. Actually, here in Soul we don't have a nightshift. We're all on waking-time-only contracts. That's not to say we never work during the

2

night. Occasionally, if Jessica is tossing and turning in the early hours of the morning, grappling with some kind of existential angst, one of us might be called to offer a spiritual insight or simply a calming thought. That's not often nowadays. Jessica has plenty of sleepless nights but the folk in Pre-Frontal City rarely ask Soul for advice.

I like being at work early, having the chance to get things in order before the others arrive, but that morning someone was there before me. I negotiated the bead curtain in the corner of our open-plan office and entered Alfred's domain. The small sparsely furnished room was lit by a solitary candle on a low table. Alfred was sitting upright, in his favourite chair, with his eyes closed. The flickering candlelight softened his features and, with his ash grey hair and beard, he looked like a biblical character from a renaissance oil-painting. He opened his eyes and smiled;

'Colin.'

'Morning Alfred, how are you doing?'

We'd been worried about him, we weren't sure he was eating properly; his clothes seemed to be too big for his small frame and he was using a piece of string to hold up his trousers.

'I'm fine, just fine.'

'I've brought you some glucose tablets.'

'Very kind.'

I put them next to the candle and wondered what to say next. On the table by the wall was his Go board and I went over to look. I had been following the progress of this particular game over several weeks. Alfred was playing someone in the far north of the Motor Cortex, just a turn or two a day, and much of the board was now covered with black and white stones. Opposing groups encircled each other and it was hard to make out what was dead and what was alive.

'Who's winning now?' I asked.

'There's a lot that's unresolved. I would say that it's uncertain.'

The Real Time Monitor above the table stuttered into life. A jagged sequence of images splintered the peace of Alfred's room; a cup with no handle, the face of Jessica's boss, a missing shoe, a toilet door. Each one filled the screen for a second or two before being replaced by the next. The day had begun; Jessica was dreaming.

'Colin?'

'Yep.'

'Today …,' his voice trailed away, he was looking down at the paper bag, absentmindedly feeling the outline of the packet of tablets with his bony fingers. 'Today could be … different.'

He looked up at me, his rheumy grey eyes fixed on mine.

'In what way … different?'

'I suppose one might say … he paused, 'interesting and different. Keep your wits about you, hold fast, Colin, hold fast.'

With that he closed his eyes. I knew that this meant that our conversation had come to an end and I felt my usual sense of vague dissatisfaction. Encounters with Alfred often make me feel wrong-footed; as if there's an obvious piece of information that has eluded me. I went back into the main office and noticed that the white noise of Jessica's depression seemed louder than usual. I gave an involuntary shudder. Her low mood had gone on far too long and the Executive seemed to be ignoring it. *Not Waving but Drowning.* Somebody should do something, she needed to be hauled in to the shore.

2

I don't like travelling on the Nervous System, the speed of it makes me feel nauseous. Blood is not too bad, preferably on a decent size motor cruiser or launch. Lymph is definitely the most relaxing way to move around the body; you can sit back and admire the view while someone leisurely punts you along the wide river. Down in the Thymus we're well placed for the Lymphatic Network, but that morning Fola insisted that we used the Nervous System.

'They want us up there straight away,' she said. 'It's important, we can't faff about.'

When I first started working in Soul I tried hard to get us relocated up to the Brain. The Thymus is in the middle of Jessica's chest. That means that we are a long way off from the front of her Brain where ideas are discussed and decisions made. The Thymus is real backwater, no-one ever visits us here, we are not even on the way to anywhere. Our two-roomed office sits at the end of G23, an empty barrack hut, which is next to another empty barrack hut, which is next to another, as far as the eye can see. Years ago, this is where the commando units of T company were trained. However, following decentralisation, most of them have been shipped out to other parts of the Body. A lot of the huts are empty now, save for the occasional discarded training manual or moth-eaten balaclava, and they are slowly being pulled down. There are no plans to build anything else; it's not a popular site. There is one commando unit still based here and we sometimes hear them on manoeuvres. My colleague Grace has seen soldiers while out jogging up by K49 but I have never seen any, nor do I want to.

The place is dead. No wonder Soul has no influence. Apparently, the Thymus is where Soul is normally based in Other People. I argued that we could be different, we should be where the action is, high up in Pre-Frontal City or else somewhere in the Midbrain, where at least we would know what's going on. As usual, I was over-ruled.

The Nervous System is made up of fast cable cars and trains. In the Thymus we are served by the high-speed Vagus Line and the launch platform is just outside our office terrace. Fola bundled me into the two-person cabin and moments later, we were at Medulla Central Station – the starting point for all destinations in the Brain.

Fola strode through the huge concourse that was littered with folk trying to find their right platform or, as it seemed to me, simply standing around getting in other people's way. She cut an impressive figure; tall, turbaned and dressed in a magenta and orange floaty kaftan like an African queen. She cleared a path through the crowds and I ran along behind her with an odd mixture of pride and embarrassment. Somehow, she got us to the correct platform and moments later we were in Pre-Frontal City and the vast atrium of Dominion Tower.

I had not been inside the building before. On previous trips I had travelled up to the roof using the external lift that is grafted on to the side of the block. The roof is the most interesting thing about Dominion Tower because it is where Active Consciousness or, as we like to call it, ActCon is located. If you have an important Thought, one that you want to get turned into an Action, you have no choice but to go up to the roof and take it into ActCon in person. Of course, chances are that you are not allowed inside. And even then, if you do manage to get in and speak your Thought, it invariably falls flat, over in seconds with no follow up Thoughts or Actions. It's easy to become disheartened.

The first thing that struck me about the ground floor was the cathedral-like space and a pair of transparent lifts silently ferrying people up and down. Groups of low chairs, all empty, were dotted around the marble floor; they were carefully placed between large pots of trees that stretched up their branches towards the roof.

'They're fake,' said Fola, seeing me crane my neck to look at a bunch of grapes hanging from a huge vine.

'What, the leaves as well?'

'All of it, all pretend.'

The reception area, with its sweeping counter of white laminate and walnut veneer, appeared to be modelled on that of a five-star hotel. A hotel with a security problem however; a couple of Whiteshirts, Internal Security Service guards, both carrying submachine guns, were positioned on either side of the counter. The two receptionists wore identical red blazers.

'What's with the uniform?' I murmured to Fola as we approached the female receptionist.

'You're in the corporate world now,' she replied under her breath.

'Good morning my dear, I am Fola and this is my colleague, Colin. We've been summoned here this morning. We're to meet with the Chief Executive, and apparently...' (here she paused for effect) '...we are needed urgently on a matter of Emergency Response.'

I glanced up at Fola in surprise. What emergency? And why on earth would anybody think we would be useful? Soul was rarely asked to contribute to anything going on in Dominion Tower. It made no sense.

3

Jessica Drummond rolled over to the empty, cooler side of the double bed and tried to anchor herself to a fixed point in time: *a work-day, Thursday.* It felt too early to get up but further sleep seemed out of the question as fragments of unhappy dreams floated out of reach. The familiar dread returned, as it did most mornings, rising up from the deep and lodging itself in the centre of her body like a stranded sea-creature. *What's wrong with me?* she asked herself.

She missed the warmth of a body sharing her bed; however, if anyone asked, she would always assert that she liked living on her own. She was the architect of her own time. There was no requirement to compromise, to adapt, to fit into another's schedule. No need to draw in her spikes for fear of piercing someone else's ego.

The grey dawn was seeping through the curtains as she turned over again and peered at the alarm clock; ten to seven. She switched it off and went through the daily ritual of counting her blessings; she was a healthy, thirty-eight-year-old with a reasonably well-paid job. She was comfortable living on her own and had friends, good and cheerful friends, within easy reach of her north London home. But she still felt like shit.

She padded to the bathroom and went to the toilet in the semi-darkness, avoiding the harshness of artificial light. The creak of floorboards overhead told her that her upstairs neighbour was also up and she blocked her ears from the sounds of his inevitable bathroom routine.

Returning to the bedroom it was hard to resist crawling back under the duvet, but she put on her faded blue dressing-gown and sat on the edge of the bed, contemplating the day ahead. There was only one thing to achieve: she had to finish the Performance Report.

Up and down the country, from Cornwall to Cumbria, there was a Jessica working on a report on behalf of her local Children's Social Services. The deadline had arrived when all these reports, along with reams of accompanying statistics, would be emailed to the computer of some central government inspector. They would award stars to those local councils who had performed well and issue penalties for those who had done badly.

For the past six weeks Jessica's working days had been consumed by this report. There was data to collect, spreadsheets to devise, pie-charts and bar-charts to agonise over. There were comparisons to be made, with previous years' performance, with the London borough next door. There was analysis to be written; an interpretation of the data which trumpeted the progress since last year while also acknowledging, briefly, the areas for improvement. And still, at this late stage, there were some figures that needed chasing and an executive summary to compose.

Her non-working hours were also stalked by the Performance Report; lying in the bath, sipping her morning tea, negotiating the rush-hour crowds, Jessica's thoughts were dominated by holes in the data and the optimal choice of pie-chart colours. Even her dreams were disrupted by percentages and averages and a generalised anxiety that the report, the performance of her department and indeed, she herself, were simply not good enough.

Early on, the job seemed a breeze compared to what she had been doing. Unlike being a front-line social worker, here she had some control. The numbers stayed where she put them. She could enter them into a spreadsheet and they would obey her command to join the others in totals, be turned into averages, transformed into percentages. Numbers turned up and did their thing.

When she had a caseload Jessica found that her families were often not very good at turning up. Or, to be more precise, not very good at being in when Jessica turned up. The 'social worker's knock' is famed for its lack of audibility; a gentle knock by a timid social worker who would much prefer it if her 'service user' was not at home so that she could return to the warmth and camaraderie of the office. Jessica was not one of those social workers. She would bash loudly at the knocker, yell through the letter box and even, if necessary, find a way into the back yard and rap on the kitchen window. Jessica's families would roll their eyes; 'that bloody woman' they called her. However, they mostly respected her and some even grew to like her. They always knew where they stood with her; she said it as it was. She was

9

considered to be a good social worker. But that was before the baby, the baby who changed everything.

What to wear today? she asked herself. Over in the corner the chair was piled high with clothes. Yesterday's bra lay puddled on the floor alongside her best work blouse. She fought off the urge to get back into bed. It was inconceivable that she would skive off work, today of all days. She felt the heavy weight of the department's reputation hanging around her neck. It seemed to be dragging her downwards.

She pulled the dressing-gown more tightly round her. *What to wear?*

4

The receptionist flicked her blonde hair behind her ear and studied the computer screen on the desk.

'Which department please?'

'We're from Soul.'

'Sorry – can't find that department listed here.'

Fola rolled her eyes heavenwards.

'Try under Thymus,' I suggested.

'I've got 'Thymus: T cell company 54.' Is that you?'

We shook our heads.

'How about Thymus: Residual Projects?'

'I guess that'll be us,' I said.

The woman got us to sign various bits of paper and then made each of us an identity pass.

'Please wear your pass at all times. The Executive is on the twenty-third floor. Have a nice day!'

Fola was fuming as we made our way to the lifts.

'So Soul doesn't exist anymore. Residual Projects; it's unbelievable!'

'Might just be her list.' Although, truth be told, I had read something in one of the Executive Bulletins about our name change but hadn't liked to mention it to Fola.

'No, Colin. We are not recognised. Soul has no importance in this brave new world.'

And it was a new world for me. As we glided upwards I peered through the lift's glass sides, taking in the open plan offices with their modular furniture configured in identical lay-outs. There were terminals on all the desks and small figures wearing corporate blazers hunched over them. I wondered what they were working on, what projects took priority in Dominion Tower. Judging from the bulletins, a lot of it would be about finances. Jessica was always short of money – her rent was too high for her salary. These West Side workers would be devising money-saving ideas and then competing to get them into ActCon.

'Why are we here, Fola?'

Fola turned to look at me. Her eyes flicked towards the camera in the corner of the lift ceiling; we were probably being watched and over-heard. She shrugged:

'I know about as much as you do. Something to do with an emergency. I guess we're here to provide a different perspective… maybe…'

A further reception desk greeted us on the twenty-third floor, presided over by another blond receptionist.

'The Executive meeting is in Committee Room One, down the corridor through the double doors. Please wait in the seating area, you will be called shortly.'

They didn't go in for open-plan working on this floor of Dominion Tower and the corridor was lined with office doors, each with a brass name plate. By 'name' I mean title like 'Deputy Chief Executive' and 'Head of Communications.' Through the double doors we were met with a stream of light. The waiting area outside Committee Room One had a huge panoramic window which immediately drew Fola to gaze down at the world below.

'It's a great view, you should take a look.'

Keeping a prudent distance from the glass, I stepped towards the window. The early autumnal mist was clearing and hazy sunshine bathed the rooftops beneath us. This quarter of the West Side is heavily populated with sky-scrapers, Dominion Tower being the tallest of them all. These office blocks are being added to continuously and several had cranes perched precariously on their roof-tops.

Between the buildings I could see the ravine which divides the two hemispheres of Jessica's Brain. Most of her Brain is split into two halves; the right and left hemispheres or, as we usually refer to them, West Side and East Side. West Side is where the power is. It's happened slowly, almost imperceptibly, over the past few years. Nowadays there is no power-sharing between the two halves; West Side always sets the agenda and takes the lead. Our natural allies are over on East; Soul is not popular in West.

'Look Fola. Over there is where I used to work.' I pointed across the ravine to a cluster of buildings on the East Side. Less built-up than the Left hemisphere, the streets on the Right are broad and spacious and I could just make out flashes of green from parks and gardens.

'Me too. Do you miss working in Creative Thoughts?'

'Not really,' I said, not entirely truthfully. I imagined flying over the ravine to the other side or hopping across a bridge. Except there are no bridges across the ravine, only the underground through the CorpCal Tunnel, always heaving with people trying to get to the other side in the semi-darkness.

I switched my attention to the RTM in the corner of the room. Jessica still wasn't dressed. In fact, she seemed to have gone into reverse and was now taking her trousers off. Deciding-What-to-Wear had broken down completely. At this rate, I thought, she's going to be late for work.

'Fola, my darling girl!' A loud, fruity voice filled the room as Fola turned to greet the new arrival.

'Nathaniel, good to see you!' Fola beamed and hugged the man who was as tall and broad as she was. When they embraced their two ample girths met in the middle. He was dressed in a loose purple shirt and it was hard to see where Fola ended and this man began.

'Colin, this is Nathaniel. We used to work together in Making Music, now he's the chief of East Side!'

With his long hair, tied back in a pony-tail, and unkempt bushy beard Nathaniel was the epitome of East Side casualness. He gripped my hand in both of his:

'Honoured to meet you, Colin. Tell me, how are Alfred and Grace?'

'They're well thanks, though Alfred is getting a little frail.'

13

'We often think about the four of you in Soul, I am only sorry that your department has been so depleted in recent years.'

'Efficiency Savings,' said Fola.

'Doing More with Less,' I added.

Nathaniel laughed loudly and I smiled for the first time since leaving Soul that morning.

'We got the urgent summons to be here first thing this morning,' said Fola. 'We don't know why. They asked for Alfred, but they've got us instead. What about you? I'm surprised to see you here.'

'It's a code orange emergency, didn't you know? In a code orange, the Chief Executive is obliged to invite the head of the other side to the Executive meeting. My guess is that we'll probably be blinded by science this morning. And I wouldn't be at all surprised if it's our side that gets the blame.'

'Blame for what?' I asked.

'Jessica's current mood… the depression …and it seems to be getting worse.'

The door to Conference Room One opened and Nicholas, Marcia's personal assistant appeared:

'They're ready for you now.'

Fola and I gave each other looks of encouragement and entered the room.

5

Social workers are paid to be nosy; they never stop 'assessing' people. Jessica used to enjoy working with the young people on her caseload; 'direct work' as it was called. She would draw a large chart with a circle representing the young person in the middle. Lines would radiate out like the spokes of a wheel and the child would have to say who was in their family and friends' network, who they felt close to (strong lines) or rather distant to (dotted lines) or in conflict with (jagged lines).

Jessica's chart – the one with her centre stage – would be a messy affair with a predominance of dotted lines. Nan would have been the nearest satellite with a healthy strong line, but now that line was cut in half, intersected by two small ones indicating that that she was dead. The remaining strong lines would be reserved for a handful of Uni and work friends. At the end of a dotted line would be Dad, his new wife and their baby. Jessica thought it was preposterous that he should be procreating in his mid-sixties, so he was banished towards the outer edge.

Similarly, around the periphery and also at the end of dotted lines, orbited the Past Men, the trio of Tim, Spike and Gary; boyfriend, cohabitee and husband respectively. Jessica harboured no animosity towards the Past Men but also no yearnings for lost love. She retained a fondness for them and didn't want to forget about them completely. She would hear of their activities through mutual friends or keep an eye on their Facebook pages, gleaning information which led to an over-riding feeling of relief and a sense that she was 'well out of it.'

Then there was Mother. She was like a comet, hurtling in and out of Jessica's life; sometimes near enough to risk collision, sometimes in the cold outer-reaches. Her line was definitely jagged.

Another part of Jessica's 'assessment toolkit' was the Three Houses exercise. Ethan or Finley, Maisie or Eva would be sat down and given a picture of three houses represented by blank rectangles, each with a brightly coloured roof. These were named 'The House of Worries', 'The House of Good Things' and the 'House of Dreams'.

Ethan or Finley, Maisie or Eva would be encouraged to draw something in each of their houses. They would fidget and suck the ends of their Sharpie pens, pondering how to pick a delicate path between pleasing this nice lady who, after all, smiled a lot, and not causing trouble. It was usually safest not to cause trouble.

How would Jessica fill in her Three Houses? The House of Dreams would be left empty. She couldn't contemplate the future any further than the immediate day ahead. She had no hopes or aspirations. 'Just get through today,' was her mantra.

The House of Good Things would also be left vacant until eventually, once she had been pressed, Jessica would remember that she did at least have some friends. Even the House of Worries would be a struggle to complete. Work would obviously dominate here, the Report in particular. It wasn't that Jessica spent a lot of time feeling anxious. Mostly she didn't feel anything at all other than extremely tired. Everything was a struggle; today, even getting to the bathroom and wiping her face with a damp flannel seemed a Herculean task and choosing what clothes to put on felt quite beyond her capability.

6

The meeting was taking a break; a couple of people were standing and stretching while, further down the long oak table, clusters of heads were bent in quiet conversation. Someone was fiddling with the blinds; the golden morning sunshine being extinguished and replaced by a cool gloom.

I did a swift head-count and reckoned that there were about fifteen people present. One or two looked in our direction, but we were largely ignored. Nicholas, Marcia's assistant, found us some chairs and, after some shuffling along one side, a small space opened up and we took our places.

I recognised a few of the faces from the bulletin: heads of West Side departments - Working Memory, Looking Good in Front of Other People and Problem Solving. Fola seemed to know several of them and she greeted them warmly, receiving strained smiles in return. A few wore the West Side corporate blazers while one woman was in full military uniform, presumably Chief of Staff for External Security. I remembered that the West Side had a close relationship with Internal Security and wondered who, among the people that I did not recognise, was representing the Whiteshirts. I felt an increasing sense of unease. What were we doing here?

The woman standing at the far end was the Chief Executive, Marcia. She seemed to be listening to a muscular bald man and, at the same time, directing the person at the blinds:

'No, pull it right down. Not like that, use the other string.' Her voice was sharp and the man laughed nervously.

She was smaller than I had expected. I'd heard the stories; her determination to push her way to the top, her ruthlessness in the face of opposition. I'd seen Marcia's image many times in the bulletins or the Executive Briefings describing the latest round of initiatives or efficiency savings, and for me she had become something of a pantomime villain. Yet here she was; a slight, well-groomed woman of about my age. She wore a pale grey suit with a well-pressed white blouse beneath and her hair was dyed a shiny blond, forming a tight helmet around her head. The only flash of colour was from her long, manicured nails and I was drawn to those scarlet talons, both fascinated and repelled at the same time.

The room was bland; pale walls, dark parquet flooring and a couple of artificial ferns in the corners. I had my back to the windows so didn't have a chance to admire the view before the blinds came down. On the wall opposite was a large photograph showing a seated Marcia surrounded by her executive team, about half of whom I matched to people in the room.

She came over and touched Nicholas's arm lightly.

'We need caffeine urgently, Nicholas, will you sort it?' Now her voice was warm and conspiratorial as if she had just asked him to undertake a task of major significance, just for her. The meeting resumed.

'Before we go to our main agenda item, I want to return to Office Reconfiguration.' Marcia immediately had the attention of the meeting. 'During the break I have reconsidered our options. We cannot postpone making a decision on this. The Department of Certainty must move out of Dominion Tower: the space is needed for Following Twitter.'

I caught the sudden intake of breath and rise in tension. There was the briefest flicker of eye-contact across the table and the head of Problem Solving cleared his throat:

'Marcia, I don't think I just speak for myself when I say that this could use further discussion, Certainty has already been cut down to one person and a desk, she hardly takes up much room. That department has always been close to the Executive....'

Marcia interrupted him with a bright smile:

'Thank you, Sean, I am fully aware of what's happened in the past. The point is that the Outside World is changing very rapidly and we must adapt to survive. Certainty is an anachronism, nothing is certain, everything is relative. I'm sure Nathaniel can find space for her over in East. If not, she can go back to the Cerebellum,' Marcia continued, ignoring the raised eyebrows; 'I do sometimes wonder whether you all share our vision for the future and our need to be a forward-looking and flexible organisation.' Her voice had become slower; every syllable articulated precisely; it was as if she was talking to a group of recalcitrant children.

'Now I must move us on to the main agenda item for this morning, You all know Nathaniel and this is Fola and ...... her colleague from Residual Projects.' I sensed Fola drawing herself up, her physical presence ballooning next to me. Oh God, Fola, I thought, examining a patch of the table in front of me, don't take her on.

'I would like to know,' Fola's low musical tones filled the room, 'exactly when it was decided, without any consultation, that our department should have a new name.'

Marcia sized Fola up:

'If you'd bothered to read our Executive bulletins, you'd know all about that. Soul also has to change and adapt to keep up with the real world.'

I knew that Fola was itching to respond, hers and Marcia's view of the real world were far apart. But Marcia was continuing, her voice brusque:

'As I was saying, the main agenda item this morning is that we are in a code orange emergency. I have asked Julia to talk us through this.'

A tall red-haired woman got up and stood at the side of the screen.

'Who's she?' I muttered to Nathaniel.

19

'One of the Midbrain boffins, recently promoted to Chief Scientific Adviser.'

The screen sprang into life and a table appeared containing a range of letters and numbers. Down one side were a series of dates over the past few weeks and across the top appeared the words Serotonin, Norepinephrine and Dopamine. Julia was showing us how these figures were going up and down. I was just taking this in when she switched to another chart, this time, rather than words at the top, there were a sequence of letters like BDNF and GABA.

I soon lost the drift of this and began watching the RTM which was inserted into a small corner of the screen. It looked like Jessica had finally made a decision about what to wear and was, at last, getting dressed. The early morning light filtered through her bedroom curtains in white and pale cream vertical bands, the folds a contrasting golden brown.

There's much to like about Jessica's home. Her flat takes up all the ground floor of a modest Victorian terraced house. The front room is her sitting room. This is best in the late afternoon when the bay window catches the sunlight and the motes of fine dust prance and whirl. The next room is Jessica's bedroom; small and dark, but with the bedside lamp it is transformed into a cosy boudoir. Then there is the windowless bathroom squeezed in under the stairs leading up to the flat above.

My favourite room is the kitchen at the back of the flat which Jessica painted a lovely lemon yellow when she first moved in. A pine table, the grain of the wood quite unique, sits by a large window overlooking the small garden. Sometimes there are squirrels.

I realised that Julia had stopped talking. Her final table was labelled 'The last 24 hours,' and a number of the columns were shaded red. She sat down and looked expectantly at everyone.

'Is that it?' asked Marcia.

'I've finished my presentation.'

'What are you trying to tell us? What's the bottom line?'

'The bottom line?' repeated Julia.

'Yes, the bottom line. What all this actually means, what you told me this morning, before the meeting.' Marcia was starting to sound annoyed and Julia bit her lower lip.

'I thought I'd explained the recent changes in activity of a number of different neurotransmitters.'

'So?'

'So…. we have advised a level orange emergency. Our research suggests that this chemical imbalance is something we all should be worried about. Statistically there is a significant risk of self-harm.'

There was a pause while everyone took this in.

'May I ask a question?' A small man inclined his head towards Marcia. 'Go on.'

'The Professor, head of the Thalamus,' muttered Nathaniel, 'another boffin.'

'What's your evidence, Julia? How do you correlate the current chemical environment with this increased risk of self-harm?'

'We've examined historical records. The last time we experienced this level of neurotransmitter activity was immediately before the Paracetamol Incident of 1997.'

An audible gasp of surprise went around the room. I had not heard any talk of the Paracetamol Incident for many years. It was as if its very mention might rouse unruly demons from their sleep.

'I see,' said Marcia, 'I suppose nowadays we have better scientific information. I take it you're working to remedy the situation.'

'Working …in what way?' Julia looked perplexed again.

'Getting the levels right… Serotonin and what not.'

'Might I explain?' said the Professor. 'Julia and her team in the Hypothalamus, are like the weather forecasters in the Outside World. They can monitor what's going on, but I'm afraid that they may not be able to control the chemical weather, so to speak.'

Nathaniel stood up and walked to the head of the table.

'Marcia, if you don't mind, I'd like to say a few words.'

Marcia looked like she was about to say something but then gave a cursory nod.

'Thank you, Julia, a very clear analysis.' Julia gave him a grateful smile while Nathaniel continued: 'I agree that we have a problem and one which we have not seen for twenty years. Jessica is sad and unhappy; people who know these things on the Outside World would probably say that she is seriously depressed.'

'Aren't you just playing with words?' The Professor leaned forward. 'Terms like unhappiness and depression are simply layman's talk for the chemical situation that Julia has so eloquently described.'

'No,' said Nathaniel slowly, scratching his beard, 'all we've heard this morning is that there is a correlation between Jessica feeling low and the chemical cocktail you guys down in the Hypothalamus have been monitoring.'

'Our research indicates that it is more than simply a correlation,' said Julia.

'Are you saying that Jessica's unhappiness is caused by a chemical imbalance?'

Julia screwed up her eyes.

'I would say that a direct causal link has been established.'

'Bollocks!'

'This is not helpful,' interrupted Marcia, 'we are in a state of emergency with an apparently high risk of self-harming behaviour. We have to do something and I am authorising Julia's team to take any means necessary to bring us back to a normal state-of-affairs.'

She spoke as if the mere act of her authorising something was enough to remedy the situation. She's mad, I thought, quite mad.

'So more chemicals,' said Nathaniel.

'Yes,' said Marcia.

'Actually, it is quite complicated,' said Julia. 'I have some more slides which will illustrate the complexity of the relationships, shall I move on to those now?'

'No,' said Marcia and Nathaniel together. They glanced at one another and I caught a hint of an earlier alliance, friendship even, which had been worn away by the tensions between East and West.

'Talking of chemicals....,' Marcia said, 'I did ask for caffeine to be brought in. Chase it again, please Nick.'

22

'I can give you a dozen reasons why Jessica is unhappy,' said Nathaniel, 'her job, the wretched Performance Report...'

'We don't want to hear that stuff,' interrupted Marcia, but Nathaniel continued:

'.....And then there's what happened to her when she was a kid. Mother and the drinking...'

'That's enough! It's not appropriate to raise these things here. Negative Thoughts will get into Active Consciousness and you'll make a bad situation worse.' She was angry now and had stood up facing Nathaniel on the other side of the screen. 'It would be more useful if you put your own house in order.'

'I'm just saying that we should commission a proper survey of the reasons and do something about them.'

'That's just delaying things. Delay is completely unacceptable, I want the chemical response to start immediately. Furthermore, all Thoughts going into ActCon must be first cleared by my office.'

'What, all of them?' asked the head of Problem Solving, 'Even work-related? That will really slow us up.'

'Okay, all Thoughts that are not work related.'

Nathaniel shook his head and returned to his seat to gather up his papers.

'I've said my piece, Marcia. There's no point in me staying. I will get a report prepared from our side on the causes of Jessica's depression. It will include some proposals for action.'

With that, Nathaniel left the room. There was an awkward silence while everybody hoped that someone else would say something.

'Don't you want to know the real causes of Jessica's unhappiness?' This was Fola: everyone looked at her, in awe of her audacity. I sunk lower in my seat.

'We know the cause,' Marcia had adopted her 'talking-to children' voice again. 'We've just had it explained to us by our scientific adviser.'

Then the collision happened. It was at the exact same moment that I asked myself, yet again, why we had been told to attend the meeting. The noise was like thunder right above one's head, but short-lived, like a motorbike backfiring. Dominion Tower trembled. Everything on the table slid off and landed in a chaotic heap. The picture of Marcia and her gang crashed to the floor scattering splinters of glass. I looked up at the RTM; for the briefest moment I thought I saw a raised hand coming towards Jessica's head. The hand vanished immediately and a view of Jessica's kitchen work surfaces came onto the screen; there seemed to be something wrong with the monitor as everything was spinning uncontrollably.

'Jessica's been hit!' someone shouted.

Fola grabbed my arm and swore softly.

The sound of pain filled the room; nee-naw, nee-naw, a wailing siren making it impossible to think. The building stopped swaying and the RTM went dead. I gripped the edge of the table and closed my eyes, willing myself not to be sick as the bile rose from my stomach.

7

At weekends, Jessica generally wore jeans and a t-shirt, adding a jumper or fleece in winter. This was her default setting, minimising the need for mental activity too early in the morning. The colours tended to be muted; browns, greys and navy. She had fallen into these choices in recent months, but it hadn't always been the case. She used to seek out colour. She would scour the charity and nearly new shops, landing a pink cashmere jumper or a purple leather jacket. A comedy night meant bold dressing – mad or bad. Colour created confidence; she needed to be seen, to be taken account of. That was a while ago. She hadn't done a comedy gig for over six months.

Her work wardrobe could be described as capsule. It was built around the clothes she used to wear for court appearances; black trousers and a smartish jacket. It could get very hot in the office so that meant a blouse or high-end t-shirt. The choices were limited but that didn't make it easier for her to pick out three items to put on. Eventually she settled on the same clothes that she had worn the day before, even though they were not very clean and needed a good iron. She decided that she would wear her black coat, the one that she had bought for Nan's funeral. That would off-set the overall air of shabbiness.

The best thing about Jessica's morning routine was her mug of strong tea. It was an integral part of her waking process. Not only did the liquid serve to kick start her brain cells, there was something comforting about the physicality of the hot mug. She would hold it in both hands, feeling the warmth seep through the china and radiate up her arms.

That morning she couldn't face eating any breakfast however the need for some caffeine was particularly strong. The kettle boiled and she splashed water into the mug. She flicked the soggy tea-bag towards the bin It missed, landing on the floor. She bent down to retrieve it and, as she straightened up, she hit her head hard on the corner of an open cupboard door. There was a loud crack. For a moment it felt as if she had been struck, the room span and she sat down and closed her eyes. The pain was overwhelming and blocked out all other thoughts. She felt her throbbing head; no skin was broken but there would be a bruise, for sure.

The world was not kind. Everything was lined up against her. Nothing was fair. She was completely alone and no-one cared about her. There was no point in going on.

8

'Attack or accident?'

Marcia shouted to Military Woman who was speaking into a mobile phone. The pain siren continued its incessant braying as we began picking up papers and bits of broken glass off the floor.

'It's looking like an accident, Ma-am,' she said to Marcia.

'Any casualties?' Julia asked.

'Too early to say…'

'Can't we do something about that God-awful noise?' said Marcia.

Military Woman talked some more into her phone and the siren's strident wail quietened down to something more like a sob.

'Look over there!' Someone was opening the blind. 'A crane's come off that building.'

We gathered round the window; at ground level there was a crane lying on its side like a dead grasshopper. We could see that it had fallen from the roof of the office block opposite us; it had ripped the corner of the high-rise building, exposing the top four floors to the elements. Windows were shattered down the side and raw bits of steel were hanging loose.

'The new Financial Services Building. At least it was empty,' said Nicholas.

'But what about the poor people on the ground?' said Fola.

Military Woman came off the phone.

'Definitely accidental, Ma'am,' she said.

'Caused by?' asked Marcia.

'Spatial awareness problem, by the look of it. Collision between top of head and cupboard door.'

'We're in code orange, I expect everyone to be on full alert. This is carelessness on someone's part.'

There was an exchange of looks round the room.

'Marcia,' said the Professor, 'Accidents do happen... there's nothing to be gained in finding someone to blame.'

'It's negligent and it's unacceptable... Nicholas can look into it.'

Nicholas frowned and I thought about how Marcia found so many things unacceptable. I had a list of unacceptable things too. It was unacceptable that Soul's personnel had been reduced to four. It was unacceptable that we were stuck down in the Thymus. It was unacceptable that Jessica never read poetry any more.

'Any damage to the East Side?' someone asked.

'Not that I'm hearing,' said Military Woman, 'Looks like West Sector nine took the direct hit.'

'ActCon is dead!'

Julia flipped a switch so that the RTM now filled the entire projector screen. The monitor stuttered and then came back to life and now there was a view of the kitchen floor which Jessica seemed to be examining closely. Beneath the screen were the words *Current Mood = very low.*

'Fucking hell,' said Sean under his breath.

'ActCon's on lockdown,' said Military Woman. 'I have a team trying to force their way in... should be less than a minute.'

'What are they going in with?' asked Sean, 'Something simple I hope?'

'Just a repeat of the 'drink tea' command.'

'Good, we're all desperate for caffeine here.' Marcia spoke lightly but it was obvious that everyone was on edge. Military Woman was looking ashen while Julia and the Professor were talking together urgently. The Professor took out his phone.

'The collision will have had an impact on neurotransmitter levels,' said Julia. 'It's likely to mean a higher level of risk.'

'That's all we need,' said Marcia.

'We're in, Ma'am,' said Military Woman. The RTM showed that Jessica had stood up and was now nursing the mug of tea. Everyone breathed out.

'Marcia,' said the Professor, 'my team are putting a Thought into ActCon to say that Jessica should stay at home and not go to work this morning.'

'What have I just said? All Thoughts must be cleared by this office.'

'Sorry… I'll ask them to hold…'

Sean shook his head:

'We can't miss work today, there's a deadline to meet, she has to finish the report we've been working on it for weeks. Today's the day.'

A pause, no-one moved.

'Wouldn't it be best if she went to work as normal?' This was from the head of Looking Good in Front of Other People.

Marcia hesitated.

'She should go to work,' said Marcia with an air of finality, and then to Sean: 'Send two Thoughts into ActCon… one reminding her what she's got to do for the report and the other saying she'll feel better once she gets to work.'

'Ma'am,' said the man with the bald head, 'I think, until we know otherwise, that we should treat this incident as an act of sabotage, a terrorist threat, even. Shall I ask Internal Security to investigate?'

'Thank you, but no need,' said Marcia, all charm and smiles, 'we can manage up here. This meeting is now over. Nicholas, treat that investigation as top priority; I want a report on my desk by the end of the day. Julia, I'd like you to make sure that serotonin and the other stuff returns to normal.'

Fola snorted, rather too loudly.

Marcia turned to face Fola and me. 'You two, I'd like a word with you, come with me.'

Marcia had a corner office with windows on two sides. At first sight it looked as if she had been burgled as the contents of her desk lay strewn on the floor. She called for Nicholas and we stood, mildly embarrassed, as he scurried about tidying the room. Once he had left Marcia sat down on one side of the large desk and gestured for us to sit opposite her.

29

'So, what did you make of this morning's meeting?' Marcia adopted a friendly tone, as if she were amongst colleagues.

'We should treat the situation as an opportunity,' said Fola eagerly. 'Nathaniel is right, this is a chance to do something about the reasons why Jessica is unhappy. We are ready to help in Soul; we have a number of interesting proposals with respect to Quality of Life.'

Marcia frowned while I willed Fola to shut up, but she continued:

'This could be the time to give serious consideration to moving out of London…'

'That's not why I wanted to see you,' interrupted Marcia, she began fiddling with her pen, turning it round and round in her fingers.

'Do you think that there is a real possibility that Jessica could hurt herself?'

'I guess it's a *possibility*, it's happened before.'

'What about death?'

'Death?'

'Yes, death,' repeated Marcia, her eyes narrowed to a frown as she looked across at Fola, 'do you think there's a chance that Jessica could die?'

'All humans die, sooner or later.'

Marcia pursed her lips:

'What I want to know is… has Alfred made any arrangements?'

'What do you mean, arrangements?'

'Does he have a plan, does he have any information … for Soul to carry on living… if the worst should happen?'

We both stared at Marcia. Fola cottoned on before I did and began to laugh with a deep belly guffaw.

'Oh you mean… like a Heavenly Aeroplane!' Fola began singing:

'All you thirsty of every tribe
Get your tickets for an aeroplane ride,'

'That's enough, Fola.' Marcia reddened, but Fola carried on:

Jesus our Saviour is coming to reign
And take you up to glory in His aeroplane.

'You'd like a ticket for the Heavenly Aeroplane!'

'I said that's enough.'

There was no stopping Fola, she carried on laughing and said:

'You think that Alfred has a plan... that down in Soul we will be saved, while you all die.... we'll take off to heaven and leave the rest of you stranded!' Fola looked at me and I couldn't help smiling too. The image seemed so surreal.

'No, there are no plans. Though it would be very splendid if it was just like the song. We could issue tickets...' continued Fola, singing again. '*And take you up to glory in His aeroplane.*'

'Enough!'

Marcia jumped out of her seat:

'Merrick!' she called through the door.

The bald man who had been at the meeting appeared.

'Yes ma'am?'

'This woman needs to learn some manners, take her away.'

'The Oubliette, ma'am?'

'Yes, the Oubliette, I may need her later, for now I want her out of my sight.'

'What about him?'

'The poodle?' she said, looking at me. 'He's harmless, he can go and report to Nicholas and help with his investigation.'

It all happened so quickly. Merrick took us both by the arm and ushered us out of Marcia's office. A couple of Whiteshirts appeared out of nowhere and bundled Fola into one of the lifts. She looked confused and disorientated but before the doors closed she turned back:

'Hold fast, Colin,' she said. 'Hold fast!'

The door of the other lift opened; the caffeine trolley had arrived.

9

I didn't know what to do; I stood for a while staring at the lift doors in the hope that Fola might reappear. I imagined her laughing and cheerfully explaining that Marcia had been joking and that everything was back to normal. But the doors stayed shut and the area emptied save for the blond receptionist and a small thin woman pushing the caffeine trolley.

'Caff, love?'

'Please, Annie.'

'Nasty business… that bash… everyone's all shook up. What about you, dear? Nice strong cuppa?'

I shook my head, I felt sick. All I wanted to do was to get back to Soul as quickly as possible, but now I had to obey Marcia and stay put. Annie sidled up to me, she wore a pale blue housecoat that seemed several sizes too big for her and her iron grey hair was fashioned into neat wavy perm. She was an Old One, not an Ancient like Alfred, but clearly one of the early pioneers. There had been no Old Ones at the executive meeting; it looked like they were relegated to the more menial tasks in Dominion Tower.

'You look very peaky,' she said quietly, 'you alright? I can find you something to pep you up if you like.'

I didn't understand what she meant and shook my head again.

'Worried about your friend?'

The receptionist sounded curious rather than concerned or caring.

'I'm supposed to report to Nicholas,' I said, 'where is he?'

'Down the corridor, third door on the left.'

Nicholas's door had *Personal Assistant to the Chief Executive* on a brass name-plate. I gave a tentative knock and then tried again more forcefully.

'Come in,' Nicholas shouted. He sat behind a large desk, leaning back in his chair. He was on the phone:

'You heard her. She wants it by the end of today.'

A pause, the person at the other end seemed to have a lot to say.

'Can't,' said Nicholas, 'up to my eyes in it here, you wouldn't believe it.'

Another pause. I stood awkwardly by the door, looking at the desk. It was almost empty; there was a metal tray marked *IN* on one side containing one piece of paper. Its sister *OUT* tray was empty. In front of him was a pristine blotter with a pencil and a pen lined up neatly at right-angles.

'Hang on a minute, someone's here,' then to me: 'Yes?'

'Marcia says I'm to help you. Help with the investigation, into this morning's incident?'

'Really?' He sounded incredulous as he looked me up and down, then he was back on the phone: 'You're in luck, I can send someone down to help you.'

Pause.

'It's Colin from Soul. He was at the meeting. Don't swear at me Sean, I'm sure he'll be helpful. He'll add a different perspective. I'll send him down now. Don't forget, by the end of the day. Got to go now, bye.'

He put the phone down.

'What happened to your friend?'

'Marcia's had her taken away, I think she said the Oubliette?'

'Gosh… couldn't keep her mouth shut, I suppose. I'm sending you down to the twenty-first floor. Sean's in charge of the investigation. Off you go, you want Problem Solving.'

As I passed the front desk the receptionist was flicking through a magazine.

'Could I use your phone?' I asked.

She looked at me warily.

'I can connect you, which department?'

'Soul, it's in the Thymus, you might have it down as Residual Projects.'

After some unnecessary faffing she connected me to the office. Relief flooded through me as I heard Grace's voice:

'Help is at hand, Soul is here.'

I was usually irritated by Grace's idiosyncratic way of answering the phone, but not that morning.

'Grace, it's me, Colin.'

'How's it going?'

'Badly, very badly.'

I told her what had happened to Fola but cut out the bit about the Heavenly Aeroplane as I was being overheard.

'They've taken her to somewhere called the Oubliette. Do you know what that is?'

'Some kind of prison. Think it's run by the Whiteshirts. Not good, we've got to find a way to get her out. Are you coming back?'

'Can't just now.' I glanced over to the receptionist who was frowning with impatience. 'I've got to go, I'll call you later.' I passed the phone back to the receptionist and waited for the lift. For a moment I thought I was going to throw up and I leaned against the wall. I took some deep breaths to calm myself. Oh Fola, I thought, why couldn't you have kept quiet, just for once?

10

The twenty-first floor of Dominion Tower was entirely open-plan; however the various teams occupied clear demarcated areas. It was quite hard to find Problem Solving as it sat in the middle of the floor surrounded by the large Looking Good in Front of Other People team and the smaller Doing Sums. Problem Solving had marked out its territory by the use of nose-high partitions, metal filing cabinets and large cupboards which acted as physical barrier against the rest of the floor. It reminded me of those old cowboy films where the doughty settlers erect a camp, encircled by wagons, and wait for the Indians to arrive. I peered over a partition.

'I'm looking for Sean,' I said to a woman studying a document on the desk in front of her.

'In here,' she said without looking up.

'How do I get in?' The wall of office furniture appeared impregnable. The woman sighed.

'Over there – there's a gap between the photocopier and that cupboard.'

I squeezed in. Sean was talking with a group of his team. I noticed that he had jettisoned the red blazer in favour of a Killers tee-shirt. He beckoned me over:

'Ah, Colin, follow me.'

He strode over to the corner where an area had been enclosed by more partitions. Inside were a desk and swivel chair, a couple of shabby armchairs and a large couch.

'The powers-that-be have declared that individual offices are only allowed on the twenty-third floor, so this…' he stretched out his arms, 'you will note, is not an office. It's a Multiple Use Area.'

I didn't know what to say, but by now he was in the swivel chair doing half spins, first one way, then the other:

'It's fucking bad timing, I can tell you, this investigation of Marcia's. I need everyone on work today.' He ran his hand through his floppy red hair. 'You've been sent down to help?'

'I guess so…. but…..'

'What happened to Fola? She coming down too?'

I explained what had happened, again, leaving out the Heavenly Aeroplane. Sean stopped spinning:

'Bloody hell,' he said quietly, 'not Fola.'

I wanted to ask him about the Oubliette but he leapt up and disappeared back into the main office. There was an RTM on his desk and I could see that Jessica had now left the flat and was walking to the station. The view was of the grey north London pavement. 'Look up! Look up!' I wanted to shout. 'Look up at the colours of the leaves, they're amazing!'

Sean returned with a man dressed in black who had a huge stomach that hung over the front of his trousers. Throwing himself onto the couch with a sigh, the fat man began mopping his forehead with a grubby hanky.

'I could use some caffeine,' he said to no-one in particular. 'The machine was empty when I last looked, do you think they've filled it up yet?'

'Fliss!' Sean shouted to the far end of the office. 'Could you bring us four caffs and come and join us?'

A small man with a neat moustache put his head round the screen:

'Sean, I want to put a Thought into Active Consciousness.'

'What now?'

'I need a reminder about chasing the data on 14b…..'

36

'What's the point?' interrupted the fat man, 'she can't do anything about it now, can she? In case you haven't noticed, she's walking to work. Anyway, didn't you get that same Thought into ActCon three times last night? No wonder she's feeling fed-up.'

'Ha ha, very funny Max,' the man did not look amused; in fact, he looked drawn and anxious. 'Sean, please?'

Sean sighed.

'Go on then, if you want. Thoughts are allowed so long as they are to do with work. Now bugger off and leave us alone. I need this fucking investigation sorted by the time Jessica gets into work.'

11

Jessica's work was located in the Scrutiny, Policy & Intelligence Team and her job title was 'Performance & Information Management Practitioner'. Her friend Giulia said that the acronym was highly appropriate: 'We're being screwed on a daily basis while you're being paid extra to keep us in check and tell us we're rubbish.'

At first, being a PIMP seemed easy: no difficult clients to see, no late nights writing court reports, none of the nagging worry about the stuff that collected at the bottom of the 'to-do list'. Then, after a few days, she found herself thinking about returning to social work. She missed her feisty and fickle families. She had always found ways of cutting through the jargon and talking to them as human beings rather than 'service users.' Even in the direst of situations there had been that spark of British humour, often sarcastic and cynical, yet something to pick up and run with. Like a signal caught from an alien galaxy. An indicator that here was life, here was humanity and we are all on this ship of fools together.

There was not much to laugh about in SPIT. First of all, Jessica didn't feel like part of a team. Her nearest colleague was Marie, an earnest young woman who had a pink crocheted coaster on her desk. Marie was Jessica's counterpart in Adult Services and she spent her days gathering information about hospital discharge times and the costs of care packages for the elderly. Although they shared an office, they rarely met, as Marie preferred to work from home so that she could walk her Bichon Frise at lunchtimes. This meant that it was quite possible to go through the day and not talk to anyone at all. The days were long ones too; a strange phenomenon was that the office clock seemed to get stuck every day at around 3:30 pm. She drunk more tea.

38

Performance Indicators are hungry for quantifiable data; they need to measure something that has an answer like 17.4 or 8 months. As she harvested the statistics from the social work teams Jessica began to question the usefulness of the information. The 'how many' and 'how long' questions might work in a factory that made frying pans but were they really appropriate for social work?

She put this question to Darren, chief PIMP and head of SPIT, during her first, and only, supervision session.

'Maybe we could do some qualitative research,' she said, rather pleased with herself for coming up with a technical term. 'We could ask a group of foster kids what they feel about their foster placements. Not a huge survey, just a few targeted questions. You know, whether they feel safe and settled and part of the family. It could run alongside all the stats we're collecting.'

Darren smiled broadly.

'Great idea,' he said, while actually thinking 'over my dead body'. He wasn't a social worker and didn't have much of a clue about how social workers spent their days. His background was finance and he had a keen suspicion of touchy-feely surveys and the unquantifiable subjective gloop of their so-called results.

'Yep, great idea,' he repeated, scratching his designer goatee-beard, 'though it will have to sit on the back-burner just now. The government's performance framework has to be our number one priority. But you're thinking outside the box. I love that,' he lied.

Jessica returned to badgering the teams for their statistical returns. She told herself that she would give it six months.

That was eight months earlier, and she was still there.

12

I was not used to hearing about work. Generally, down in Soul, we tried to distance ourselves from anything to do with Jessica's new job. After ten days of Jessica being a PIMP, Fola set up a meeting with Nathaniel and together they got a Thought into Active Consciousness to the effect that Jessica should leave the new job and go back to being a proper social worker. They put in a lot of preparation into this Thought and had all their arguments marshalled. Fola told me that they had even garnered support from Sean and his team in Problem Solving, they had provided evidence to show that collecting numerical data, like the number of visits a social worker makes, doesn't tell anyone whether she is making a positive difference to a child and their family.

Marcia was furious that the debate hadn't taken place in the Executive first. She told Problem Solving to come up with some ideas for more interesting work that Jessica could put to her boss. When that didn't get anywhere, Marcia decreed that Jessica should stay put and get on and do the job that she was hired to do. After all, it was better hours and more money.

Fola had returned to Soul feeling powerless and dejected.

'We must leave it up to them now,' she said. 'If we get involved in Jessica's work it will destroy us all.'

Since then Soul had kept out of anything to do with work while Marcia had used this victory to strengthen the influence of West Side over East.

A woman in a red blazer entered with a tray of caffeine which she plonked down on Sean's desk.

'It's not my job to make caffeine for everyone, couldn't you have asked him?' she nodded at the fat man, 'and will this take long? I've got a mountain of work to get on with.'

'Thanks Fliss,' said Sean, taking his place back in the swivel chair, 'no, it won't take long. Introductions…. Fliss and Maxwell - this is Colin from Soul.'

Maxwell nodded in my direction, took a large mug out of his jacket pocket and poured the plastic cup of caffeine into it.

'Can I have that one too?' he said to me.

I nodded. I was staring at the woman; she looked familiar.

'You work with my little sister,' she said.

'Grace? You must be Felicity.'

'No-one calls me that, it's Fliss. How's she doing? Is she still trying to get Jessica to move out of London?'

Grace has a white-board above her desk with a list of her 'Key Priorities.' Number one says 'Move to the country' and she has achieved fourteen Thoughts in Active Consciousness in her Progress-So-Far column. All that means is that Jessica has been aware of fourteen, mostly fleeting, Thoughts about moving out of London. Four of these actually turned into Actions and Grace is labelling these as 'Next Steps'. One was reasonably genuine and it was when Jessica went on a day trip to Whitstable and spent time looking in estate agent's windows. The other so-called 'Next Steps' were the three occasions when Jessica purchased 'Country Living' magazine.

'Yes, she's had some Thoughts into ActCon…'

'Waste of time,' interrupted Felicity, 'no-one in West wants to leave London.'

'Oh, I don't know,' said Maxwell. 'Might be quite fun… Jessica could become a country matron and join the WI, take up golf and bridge.'

Felicity snorted. 'Not if I've got anything to do with it.'

Looking at Felicity, I could see the family resemblance to Grace; the same brown eyes and dark hair: however this slightly older woman was thinner and sharper in her features. While Grace's hair was long and swept up in a straggly bun, Felicity had hers cut short in a neat bob. Grace favoured jeans and a sweatshirt while Felicity wore a knee length skirt and the corporate red blazer.

'This is all very jolly,' said Sean, 'but as Fliss says, we've got a hell of a lot of work to do today ...'

'Any biscuits?' asked Maxwell.

Sean gestured to a tin on his desk and continued:

'You felt the crash down here. Sector Nine took a direct hit. A crane fell off the new Financial Services Building, no casualties. Marcia wants to know the cause by the end of today. My plan is that we give her an answer now, before Jessica gets to work. I need you both on the Performance Report once she gets in.'

'If no-one was hurt why is she so interested?' asked Felicity.

'She thinks it was sabotage,' said Sean.

'Why's he here?' Maxwell gave a nod towards me; he had rested the tin on his stomach and was steadily working his way through the biscuits. Crumbs were collecting in drifts down the front of his jacket.

'Marcia thought I might be able to help, give a different perspective. But I don't think I can, I need to get going. Sean, can you tell me, where exactly is the Oubliette?'

'Amygdala Fort, beneath the Archives. There's nothing you can do.'

'Can't you do something?'

He shook his head.

'Who is it this time?' said Felicity.

'Fola.'

'Oh no, poor Fola.'

'Abandon all hope,' muttered Maxwell.

'Maybe if I went down there, I could get to see her?'

'Visiting times are between two and four every day,' said Maxwell.

'Really?' I said, suddenly hopeful.

'Of course not,' said Maxwell with a sneer. 'The clue's in the name: oub-li-ette. People who end up there are forgotten about.'

This sweaty man was starting to annoy me with his sarcasm and his snide comments.

'Nathaniel's your best bet,' said Sean. 'Wait for all this emergency business to die down and then go and ask him to pull a few strings.'

I felt a surge of relief. Nathaniel was a close friend of Fola's, he would sort this out. I made up my mind to go over to East Side to see him as soon as I was able.

'Anyway,' said Sean, 'a terrorist act of sabotage, says Marcia.'

'It was probably just an accident,' said Felicity.

'Freud said there's no such thing as an accident,' announced Maxwell.

'It looks like Marcia agrees with Freud,' said Sean, 'what's more, the bash-on-the-head upset Jessica's emotional stability. Seems she's more likely to top herself now.'

'What, seriously?' asked Felicity looking unconvinced.

'That's what Nick says,' Sean stretching over to take the last biscuit, 'although you can't believe a word he says.'

'We're all going to die... we're all going to die,' chanted Maxwell.

'Come on you two, focus,' said Sean, 'we get this done and then you can both get back to checking the stats.'

'Let's review what happened,' Felicity was saying. 'Jessica was making a cup of tea as normal, dropped the tea-bag... bent down to pick it up and hit her head on the door... I don't see how anyone could engineer that to happen.'

'Difficult, but not impossible,' said Sean.

'Opportunistic,' said Maxwell, 'someone saw that the cupboard door was open and in a fraction of a second set it up.'

I shook my head, it all seemed very unlikely to me.

The man with the moustache appeared round the screen again.

'Sean?' he said.

'Piss off, Will,' said Maxwell. 'Sean told you, we're in a meeting.'

The man took no notice:

'I'm sure that there's a mistake on the third page.'

'For God's sake!' said Maxwell.

'Jessica needs to remember to check it, I need to put a Thought into ActCon.'

'What, another one? Can't it wait until she gets in?' said Sean. 'She'll be there in forty minutes, she must be nearly at the station.'

We looked at the RTM and saw that Jessica was trudging towards the junction. On the far side of the road was the underground station. Thirties architecture, quite beautiful in its own way, and always going un-noticed.

'She'll be busy later, I may as well send a Reminder in now. Please?'

Sean sighed.

'Go on then, but it's the last one before she gets to work.'

The man left and I marvelled at how easy it was for Problem Solving to get Thoughts into Active Consciousness, while for us, down in Soul, it either takes weeks of planning or else we have to wait until Jessica's lying awake in the middle of the night and sneak a Thought into ActCon while no-one else is around.

'One approach,' Maxwell continued, 'could be to find out who Marcia wants to blame and say it's their fault. That would put Nathaniel in the frame.'

'That doesn't seem fair,' I said.

'No,' conceded Sean, 'but it has the double advantage of being quick to achieve and acceptable to Marcia. What's more, there'd been a dust up between Nathaniel and Marcia at the meeting and he left before the end.'

Sean got up and wrote *Nathaniel?* on the small whiteboard on the wall.

'Can't see why,' said Felicity.

'Long-term disagreement with Marcia, angry with her at the meeting…. Maybe he hoped that Dominion Tower would fall down… I could live with Nathaniel being our number one suspect…. And Marcia will like that result.'

I didn't like the way this was going. 'Nathaniel said he was going back to East Side to do research on what was causing Jessica to be depressed. He wasn't going to hang around and commit acts of sabotage.'

'I agree, don't buy it,' said Felicity turning to me. 'When Jessica dropped the tea-bag, which hand was it in?'

I shrugged.

'We can check it on the Replay. I'll set it up… I guess about half-an-hour ago,' said Felicity as she put the RTM in playback mode. It said minus 29 minutes at the top of the screen and we watched as boiling water was poured over a tea-bag in the pale blue china mug. Jessica picked up a spoon, gave the tea a stir and squeezed the tea-bag against the side of the mug. This was the same action that Jessica carried out every day. All that was needed was a 'Make tea' command and Jessica went into automatic mode for the rest.

She fished the tea-bag out using the teaspoon and opened the pedal bin with her foot. Felicity pressed 'pause'.

'Right hand ...definitely Right... so if there was a command to drop the teabag it originated from the northwest Motor Cortex... that puts Nathaniel in the clear doesn't it?'

Sean shrugged.

'I dunno, not really, he could have used his phone..... rang a contact up there. Then I suppose so could anybody. This left or right-hand business doesn't help at all.'

They fell silent. The RTM reverted to real-time mode and showed that Jessica was now standing on the escalator and sinking down to the depths of the underground station. She seemed fixated on the shoulder of the person in front of her. A navy wool coat with a fine dusting of dandruff.

'May as well see the rest of this,' Felicity leant across and switched the RTM back to replay mode.

We watched the tea-bag falling to the floor with a splat and Jessica bending down and getting up again. There was a loud bang and the screen went blank. But there was something else, something in the split second before the screen went dead.

'Did you see that? ... I thought so!' I said.

'The hand?' said Felicity. 'I'll play it again and slow it down.'

She reset the dial and we watched transfixed as Jessica straightened up slowly, the bang happened, everything shook and then, fleetingly, a hand came out of nowhere and hit her head. This was immediately followed by the screen going black. Felicity replayed it: bang – hand – blackness and again: bang – hand – blackness. The fourth time Felicity froze the screen and we could clearly see the hand, fuzzy and indistinct, but a hand none-the-less. It was if someone had materialised out of nowhere and hit Jessica hard on the side of the head. It made no sense, no sense at all.

13

'What the hell was that?' said Maxwell.

'That,' said Sean, 'was a flashback, you don't often see them.'

'Bloody hell.'

'I don't understand,' I said, 'where did it come from?'

'Deep in the Archives, would be my guess,' said Sean. 'It'll be a Memory triggered by the bang on the head.'

'Weird,' said Felicity.

'Very,' agreed Maxwell.

'Nathaniel said something about Jessica's past… childhood stuff,' I said.

The others went quiet. We could hear sounds from the other side of the partition; phones ringing and the whir of the photocopier. I tried to rack my brain for information from when Jessica was a child, but like all Newbies I knew very little. We began our lives while Jessica was growing up and we spent our early years in the kindergarten of the Cerebellum. We were learning stuff; however, we were sheltered from a lot of the day-to-day. The Old Ones were in charge and they protected us. They made sure we didn't see anything too disturbing or traumatic.

'Why is this never talked about?' asked Felicity quietly.

Sean moved his chair closer to the sofa and lowered his voice:

'Restricted Access; some of Jessica's childhood Memories are restricted. You need special clearance from Internal Security.'

'What's the point of that?'

'So they don't get into ActCon,' said Maxwell,.'The likes of us are not trusted to keep quiet.'

'But …' Felicity shook her head.

'It's only dangerous memories,' said Sean, 'the ones that cause pain if they get into ActCon.'

'Well, that one got in this morning.'

The RTM made a ping sound and we all turned to see the face of Marcia's Personal Assistant.

'Good news,' announced Nicholas.

'Doubt it, Nick.'

'You're stood down from the investigation; Marcia has looked into it herself.'

Felicity caught Maxwell's eye, he shrugged, neither of them looked surprised.

'Well that's just fucking hunky-dory. Who's in the frame?'

'Can't say, I'm afraid.'

'Come on Nick, it's the least you can do after wasting my time.'

Maxwell mouthed 'Nathaniel' to Felicity.

'Well, let's put it like this; Marcia has put out a warrant for Nathaniel's arrest if he comes over to West Side.'

Maxwell grinned and started to brush the biscuit crumbs off his jacket and onto the floor. Felicity shook her head.

'I've got to go, Sean, something's up.' Nicholas disappeared to be replaced on the Real Time Monitor by a view of black dust and grey metal.

It took me a moment to work out what Jessica was looking at, then I realised it was the rails of the underground line; she was down on the platform, waiting for the train. As she looked down at her feet we could see that the toes of her black boots were about three inches from the edge of the platform. A Thought was playing:

'You could do it, just end it.'

'Fucking hell!' said Sean.

There a low rumble and a whoosh of air as the train approached. We could see the front of the train hurtling towards Jessica, accompanied by a roar.

'Do it now… jump.'

Everything seemed to slide into slow motion. The train got closer and closer and I shut my eyes. A woman's voice came over the tannoy system:

THREAT TO LIFE; CODE RED EMERGENCY … THREAT TO LIFE; CODE RED EMERGENCY.

14

As she stood in the underground Jessica realised that she could not recall anything at all about her walk from the flat to the station. It was as if she had been vaporised by an alien force at her front door-step and then rematerialized on this southbound platform. Her head still ached dully from where she had hit it on the cupboard door and she felt nauseous. The message board showed that a train was imminent and commuters were gathering, positioning themselves in clumps where they judged the tube doors would open, each person seeking a strategic advantage over the next.

The message board changed to TRAIN APPROACHING and a low keening sounded way down in the tunnel. The noise got louder and louder as Jessica moved closer to the edge and over the yellow line. *You could do it, just end it.* For a moment she was startled at the clarity of the voice in her head. As the train approached she readied herself and snatched a breath. It came again: *Just do it now... jump.* Then another thought followed fast: *No, not now ... do it later ... on the way home. Finish the report... you've got this far... do it on the way home.* The train stopped and the doors slid open in front of her.

15

THREAT TO LIFE; CODE RED EMERGENCY.

The voice was devoid of emotion but carried an urgency... a call to action, but exactly what kind of action wasn't clear. I opened my eyes and followed Sean, Maxwell and Felicity into the main office. Small groups of people were staring at a Real Time Monitor mounted high up on the wall. No-one said anything and I could hear someone crying on the other side of the partition. Jessica had her eyes shut so it wasn't clear where she was or what was happening. It wasn't until the RTM showed the inside of the tube train that my heart stopped thumping. Jessica was standing in the main body of the carriage holding on to a vertical metal bar.

'Thank God,' someone said.

The woman on the tannoy stopped abruptly.

'Okay everyone,' said Sean, 'back to work.'

No-one seemed inclined to move. A young man piped up:

'Do you think she'd have done it, Sean? Really jumped?'

'I don't know... the important thing is that she didn't.'

'Looked pretty close to me,' someone else said. 'Where did it come from, the Thought.... the Thought telling her to jump?'

They looked at Sean expectantly, he shook his head.

'Don't know... makes no sense.'

William burst into the office, he was flushed and out of breath.

'It was me,' he said, 'I stopped her!'

'What?' said Maxwell.

'I stopped her… stopped her from jumping. I was already in ActCon. I had a Thought ready on the report and I stopped her. I saved her life… our lives!'

The team gathered round him and there were hugs and 'Well done mate' and pats on the back.

'Good work, Will,' said Sean.

'Might have been better without the 'do it on the way home… finish the report,' bit,' said Maxwell.

'I was thinking on my feet, and if this is going to be Jessica's last day she may as well spend it doing something useful.'

'With the Performance Report.'

'Exactly!' said William, Maxwell's sarcasm missing him by a mile.

'Back to work everyone. Jessica will be in the office in about thirty minutes and we need to be ready to pick up on the report.'

Sean's voice was upbeat but I could see from the set of his mouth that he was anxious. Maxwell and Felicity followed him back into his office space and I went too, not knowing what else to do.

'Bloody idiot,' said Maxwell.

'Who, Will?' said Felicity.

'Of course, Will. He thinks his Performance Report is the most important thing on earth.'

'Yeah well, it looks like he saved the day.' said Felicity.

'He hasn't saved the day… he's just postponed the hour… you heard his Thought: 'Do it on the way home'. We're going to have go through all this again when Jessica goes home.'

'Oh God,' sighed Felicity, 'I can't bear it, what's going on? We should do something.'

'Like what?' said Sean.

'We're supposed to be Problem Solving – this is a bigger bloody problem than the wretched report,' said Felicity. 'We need to find out who put the jump-in-front-of the train Thought into ActCon. Maybe Will saw something when he was up there.'

'I'll speak to him,' said Sean, 'but Internal Security will be on the case, they won't take kindly to the likes of us sticking our noses in.'

'What I don't get,' said Maxwell slowly, 'is how it could be anyone's interest to carry out a suicide mission. Why would anybody want Jessica dead? It would be the end of everything.'

No-one spoke for a while. Sean shook his head and sighed:

'The only way it would make sense would be if someone was in a load of pain and it was the only way out. The only way for the pain to stop. I'll take both of you off the report this morning. Max, go up to ActCon and see what you can dig up. See if someone knows something about the bang on the head business too. Maybe they're linked, could be the same person. Fliss, go over to East and see Nathaniel. He said he was looking into the causes of the depression. See what he's come up with. Tell him what we saw on the RTM, the hand business, it could help.'

'I'll come with you, Felicity,' I said, 'I used to work over there.'

'Good, we'll take the CorpCal.'

16

The CorpCal is the underground line between West and East Side. The last time I was on it I vowed never again. It's a nightmare, always full of people being shoved into carriages like dumb beasts on the way to the abattoir. You spend the journey standing up with someone else's warm breath in your ear. Invariably the lights go out half-way across and, just as you think that you are plummeting down to Hades, you're catapulted back up again, leaving your stomach somewhere far behind. Not a pleasant experience.

It wasn't like that this time. Working in Dominion Tower brings special privileges and Felicity had two passes for First Class. The Premier Waiting Lounge was large and airy with sofas in black leatherette. On one side was a wall of glass and we could see the poor sods in Economy being herded into the dilapidated carriages; they gazed at us reproachfully.

There were a couple of Whiteshirts at the security gate. I was suddenly aware that I was the only person in the lounge not wearing a corporate red blazer.

'Passes and ID,' grunted the larger of the two. He scrutinised mine for what seemed like an eternity.

'Thymus, eh? Why d'you come this way?'

'I've been to the Executive ... on business,' I didn't sound convincing, even to myself.

'He's with me, officer,' said Felicity with authority, and then to me, under her breath, 'Looks like Marcia has ordered extra security, it's not usually like this.'

A voice came over the loudspeaker:

'All customers are reminded the current risk level is Code Red. Please be vigilant at all times.'

We found our seats and a short while later we were plunged down into the darkness. Last time, in Economy on the CorpCal, the noise was deafening, but today it was possible to have a conversation above the low hum of the engines.

'So....' said Felicity, looking up from her magazine, 'I was sorry to hear about Fola. She came up to Problem Solving a few weeks ago and had an argument with Sean about the Performance Indicators. She said he had no integrity... working on the PIs. He was lost for words for once. She's amazing, isn't she? I didn't agree with her but I had to admire her spirit.'

'I didn't know that... didn't know she was still trying to make you guys see sense. Thought she'd given up.'

'Well, she's fighting a losing battle, isn't she? Performance Indicators are Jessica's job; may as well make the best of it.'

Felicity stuffed the magazine forcefully into the pouch of the seat in front of her. I didn't want to end the conversation there.

'She's right, you know, about Sean,' I said.

'What do you mean?'

'Sean was part of the original lobby trying to get Jessica to leave her job. He gave us the lowdown about the Indicators. He said, back then, that all they do is count what can be counted. He said they don't give information as to whether a kid in care or a child being abused is having a better life than they had before. He seems to have forgotten all about that now. He blows with the wind, does your Sean. Performance Indicators are not all they're cracked up to be.'

Felicity pursed her mouth and raised her chin.

'They're better than nothing at all,' she said sharply. 'There has to be some way of telling whether the service is getting better or getting worse.'

We sat in silence for a while and then a voice came over the intercom telling us we'd shortly be arriving at East Central Station.

'Well anyway,' said Felicity, 'Sorry about Fola. From what I've heard, the Oubliette's not a good place to be.'

'I'd like to try and find her.'

The train started to slow down as we approached the station. Felicity shook her head.

'You'll not get inside Amygdala Fort,' she said, 'or... let's say... you might get inside but you won't get out again. It's the headquarters of Internal Security, the most secure place there is.'

The train came to a halt; we had arrived at the East Side.

17

If you were dropped by parachute on top of Jessica's cerebral hemisphere you would know immediately whether you were on West or East Side. The West is all concrete, chrome and glass, the old buildings have been pulled down and high-rise office blocks have been put up in their place. Most of the parks have been bulldozed and the only remaining green space is a carefully manicured patch of lawn outside Dominion Tower where a few beds of garish annuals are replaced every season.

The East has elegant buildings in a Georgian style and garden squares with tall trees and wild, overgrown corners. There's a sense of space and you feel that you can breathe.

I worked in Creative Thoughts on the East Side all the way through Jessica's teens and into her mid-twenties. It was different back then; we worked hard but we had fun. In those days Jessica read and read, and not just the *Saturday Guardian* and the Sunday colour supplements. One of her A levels choices was English Literature so we had Shakespeare, we had Dickens, we had poetry; John Donne and George Herbert, Emily Dickinson and Stevie Smith. She still has a few battered copies on her bookshelf and I sometimes catch a glimpse of them as she walks past. Once or twice I've tried to send a Thought up to Active Consciousness to take a *Selected Poems* off the shelf and have a look at it. It has never worked though; by the time I get my Thought up there

Jessica is on the sofa watching television and it comes back unheard and stamped: 'Not Relevant to Current Situation.'

There was much more collaborative working in the old days; when Jessica had to write a literature essay, a couple of people would come over from Problem Solving in West and work with us in Creative Thoughts. There were no red blazers back then and everyone mucked in together. The place was buzzing with new ideas and in the evening, there would be music and dancing and late night arguing about politics and religion. Those were the halcyon days of the East Side.

'The trouble with this place,' said Felicity as we picked our way over the potholes in the pavement, 'is that no-one ever gets things sorted.'

She was right; the East Side always looks shabby compared to its neighbour on the other side of the ravine. Poor funding combined with a lack of will meant that the fabric of the place was steadily deteriorating. As we approached the Civic Centre I could see that paint was peeling off window frames and doors and some purple buddleia was sprouting from the guttering.

'The East's much poorer,' I said. 'It just doesn't get the same share of resources.'

I knew that it was more than that, the East Side's management was lackadaisical compared to the West's and no-one took an interest in the maintenance of buildings or the repairing of roads.

The Civic Centre on Ninth Avenue is modelled on a Victorian Town Hall. Double fronted and three stories high, it even boasts a central clock tower. (The clock always stands at ten to three.) And that morning, unlike Dominion Tower, the East Civic Centre had no security to speak of at all.

'Don't they know we're in a Code Red?' said Felicity as we were waved past a smiling doorman. The lift was out of order so we had to walk up the three flights of stairs to the Managers' Floor. Felicity strode up the stairs taking two at a time; another jogger, I decided, like her sister. Thinking of Grace reminded me of my reason for needing to see Nathaniel. I decided that I would leave Felicity to save the world; my only purpose was to get Fola out of the Oubliette as quickly as possible. I started to rehearse in my head what I was going to say.

When we arrived at the third floor all the offices were empty. We found a scribbled note on the door of a secretary's office; 'Back Soon' was all it said. As we settled down to wait I shut my eyes to rest and to think; Fola's silly song kept interrupting my train of thought:

'All you thirsty of every tribe

Get your tickets for an aeroplane ride'

'Look Col, mirror!'

I opened my eyes with a start. Everyone has a thing for mirrors. A call goes up: Mirror Moment is broadcast on the RTM, or maybe simply 'Mirror!' and we all down tools and stare at the screen. It's like when the astronauts came back with the first pictures of Earth; the blue and white marble floating in indigo space. People said 'That's us – that's where we are.' Well, that's how we feel when Jessica looks in the mirror.

Felicity and I focussed on the RTM; Jessica was in the ladies at work. She came out of the cubicle and turned on the tap, then it was Jessica's face that filled the screen. The engineers in Vision always focus on her eyes. For them, they are the most important part of her outside body. Come to think of it, they do the same whenever Jessica sees another person – in real life or in a picture – it's eyes first and then the rest of the face. It's like they have a fixation with eyes.

That day the brown eyes were dull with no sign of sparkle, a valley of darker skin underneath each eye. The nightmares have been waking her up too early, I thought, not enough sleep. The skin looked pallid and slightly sweaty with the left cheek mole more obvious than usual.

'What happened to 'put-on-makeup' this morning?' said Felicity. 'And shouldn't it have been a hair-wash morning? Look at it.'

The hair hung down to the shoulders forming two drab curtains either side of the face. Some months back Looking Good in Front of Other People had insisted on blonde highlights and the remnants of these were visible from the ears downwards while higher up and on the scalp the hair was its natural brown colour. When it is clean, the hair has some bounce and stands up a bit. Looking Good got the purchase through of some waxy product which is supposed to help the hair 'have body', whatever that means. It hardly ever gets used though, and that morning the hair sat flat and listless.

The best work blouse had been rescued from the floor and it looked reasonably clean but there was a crease on the right-side collar so the corner turned up.

Oh God! I look like shit.

Jessica splashed some water on her face and made her way back to her desk. Meanwhile the song looped round my head:

Jesus our Saviour is coming to reign
And take you up to glory in His aeroplane.

Felicity stood up and began pacing up and down.

'Where is everybody? This is hopeless.'

'Dunno, they probably won't be long.'

She stopped pacing and stood in front of the RTM.

'She's going through the Report, she's getting to the part that I wrote.'

Jessica was sitting back at her grey plastic desk. She was reading from a piece of paper but occasionally her gaze would switch to a computer screen showing a number of tables and figures. Then the view changed again as she looked out of the window. We saw a car park and a lonely tree, almost bare in the Autumn sunshine. A gust of wind gathered some of the remaining golden leaves, swirling them in a great arc and scattering them over the cars.

Fall, leaves, fall; die, flowers, away;
Lengthen night and shorten day;
Every leaf speaks bliss to me
Fluttering from the autumn tree.

I was jolted out of my reverie by Felicity's sigh of exasperation.

'What's she doing? She should be concentrating; she hasn't got time to look out of the window.'

'It's really important to you, isn't it?'

'What do you mean?' Felicity turned away from the screen and looked at me in surprise.

'This, the report… the whole performance business … this stuff… you really care about it.'

'Of course I care about it. We all care about it. We've been working on it for weeks.'

I shook my head. It seemed such a waste of time.

'It's got to get finished today,' Felicity turned back to the RTM which again showed the car park and the tree. 'for God's sake! How are we going to get it done if she keeps staring out of the window.'

And then, as if on cue, we heard a Thought: *'Must concentrate, must concentrate.'* Jessica went back to reading the report.

'That's probably William. Thank God someone's got their wits about them.'

Felicity sat down next to me and I closed my eyes again.

'You've got no idea, have you? What do you do all day, down in Soul?'

'Oh, this and that.' I kept my eyes shut.

'What sort of this and that?'

'We work on projects…'

'What, like trying to get Jessica to move to the country?'

'That sort of thing…'

The truth of it was that the four of us did very little of consequence. Alfred spent most of the time meditating or asleep. Fola tried to broker deals with other departments while Grace made lists. My role was as a general lobbyist, working with Fola to influence the decision-makers in Pre-Frontal City and get our ideas into ActCon. The other thing I did was notice stuff. See the beauty in ordinary things; the reflections on Jessica's iPhone screen or the billowing clouds of caramel in a cup of tea after the milk is added. I usually try to get these moments into ActCon too, but I've had very little success.

In the old days, when we were a larger team, I had the Poetry Portfolio. Not writing it, but selecting and filing our favourite pieces. I didn't bother to tell Felicity all that. I didn't think that she would understand.

'What else? What other projects?'

'Fola's working on Cultural Activities. That trip to the Barbican was one of hers.'

'Hamlet? That was cool…we watched all of it on the RTM. To be or not to be.'

I opened my eyes. I suddenly felt cold.

'God, Fliss, do you think that's where it comes from?

'What?'

'Jessica's suicidal thoughts... d'you think she's picked it up from seeing Hamlet? How does it go?

To die: to sleep;

No more; and by a sleep to say we end

The heart-ache and the thousand natural shocks

That flesh is heir to.'

'Good memory.'

'It's what I do, remember verse, but no-one ever asks me for any. There's no call for it these days. What d'you think? Is she being Hamlet?'

'I can't imagine people feel like killing themselves just 'cos they've seen a bit of Shakespeare. Isn't the point the heartache and the thousand natural shocks?'

'You're right, but it's a bit of a coincidence.'

Neither of us said anything for a while. The RTM showed the view of the tree again. A couple of pigeons were having an argument with a flurry of flapping wings, shaking down more leaves to anoint the cars.

'Fola should organise some more Shakespeare. It was great last time.'

'Trouble is,' I said, 'she had to work with Looking Good in Front of Other People. It was only with their help that it got into ActCon. She said never again.'

'Are you waiting for Nathaniel?' A cheerful woman was standing over us. 'He's downstairs in a Brainstorming Meeting – it's in the old council chamber. You should go and find him.'

18

Jessica hit a rhythm of reading the draft report, making minor changes and then staring out of the window. Marie, the other PIMP, was on leave, so Jessica spread her papers across the adjacent desk; organising them into small piles relating to each of the performance indicators. Most of the report was ready, but there were still some missing statistics. There were a few holes in the figures regarding young people in care; whether they had kept out of trouble and whether they had passed their GCSEs.

She found that she could think about the report in front of her and almost nothing else. She was still in a state of shock from the knowledge that she had nearly killed herself at the station. Would anyone care if she had gone through with it? Nan would have cared, but she was dead. Jessica was forced to acknowledge that her parents would suffer, although not enough to cause permanent damage. Her father had too much invested in his new family. Her mother had too much invested in herself.

She thought idly about her previous relationships, the Past Men. Not failed relationships exactly. Jessica would not have said that the Fiat Punto that she driven for fourteen years was a failure. She had loved that car, but at the end it didn't work very well. It became more trouble than it was worth. And so it was with Tim-Spike-Gary. She was quite fond of them all and of the good times, but they all had built-in obsolescence. Tim, the teenager, the first love before University, that petered out over the distance of 120 miles apart. Spike, the Go player and Uni boyfriend: obsessive, lazy and intelligent. They clocked up eight years of living together before he packed in this job and went off to Japan to study Go. And Gary, heating engineer and husband. When Jessica found out about his affair she expressed her fury with ice-cold sarcasm. She also felt a spasm of relief but kept that quiet.

They had met on a flight home from Barcelona. They had both been on a city break with their respective friends and had ended up sitting next to each other. Gary clearly didn't like flying and gripped the armrest, white-knuckled, his forehead beaded with sweat. She kept up a barrage of idle chat during take-off which continued through much of the flight. She went into social-work-mode; winkling out information about the perils of installing boilers before moving on to his early childhood experiences. Answering her incessant questions meant that he could no longer focus on every change of engine noise and dip in altitude. Nor could he scour the clouds for alien flying objects set to collide with their plane. He survived the flight and they swopped phone numbers before landing in Stanstead.

On their first date he was her 'bringer'. Her five-minute open-mic slot in a seedy pub was dependent upon her bringing someone who would a) buy a drink and b) remain for the entire show. Gary had never been to a stand-up comedy gig before and was amazed and impressed. Not especially by Jessica's performance – she forgot a whole middle section of her script and came off after three and a half minutes. He was impressed by her courage to stand up in front a couple of dozen people with the spot-light shining down on her. Impressed by her sheer bravery.

She had married Gary. Not a full-blown wedding with bridesmaids and a string quartet. Theirs was a witnesses-only affair in Wood Green registry office followed by a Chinese. Gary, who saw Jessica through the prism of stand-up comedy thought that she was brave, bold and brilliant. Jessica saw Gary as not-Spike and basically easier, like moving from a manual to an automatic. What she hadn't banked on was him rekindling an old romance with a childhood sweetheart. Those were the actual words that he used: he said, 'I'm sorry Jess, but I've been seeing a childhood sweetheart.' Jessica mused whether he had taken to reading 'Mills and Boon.' Then she imagined them tucking into sherbet fountains and curly wurlies behind the bike sheds. Good, she thought; material, and she mined that seam shamelessly in pubs across West London over the following six months.

What would the Past Men have said about Jessica? Tim would have said she was hard to reach. Spike complained that she was emotionally aloof and unfathomable. Gary would only say that he was sorry. All three would be shocked to hear that Jessica had thrown herself in front of a train. Shocked but not entirely surprised. They would survive, she thought.

She looked out of the window again and then tried to pull herself back to work. She wanted to get up from her desk, put on her coat and walk out,

64

never to return. But each time a counter thought seemed to pin her to the chair and tell her that the most important thing to do was to finish her report. Nothing else mattered. She watched the leaves being blown around the car park. Not long now. She would end it on the way home.

19

The council chamber is a large wood-panelled room with a raised dais at one end where a previous Head of East Side used to sit, presiding over council meetings. I had mixed memories of the room from when I was in Creative Thoughts. In the days when Jessica tried writing poetry – must be twenty years ago now - we would do lunchtime performances in the chamber to our colleagues from other departments. We would try out our latest endeavours and, even if I say so myself, they generally went down very well. That morning I was reminded of the butterflies that invaded my stomach before every performance, that and the smell of cheese sandwiches competing with floor polish.

'What a racket,' said Felicity.

I could barely hear her above the hum of excited chatter. There must have been over thirty people in the room, divided into four roughly equal groups, each one occupying a corner of the hall. Paper covered one of the walls with the over-arching title: WHY IS JESSICA DEPRESSED? written in black marker. Every now and then someone would leap up from one of the groups and stick a coloured post-it note on the wall.

I went over to the wall to take a look; the largest number of post-it notes were yellow. They were spread higgledy-piggledy under the heading WORK and they included the phrases: *no real value, boring* and *too much pressure*. A whole subsection was entitled *The Death of the Baby* with a cluster of notes beneath with words like *fallout, impact* and *loss*.

'I don't think it's as bad as it used to be.' This was from a woman with very blue eyes and long fair hair which cascaded over her shoulders. Her name-badge said *Josie - Daydreaming* which made me smile.

'What's your evidence for that?' asked Felicity sharply.

Josie Daydreaming looked taken aback.

'Just what I'd heard...' she said vaguely.

'What about when Jessica was young, was mother drinking a lot then?' Felicity was taking control of the group.

'It was a problem. Sometimes Mum would be drunk when Jessica came home from school,' said Nathaniel.

'Any violence? We believe that Jessica has been hit in the past,' said Felicity.

'And your evidence is ...?' said Nathaniel.

Felicity told the story of the slow-motion replay of the morning's collision and how the mysterious hand appeared a split second after the blow on the head.

'It was probably a flashback, triggered by a past event,' said Felicity with an air of authority.

'I don't understand,' said Josie Daydreaming, 'did someone hit Jessica this morning?'

'No, of course not, she was on her own in the kitchen, the point is that for a brief moment she had a sense that she had been hit by someone.'

'How can that happen?' Josie directed this to Nathaniel.

'It's a strange phenomenon, the flashback,' he said. 'In the case of this morning it was probably the result of someone in Pituitary panicking. As soon as the bang happened whoever was on duty must have hit the 'What the Hell?' button.'

'The 'What the Hell?' button?'

'Yep, as in 'What the hell just happened?' That sends an immediate search through all the archives. The idea is that the process throws something into ActCon which could explain the current situation. So, this morning the archives were searched for 'bang on the head' and if the first thing they came up with was 'hit by a hand,' it was probably closely followed by 'hit by cupboard door' so it wouldn't have stayed in ActCon for long.'

'I saw it, the hand, I mean,' a small woman in glasses was suddenly animated. 'I was watching the RTM, I thought it was most peculiar.'

'I saw it too, at the time,' I said. 'It's strange how it was an image... a picture of a hand rather than a voice saying "hand"'.

'Not that strange,' said Nathaniel. 'A lot of the memories in the Archives are in a raw form and haven't been processed.'

'Sean said that some of them are Restricted Access,' said Felicity.

'That's true; Internal Security keeps those in Amygdala Fort. But you can apply for access, if you know what you're looking for.'

'Amygdala Fort,' I said, 'where the Oubliette is?'

Nathaniel nodded and might have said more when one of the group interrupted:

'We should do a post-it note! *Violence in Jessica's past.*'

'Yeah, but what should we put it under? We don't know for sure that she was hit by Mum so it shouldn't go under Family, could've been Gary.'

'Gary had his problems but I'm sure he never hit Jessica,' said Nathaniel.

'I can tell you for certain that Gary was not violent,' it was the woman in glasses again. 'I was in Human Relations throughout the marriage and I don't ever remember him even getting angry. Same goes for Tim and Spike.'

'Put it under Miscellaneous for now,' said Nathaniel.

The woman in the tracksuit came over to our group:

'Jessica's making coffee,' she said. 'Should we stop a bit earlier so that we can all grab some caffeine?'

'Good idea,' said Nathaniel, 'just give them a few more minutes and I'll wind things up.'

There are four RTMs in the Council Chamber, one in each corner, so we could see that Jessica was in the kitchen area along the corridor from her office. She was leaning against the work top waiting for the kettle to boil. Christopher-from-Finance came over and took a mug out of the cupboard. He smiled at Jessica.

'How's it going?' he said.

'Nightmare,' said Jessica. 'I'm still waiting for the stats on GCSEs.'

'GSCEs?'

'The government thinks that kids in care should get better GCSE results. I'm going to recommend that from now on we only take brainy kids into care.'

Jessica made her coffee and threw the teaspoon into the sink with a clatter.

'Joking,' she said and made her back to her desk.

'Oh well... good luck,' Christopher-from-Finance called after her.

I liked Christopher-from-Finance; he always seemed cheerful. I turned to the woman in glasses.

'Are you still in Human Relations?'

'Yes, why?'

'Couldn't Jessica make a bit more of an effort... with Christopher-from-Finance?

'He's not her type... and anyway, there's an embargo on dating just now.'

'She doesn't have to go out with him... just be a bit friendlier.' I wanted to ask more about this embargo on dating; I didn't remember Soul being consulted, but folk were stacking up their chairs, and the track-suited woman came to collect the flipchart.

'Thank you everyone, for all your hard work this morning. Lots of great ideas,' Nathaniel's upbeat voice carried round the room.

'What happens next?' asked Felicity in a loud clear voice.

'We'll collect all this and get it typed up. Should get it out to you all very soon.'

'I thought you said East Side were doing research,' muttered Felicity, 'this isn't research, it's just getting a load of people's opinions. To quote my boss, I'd say this was a FWOT.'

'A what?'

'A fucking waste of time.'

I watched someone carefully unpick the sheets of paper from the wall and lay them down in a pile on the floor. Felicity was right, although it pained me to agree with her. There was no urgency in Nathaniel's brainstorming exercise. I remembered Marcia's 'delay is unacceptable.'

71

We were caught between Marcia's knee-jerk response of ordering chemical cocktails and Nathaniel's laid-back faffing-about.

'We'll go and talk to him.'

Nathaniel took us back upstairs to his office and called for some caffeine. His was a sunny room with a large window overlooking the park. It was the sort of room that you'd like to be left alone in. Behind the large mahogany desk was a tall overflowing bookcase with more piles of books on the floor. From a quick glance I spotted glossy tomes on Renaissance painting, Autumn leaves and the songs of Leonard Cohen. Smaller books were crammed in horizontally; books on how to knit, play the guitar and dance the Tango. He had a poetry collection too, not as extensive as mine, although I could see several *Selected Poems* of the favourites. The walls were full of pictures and postcards; Van Gogh's 'Sunflowers' nestled next to a view of Tobermory, while a small drawing of some praying hands was stuck over the corner of a large canvas of a damp Ophelia. In the corner were a music stand and a small keyboard. Fola would like this room, I thought, as I sat down on the purple velvet sofa next to Felicity.

'Fola's in trouble!' I blurted out. I told him what had happened; the story of Marcia and the Heavenly Aeroplane, of Merrick and the Oubliette.

'Poor Fola! Marcia's gone mad,' said Nathaniel when I had finished. 'You know she's got it into her head that I caused this morning's collision.'

'She must be seriously worried if she's planning her escape to heaven,' said Felicity. The drinks had been brought in and she nursed her mug in both hands. 'She must think that suicide's a real possibility.'

'And that was before all that 'Just Jump' business at the tube station.' Nathaniel shook his head. 'Don't forget that Marcia always likes to have a plan B. Her attempt to find a way of saving herself is typical. She likes to have all the bases covered.'

He stood up and looked out of the window; he then turned back towards Felicity:

'Sean's sent you over here to help?'

'Col told us you were doing research... into the reasons.'

72

'You saw downstairs…' Nathaniel sat down heavily. 'There are lots of factors which contribute to her current mental state… It's hard to know where to start.'

'We need a plan,' said Felicity suddenly eager. 'We need to prioritise the most likely contenders and draw up an Action Plan. A plan with proposals for what to do next.'

Typical West Side thinking, I thought. Chop everything into bite size pieces and turn them into a list. That will solve everything.

'What about the suicidal Thoughts?' I said. 'We still don't know who's making them.'

'Max's working on that,' said Felicity, and then to Nathaniel: 'Max works with me in Problem Solving. He's gone up to ActCon to see if anybody saw anything suspicious.'

'I'm interested in the hand… that business about Jessica being hit in the past. That's new information. Could be important.'

'Yes, that's what we thought… we hoped you might know something about that,' I said.

Nathaniel shook his head. 'Only what I said downstairs …'

'What about asking an Old One?' interrupted Felicity. 'They'd know, wouldn't they? They should remember what happened when Jessica was a kid.'

'Well yes, they should, but you know they don't like talking about the past. Anyway they are notoriously unreliable. It all gets muddled up with their previous lives. No, you'd have to go down to the Memory Archives if you wanted to find out more.'

'But it's Restricted, isn't it? Would we get to see that sort of stuff?'

'I could give you a Letter of Authority, Internal Security would accept that.'

'That's settled then,' said Felicity turning to me. 'Col, you go down to the Archives and see what you can find out. I'll help Nathaniel sort out this stuff.'

'I can't go on my own,' I said. 'I don't even know where Amygdala Fort is.'

'It's on Hippo Island,' said Nathaniel. 'There's a train and then you'll have walk across the causeway. It's quite straightforward, I'll draw you a map.'

'But what am I going to do when I get there?' I knew that I was sounding pathetic and I caught Felicity's raised eyebrows as she glanced at Nathaniel.

He was now sitting behind his desk writing:

'I'm putting down that you need access to all records that relate to Jessica being physically hit.'

'You might need to be more specific,' said Felicity. 'That could include being hit by a falling branch or a beach ball. Say "being physically hit by another human," and add "from any time from birth to the present day".'

'Good plan,' said Nathaniel, quite happy to accept orders from Felicity. 'All you have to do, Colin, is take this letter to the Archives.'

'Then what?'

'They have a viewing room; you'll be able to watch the Memories there. Sometimes they'll give you a copy to take out, but they probably won't with this. You may just have to write down what you see.'

'There you are, easy-peasy.' Felicity sounded mildly sarcastic.

'What about Fola?'

'I can't do anything about Fola just now. It needs Marcia's authority. Normally I would go and talk to Marcia and win her round, but not today. Not while she's got a warrant out for my arrest. I'm sorry, I truly am.'

And he did look sorry, so sorry, in fact, that I started to feel sorry for him. It was only later that I felt that he had let Fola down. He was her friend after all. He should have tried harder. Nathaniel saw my face and added, 'When this blows over I'll do what I can. The Oubliette is somewhere inside the Fort. While you're there you may get a chance to see her, at least.'

The track-suited woman came into Nathaniel's office with the large bundle of flip chart paper from the brainstorming exercise. Felicity took them off her and began arranging them around the floor. I had

Nathaniel's Letter of Authority in my backpack along with his roughly drawn map and was ready to leave.

'Bye then,' I said.

'Bye.'

Felicity didn't even look up.

PART TWO

BEFORE NOON

1

Jessica was accustomed to fear, it visited her before every gig. Hovering over her bed the night before as she tried to sleep; a dead weight in the base of her stomach followed by an early-morning bout of diarrhoea. Perhaps the shit-scaredness was part of the pull; the nausea before she went on stage was soon followed by an adrenal high as she came off. Then there were those precious moments when she made the audience laugh. Nights when they gave her something back that she could use. Serve, volley, smash. Those were the best times, when she relaxed and enjoyed herself. They made up for the hours of working on her script, learning her lines, the phone calls persuading yet another friend to come along as her 'bringer', the long tube rides to West London pubs. Not wanting to be recognised by anyone to do with work, she called it not pissing on her own doorstep, she spent hours travelling to the far western reaches of the Piccadilly and Central lines. Those rare occasions when she felt she was flying were some compensation for the bored, drunk and heckling crowds, the gig to two people on their phones, the standing in front of a motley collection of empty chairs as the meagre audience used her slot to go to the bar. Or perhaps a full crowd, raucously voluble, waiting for their mate to come on, willing her to finish, not quiet in their impatience.

She had developed a taste for being on stage in college, performing in late-night comedy reviews. Once she had left, she continued a bit of Am Dram but was put off by the tedious narcissism of her fellow actors. But, by then she was addicted, hooked on the combination of terror beforehand, followed by exhilaration once it was all over. She was always chasing that moment of flow, those few sweet minutes when she felt physically lifted up by the attention in the room.

Jessica knew that it worked best if she relaxed and was herself. It was the same with social work; breakthroughs happened when she was being natural, one human to another, rather than talking at desperate people in a social-work-voice. There were plenty of scary situations; the mentally-ill mother gripping her new baby too tightly, the drunk and angry father following her into the lift. They were not the worst scenarios, although they were anxiety-provoking enough. For Jessica the hardest times were those when she felt helpless in the face of tragedy. The middle-class adopters explaining why they no longer wanted to look after four-year old Sam. How he didn't want to be rescued and fixed by them after all. How he was simply too difficult. And then her explaining to Sam that he would be moving yet again and that these people wouldn't be his 'forever family' after all. That was a bad time, like when the baby died, but she preferred not to think about that.

As she sifted through the statistics and watched the leaves fall, Jessica told herself that fear was no stranger but rather it was a familiar acquaintance. She knew that when the time came she would feel scared but she would do it anyway. She would jump into the darkness and fall into the embrace of total nothingness, grateful that it was all over.

2

As I boarded the train heading south to Hippo Island I felt excitement tinged with apprehension. I had been given a task to accomplish on behalf of Nathaniel and Felicity. I was a secret agent, journeying behind enemy lines, with an important job ahead of me. All I had to do was to access the Memory, make some notes, and get back to the East Civic Centre. And then there was Fola; Nathaniel had said that he would get her out of the Oubliette once things had died down, so she would be alright. Maybe Internal Security would let me see her so that I could reassure her that she had not been forgotten.

I had managed to call Grace from Medulla Central.

'And what about Fola?' she asked after I had explained my mission to Amygdala Fort. 'Alfred's taken it very badly. He says she won't survive the Oubliette.'

'Tell Alfred it will be okay,' I said. 'Nathaniel says that he will get her released, once the Emergency is over.'

My positive feelings began to dissipate during the journey. It was still only late morning but outside it seemed more like twilight, the sun muffled by low cloud. The rolling stock was old; the velvety fabric on the seats worn and frayed and several light bulbs were missing from the coach-style lanterns. Someone had scratched 'Help Me' on the wooden panelling by my right elbow; too late now, my friend. The carriage swayed from side to side, juddering over the points. It was almost empty save for a couple of thick-set men in dark overcoats, sitting in the far corner and talking earnestly in low voices.

Nathaniel's instructions were that I should get off at Fornix Junction. There were no announcements so I peered through the dirty windows whenever we slowed down; alert for any sign of a station. The area was semi-industrial; mostly lines of flat-roofed low-rise buildings connected by a network of overhead cable cars. The train came to a wheezing halt and *Fornix Junction – alight here for Hippo Island* came into view. The two men at the end of my carriage stood up, one of them glanced in my direction and said something to his companion who sniggered. I held back for a moment, allowing them to get in in front of me, before making my way down the platform towards the large sign saying *Causeway for Hippo Island.*

Hippo Island is not technically an island at all but rather a rocky outcrop surrounded by marshland. *Beware of the marsh,* Nathaniel had said. *There are areas of quicksand which can swallow you whole.* Then he had laughed one of his deep belly laughs.

The Fort takes up about a third of the area of the island and appears to grow out of the granite rock. This is no medieval-style castle with gothic arches and crenellations; Amygdala Fort is a purely functional structure. Its smooth thick walls with four rows of tiny windows have a clearly defined purpose; to keep what's inside in, and what's outside, out.

The causeway is about 300 meters long and two meters wide. At the Fornix end is a security post. The female Whiteshirt guard laughed and joked with the two burly men and I was in danger of catching up with them. Eventually they walked on and it was my turn. She took Nathaniel's letter and my ID and went inside her hut to make a phone call. I could see her reading parts of the letter down the phone. What would happen, I wondered, if I was turned back at this point? I realised that my foremost feeling would be one of relief. Eventually she came off the phone and gave me back my papers.

'Okay,' was all she said.

By now the two men were far ahead of me and I felt alone and exposed as I walked along the causeway. At three points along the track were tall metal pylons supporting the cable system linking the island to the mainland. Rather like a ski lift, there were two lines of parallel cables running between the pylons. However instead of chairs the cables had boxes suspended every few meters. One cable was taking boxes to the island while the other was bringing them back towards Fornix. The wires emitted a low buzzing sound with a clattering noise whenever the cable reached one of the pylons. The boxes were the size of small coffins and I wondered whether the ones leaving the island contained dead bodies.

As I approached the end of the causeway, it became clearer that Hippo Island was made up of two distinct lumps of rock, both supporting a large building. Amygdala Fort was to the left and Hippo Campus to the right. Hippo Campus was on lower ground than the fort but it was dominated by a tall office building of steel and glass. The cable system which hung over the causeway entered one of the sides of the tall offices, about two thirds of the way up. Coming out of the other side of the building were pair of cables linking up to the Fort and I could see another line of boxes being ferried back and forth connecting the two halves of Hippo Island.

At the end of the causeway were two signs. The smaller of the two, on the right, directed people across a footbridge to Hippo Campus; described on the sign as *The Brain's Premier Location for Processing and Storing Memories*. The sign on the left, which appeared to have been freshly painted, declared *Amygdala Fort, Operational Headquarters of the Internal Security Services, Authorised Personnel Only*. Beneath that was a paragraph in smaller print explaining that I was about to enter a restricted area and any unlawful trespassing or violation of ISS rules would be met *with the severest penalties*.

For a moment I hesitated. I didn't have to do this. I could easily just turn around and go back to Soul. But Fola was here and there was a chance that I could get a message to her; let her know that Nathaniel would get her out. I turned left and reluctantly climbed the steep stone steps which led up to the fort.

3

I felt calmer once I reached the main reception area. There were no armed Whiteshirts or any other sign that the place housed a prison in the bowels of the building. It was all easy chairs and low tables with magazines. The receptionist immediately directed me to the Memory Archives on the first floor.

'Yes?' The woman behind the desk had a badge: *Yolanda: Deputy Chief Librarian,* she looked bored.

'I'm here to research a Memory.'

'Authorisation?' I handed her Nathaniel's letter. 'Head of East Side… eh? Impressive. Booth number four.'

The Memory Archives had no mahogany writing desks or leather-bound volumes round its walls. It was a bland grey room with about twenty individual booths, each one screened from its neighbour and containing a computer, monitor and a pair of headphones. I was the only one in the room save for Yolanda. I found the on switch to the computer and waited while the machine woke up.

'Let me know if you need assistance,' said Yolanda.

'It's asking me for a password.'

Yolanda sighed and came and stood behind me.

'Today's password is 'let sleeping dogs lie' all lower case and no spaces.'

'Can I have my letter back please? I need to check what I'm asking for.'

'It says *Jessica being hit by another human, anytime from birth to the present day.*'

I stared at the menu page on the screen. It was hard to know where to start.

'Get out of the way,' said Yolanda abruptly, 'it's really very straightforward.'

I stood behind her and watched as her fingers skimmed the keyboard.

'First of all, you have to choose the class of Memory… In your case it is *Action* and the type is *Hitting*. Next is active or passive… you want being done to Jessica so that's *Passive*. Time period is *0 to present*. Press *Search* and hey presto… 163 results.'

Yolanda returned to her desk and I stared at the screen in amazement. Jessica had been hit by another human 163 times. No wonder she was depressed. I got my notebook out of my backpack; it was clear that I was going to be some time.

The first memory was of Jessica being held upside down by her ankles and slapped on her bottom. In the corner of the screen it said *Approximate age = 10 seconds*. In the next one she was in a highchair and doing a lot of coughing which stopped after a thump on the back. Then there was a sequence of hand slaps which mostly followed Jessica doing something to the cat. By now I was up to number 14 and approximate age 2 years. I decided to try a few random Memories; number 100 was in the middle of a game of tag *(approximate age = 9 years)*, number 130 occurred when an over-enthusiastic friend tried to stop a bout of hiccups *(approximate age = 13 years)*. I scrolled down to the last memory of being hit; number 163 was another choking – this time popcorn in the cinema *(approximate age = 37 years)*.

I sat back in the chair. This was tedious and probably a FWOT. There seemed to be nothing sinister at all but it was going to take me the rest of the day to plough through the list. I went back to the reception desk where Yolanda was chatting amiably to a new arrival. I could hear bits of his side of the conversation.

'…dead as a doornail now. …footage from the station… yes, very likely to be classified… terrible business…nothing happening now…

this bloody song… keeps bugging me… know I've heard it before somewhere… thought I'd come down here and see my favourite girl…'

They both started giggling then stopped abruptly when they noticed me approaching.

'Go over to booth twelve, Pete,' Yolanda said to him, 'and choose the music recognition option.'

She looked at me and raised a bushy eyebrow.

'Can you help me filter some more? I've got too many hits.'

'I'll come over,' she said with an air of resignation, following me back to booth four.

'I was thinking *hit in anger*,' I said.

'No good, anger is too vague a term. Also the system will let you specify an emotion for Jessica but not for Other People.'

'Can I add *making Jessica unhappy*?'

'You can, though it won't be specific enough. What exactly are you trying to find?'

'I'm looking for Jessica being hit, probably on the head. And I mean really hit, hit so it hurts. And over the age of three.'

'Hmm. Out of my way.' Yolanda took over the keyboard. 'I don't know why you didn't say 'on her head' in the first place. That's easily sorted…' Once again, she began typing at speed. '… And *Search*, there you go; now you're down to sixty-two results.'

'You okay there, Pete?' she said with a different tone of voice completely. 'It's all set up for you… you just sing down the microphone.'

'This is still too many.' I complained. Yolanda sighed again – she did a good line in sighs but this one seemed a fraction more benevolent.

'Alright, let me see… you could add a 'followed by' and you'd need to make it very specific. How about *followed within one minute by tears from Jessica*?

'That sounds good!' I watched as she leant over me and worked her magic over the keys. 'Fourteen results – that's better. Thank you!'

'You're welcome,' she nearly smiled.

I was conscious of a sound coming from booth twelve:

'DOOby dooby, DOOby dooby – doo doo DOO. DOOby dooby, DOOby dooby – doo doo DOO. That should do it.'

The tune seemed vaguely familiar. Pete's computer gave an answering chirrup and then ...

Should auld acquaintance be forgot
And never brought to mind?
Should auld acquaintance be forgot
And the days of auld lang syne?

Pete sighed.

'Damn, that's not it. Not even close. This machine's rubbish, Yol.'

'It would help if you knew the words,' she said.

'Something about an aeroplane,' he said.

'The Heavenly Aeroplane?' I started singing:

'All you thirsty of every tribe
Get your tickets for an aeroplane ride;
Jesus our Saviour is coming to reign
And take you up to glory in His aeroplane.'

Pete swung round and stared at me:

'Yeah mate, that's it ...you're a star! Do you know the rest of it? Come over here and sing it into Yol's machine and we'll get the whole lot.'

My heart was thumping as I went over to his booth.

'You've been singing the verse bits, I'm not sure I know the words to the verses – just the chorus. Where did you hear it?' I willed my voice to sound neutral.

'I was telling Yolly. Some bint down in the Oubliette has been warbling away. It's been like the Marie Celeste in Unloading since the carry on at the station. All the boxes are coming through empty... Nothing worth sending up to Security at all. I was that bored, I thought I'd pop in here and say hello to Yolly-Dolly and trace the Aeroplane song. Go on, sing it down the microphone.'

I sung the chorus and Yolanda took control of his computer. After a few seconds there was a view on the monitor of a row of backs of heads *(approximate age = 11 years)*. In front of them was a dimly lit sea of faces, all smiling. Jessica was on stage with a load of other children singing the Heavenly Aeroplane.

'Aw, will you take a look at that?' said Pete. 'Sunday school d'you think?' he asked Yolanda.

'Primary school – end of term concert, by the look of it,' she said. I watched Pete play the Memory a couple of times. It made a change from Jessica being thumped.

'So…' I said nonchalantly, 'this woman you heard in the Oubliette… did you see her?'

'No, I didn't see her. I heard her though, through the ventilation shaft. There's a grill in Unloading and the sound travels up from down below. You mostly wouldn't want to hear those sounds… crying and suchlike. So a bit of song today made a welcome change. Hey Yol… How about you fix me up with some more songs from primary school?'

I went back to my booth. Fola was definitely here! Somewhere beneath me and still singing, so that was a good sign. Maybe, once I'd finished looking at the Memories I could find a way to see her. I found my pencil and opened up my notebook. All is needed to do was to take a record of these fourteen scenes and then find Fola.

4

The first of the fourteen showed a scene full of small children *(approximate age =3 years)*. It looked like Jessica was sitting on a tricycle when a large moon-faced boy came and stood too close to her.

'*Geroff!*'

'*No, shan't!*'

The moon-faced boy drew back his arm and whacked Jessica round the side of the head. I winced. There was then a wailing noise which must have come from Jessica. That was all. Results two and three were more of the moon-faced boy. The third time Jessica gave up her toy without a complaint but still got hit by the nursery terror. I was beginning to feel affronted by the injustice. Where was the adult in charge of all this? Could this be what was marking Jessica for life?

I hit the fourth result and an error message appeared: *Access Denied: see Administrator.* I tried 5, 6, and 7 and then all the others up to 14 and the same message appeared on all but two of them and those were more childhood scuffles. Now what, surely there was a fault with the system?

'Sorry to keep pestering you…' I needed to keep Yolanda on side. 'Now it won't let me have access to all the results.'

She frowned and came over to look at my screen.

'Ah,' she said.

'What can you do?'

'Nothing.'

'Nothing at all? But I've come all this way and now I can't see what I need.'

'I'd say it's a case of very bad timing,' she said. 'If you'd come yesterday, or even early this morning you would have had access. Now there's nothing I can do.' Then, seeing my look of incomprehension she went on.

'I had a memo this morning. I've got it somewhere here on my desk. Here it is, it says top security material needs authorisation from the heads of both East and West Sides before access is granted. You've got Nathaniel's say-so; now you need to pop back up to Dominion House and get Marcia's.'

'I don't understand, does it say why?'

'It says that in view of the current code red emergency any material deemed dangerous can only be accessed in special circumstances. There's a list of what it includes…' her voice took on a sing-song quality as she read from the list. 'General Knowledge: nothing related to methods of suicide; Music Library: no Leonard Cohen or Portishead. For us in Memory Archives it is any memory that involves any mention of suicide or that scores 8 or over on the Emotional Pain Scale.'

'So now what?' I said. 'Don't tell me I've come all the way down here for nothing.' I gave her a look that Grace calls my 'hangdog expression.' It usually works, and I could also tell that Yolanda was the sort of person who didn't like to be defeated. She screwed up her eyes.

'You won't be able to see the actual part where Jessica is hit,' she said, 'or the part straight afterwards as that will score too high on Emotion. But you should be able to see what happened immediately before. That'd tell you something.'

She came back to my computer and stood over me.

'Go back to one of the results where access is denied. You see those back and forward arrows? Press the back arrow, put *five minutes* and press *enter.*'

I chose number 10 and did what Yolanda said. There was a pause and then the sound of shouting erupted from the screen. Jessica's mother was pulling books out of the bookcase and throwing them on to the floor. Jessica (*approximate age =13 years*) was sitting on the sofa watching her. Mum's voice was strange, slurred and indistinct, and it was difficult, at first, to make out what she was saying:

'Ge' rid of these…. They're all so fucking boring… don' just sit there… help me ge' rid of them.'

This went on for some time; then she lurched round the room and stood over Jessica swaying slightly, bringing her face right up close.

'And you can fuck-off as well.'

'You're drunk mum, let me ring dad.'

Then the screen went blank.

They were all similar. Mum slurring her words and being incapable. Jessica just there, in the way, a useful punching bag for a drunk woman's anger and vindictiveness. Number 14 was when Jessica was 28. This was an outdoor scene in a supermarket car park. Mum was wandering around the place, leaning up against cars and swearing at passers-by. Jessica then had her mother by the arm and was trying to frogmarch her towards her car.

'Come on now, I'm taking you home.' Then more swearing and shouting and again, the screen going blank. I sat back in the chair. From booth twelve came the sound of children singing:

Swing low, sweet chariot,
Coming for to carry me home;
Swing low, sweet chariot,
Coming for to carry me home.

There was only one left that I hadn't yet viewed; it was the very first one. The results that I'd seen so far spanned Jessica from the age of six to adulthood and they were mostly clustered round her teenage years. They were in chronological order so this one was going to be Jessica aged six or under. I didn't want to look at it but I'd been given a job to do so I felt that I should see it through to the end.

Unlike the others all was calm at the start of the scene. Jessica (*approximate age = 5 years*) was placing two bottles on the kitchen table. She then carefully, and with a lot of effort, unscrewed the tops of both bottles. She dragged one of the kitchen chairs over towards the sink, placed one of the bottles on the draining board, climbed onto the chair and poured the contents down the sink. She repeated the procedure for the second bottle and watched the colourless liquid swirl in a vortex and finally disappear down the plughole. She turned as she heard her mother approaching:

'You fucking little bitch….'

The screen went dead.

I sat for a few minutes staring at the blank screen. I longed to be back in Soul, I needed someone to talk to. Fola was the best to talk things over with; she would just sit there and let one burble on and then she'd always say something that helped. I blew my nose hard and made some notes on the eight scenes that I had been denied access to. I was grateful to Yolanda; I had everything I needed to take back to Nathaniel and Felicity.

Pete had finished his survey of children's singing and was now back up at the desk talking with his favourite girl.

'You off then now, mate?' he said after I had thanked Yolanda for her help. 'Thank you for helping me find that Aeroplane song…. *All you thirsty of every tribe… get your tickets for an aeroplane ride…* I just love that song!'

I decided to take a chance:

'You busy, Pete?'

'Naw…' he glanced up at the Real Time Monitor behind Yolanda's desk 'She's working on that poxy report… there won't be any Memories coming through for a while.'

'I was wondering…. I've not been down here before… would you mind showing me where you work.'

'What, Unloading? Not much to look at but I'd be happy to show you round, follow me.'

After Pete had said his lengthy good-byes to Yolanda we headed down the corridor and through a door marked *Long-Term Memories – Unloading Bay*. A blast of cool air met us as we entered the room and it was soon clear why; a large part of the external wall on the far side was missing so the room was open to the elements. Above us was the whirring and clanking of the mechanism as a rotating wheel pulled a cable which stretched from the middle of the tall building in Hippo Campus to the room we were now in. Every few seconds the cable delivered a suspended box onto line of rollers at waist height and the mechanism uncoupled the box from its vertical arm. There was a branchlike set of rollers, rather like a railway siding, where a box could be pulled over and inspected. Pete wasn't bothering to give any of the boxes a second glance so they just moved in a slow procession along the rollers, shunted along by the new arrival. The track formed a large U and over on the other side I could see another inspection 'siding' at the point where the boxes queued to be launched once more out into the void and back to the Hippo Campus.

'How much do you know about how Jessica's memories are stored?'

'Not a lot,' I replied.

'Okay, stuff for storage comes across the causeway and straight into that big building in the Hippo Campus over there. They do quite a bit of filtering... cos a lot of the stuff that gets sent down is rubbish and needs to be chucked. They're pretty good over at HC. They know what needs to go straight into storage and they'll ship it straight back over to Fornix. HC keep all the smells over there.'

'Smells?'

'Yep, they don't travel well, so it's easier if HC files and logs them. Smells are always stored... don't asked me why.'

'I didn't know that.' I felt that it was a good idea to keep sounding interested.

'Did you know that you can do a search on smells? Yolanda has a special booth where you can bring in a sample and the computer will match it against what's stored over in HC, clever eh?'

'Very.'

'Come and take a look at these...' He took me over to track of rollers and pulled out one of the boxes onto the inspection table. 'Nothing in them, zilch, they're all coming over empty just now. Pity really... I'd like you to see it in action.'

Before I could stop him he'd picked up the phone.

'Hi Jasmine, my lovely, have you got anything for us over there? I've got a mate here and I want to show him how it all works.' He went over to the open space and waved. Opposite, less than a hundred yards away, I could just see a woman standing in the opening where the cables entered her building, waving in return. She looked familiar. I had grown up with a Jasmine in the Cerebellum and wondered if Pete's buddy was my childhood friend. There was a pause while he listened:

'You've got *Jessica feeling mild annoyance at the Looked After Children Team*. That'll do… It's not for us and I'll send it straight back but it will show him how it works. Number 89? Okay sugar-plum… send it over.' He put the phone down and turned to me.

'Nothing legit has come through for us since the carry-on at the station. Jasmine always lets me know whether she is sending anything across… otherwise I'd have to look inside every bleeding box.'

'What about Jessica talking to Christopher-from-Finance? I saw that on the monitor this morning, didn't that come over as a Memory for storage?'

'Dunno about that one… probably went over to West Side. Don't forget about Amygdala West… they mostly deal with the pleasant Memories. Whenever Jessica has a holiday booked one of us goes over there to lend a hand. That one probably went to them. We get the bad Memories … the ones that need to be kept securely – that's cos we've got Internal Security based here and we're inside the Fort. We've also got the main Memory Archive Computer of course. So everything that gets stored anywhere is logged onto our computer …'

I zoned out of Pete's monolog and looked round for where the grill to the ventilation shaft might be.

'Where did you hear that singing from?'

'Over there, mate, in the corner… not a squeak out of her now though …84 …85.' Pete was counting the numbers on the boxes as they came in.

I saw a metal grill a few inches above the floor and knelt down and listened. All was quiet.

'Here it is!' Pete grabbed box number 89 as it began its journey round the track. I went over and watched as he flipped open the flimsy plastic covering and took out a circular canister. 'Now, I read the label, they do the labeling somewhere up in Pre-Frontal City, and I see *mild annoyance* so I think this one's not for us. It goes straight back in the box to

Jasmine's lot in HC who will sort out where it goes next. Now, if it **was** one for us I'd send it up to Security on the third floor.'

'Thanks Pete, that's very interesting.' I went back to the grill. 'I'd like to hear the woman sing, do you think if I sing she'll sing back?'

'Well I'm not sure you really should...'

I put my face next to grill and sung as loudly as I could:

'All you thirsty of every tribe
Get your tickets for an aeroplane ride.'

Nothing happened for about ten seconds then up came the sound, faintly at first and then much stronger by the second line:

Jesus our Saviour is coming to reign
And take you up to glory in His aeroplane'.

I felt a surge of relief, she sounded okay. I tried a different song, in a similar vein:

'Keep your hand on the plough, hold on
Keep your hand on the plough, hold on
Hold on, hold on
Keep your hand on the plough, hold on.'

In return came:

'Nobody knows the trouble I've seen
Nobody knows but Jesus
Nobody knows the trouble I've seen
Glory, Hallelujah.'

That wasn't at all reassuring. I racked my brains for another song which would offer Fola some hope, but my repertoire of spirituals had run dry. Fola knew dozens and she would often regale us with then. I wished I'd listened more.

'Look mate,' said Pete, 'you shouldn't be doing this; you'll get me into trouble.'

'Okay, just one more:

Hold on, hold on
Keep your hand on the plough, hold on.'

I got up and shook hands with Pete who was, by now, looking at me rather warily.

'Thanks for showing me round,' I said, 'and for letting me hear the lady sing.'

'You shouldn't have encouraged her,' he said gruffly. 'If they make too much noise the Whiteshirts move them further underground and wall them in.'

'That's terrible!' I felt a chill of fear. 'How do they eat and drink?'

'They lower food down in a lift, if they remember, that's why they call it the Oubliette.'

I made my way back along the causeway towards Fornix. The wind had strengthened so I put on the hood of my anorak and pulled the zip right up. Overhead the boxes of Memories processed back and forth, swaying slightly in the wind. I kept replaying the last scene that I had viewed; the liquid being sucked down the plug-hole, five-year-old Jessica turning as she sees her mother approach, the look on her mother's face.

And then there was Fola. I had let her down; I should have insisted that Nathaniel get her out immediately. God knows what was going to happen to her. I had told her to 'hold on' as if she was going to be rescued and I had given her false hope. By now I was most of the way across. The plough song was in my head; I'd remembered one of the verses:

If you wanna get to Heaven, let me tell you how
Just keep your hand on the gospel plough.

I stopped dead, my mind racing. If you wanna get to Heaven, let me tell you how.

The Whiteshirt at the security post was just few yards up ahead, watching me approach.

'I've forgotten something!' I shouted. I turned on my heel and walked back towards the island. It was a dangerous, stupid, mad idea. But it might just work. If it didn't, I could be joining Fola in the Oubliette.

5

Jessica's phone rang.

'Yes?' She was supposed to announce herself and her department to the caller, but mostly she couldn't be bothered. It was Lyn, Phillipa Markham's secretary.

'You free? She wants to see you.'

'What, now?'

'She's got a window at 1:30, that okay?'

'Guess so.'

'Good, she says bring the draft report with you.'

Jessica was not surprised. Philippa Markham, as Director of Children's Services, was responsible for all the children's social workers across the borough. Of all the senior managers, Philippa had the keenest interest in the Performance Report: her career depended upon it. It wasn't just the matter of Performance-Related-Pay, although the addition to her already substantial salary was not to be sniffed at. It was a question of personal pride. She had promised that she would turn the department around, that she would steer the service out of the maelstrom of 'Pretty Bad,' through the choppy waters of 'Not Good Enough' and eventually into the calmer seas of 'Quite Reasonable, all Things Considered'. She even harboured a secret hope for a 'First Rate' but knew that she shouldn't get ahead of herself.

Jessica understood that it was crucial for Phillipa that the data showed continuous improvement on all the Government's indicators. She was also aware of the fierce rivalry between Philippa and the head PIMP, Darren, her boss. Darren behaved towards Philippa as if he had a hot-line to the central government inspectors and that a decent performance rating was in his gift. Philippa treated Darren as if he were a little bit thick. On sunnier days Jessica derived some amusement from the antics of the two managers but lately she had simply found it exhausting.

Unbeknownst to Darren, Jessica had emailed the unfinished draft to Phillipa, at her request, the previous afternoon. She had been expecting the summons to Philippa's office and was not looking forward to a prolonged discussion on the statistics. She would tell Philippa that the data was accurate and that there was nothing that she could do about it. She idly mused how Philippa would feel when she heard the news of her death; would she feel guilty when she learned that Jessica had jumped in front of a train? Would she care at all? Jessica let the thought mull around her brain for a while, then she shrugged. Darren and Philippa and the whole crew of other managers would shake their heads and say that they 'had no idea'. They would be shocked and unsettled, confused even. Then the real world would impinge and the necessity of carrying on as before would take over. The waters would close over and no-one would give her a second thought.

6

'My name is Colin and I'm here to see the Head of Internal Security.' I was breathless from the climb back up the Fort's steps but I tried to make my voice sound firm and authoritative.

'Is he expecting you?' The receptionist gave no indication that she recognised me from earlier on. I took this as a hopeful sign.

'He's not exactly expecting me… but he will want to see me.'

'You don't have an appointment? Major Grendon won't see anyone without an appointment.'

'It's very important. Can you get a message to him that I'm here from Soul? It's to his advantage that he sees me.'

She looked doubtful.

'Go and wait over there.'

I went over towards the stone fireplace and a group of low chairs clustered round a coffee table.

'… from Soul…No, no appointment… that's what I said…He says it's to the Major's advantage…don't know…Okay, bye.'

I was the only one waiting in Reception. The Real Time Monitor in the corner showed that Jessica was still reading her report in between bouts of looking out of the window. I tried rehearsing in my mind what I was going to say but I couldn't concentrate. I had a sense of being watched and noticed that above the RTM was a bunch of cameras; one was trained in my direction.

Around the marble fireside was all the paraphernalia for a real fire: tongs, poker and even some wooden and leather bellows. It seemed rather pointless as all that was in the grate was an arrangement of dusty plastic flowers.

On the low table in front of me were a pile of glossy-looking reports; I flicked through one of them. The front page said: *Internal Security Service Annual Report 2017 – Keeping Jessica Safe from Emotional Pain.* The chapters were headed: *Key Objectives, Technical Achievements, Our Links with our Business Partners* and *The Way Forward.* At the back was an appendix showing some fancy graphs and pie-charts in bright colours.

The 'Business Partners' turned out to be West Side (*some excellent joint working*) and East Side (*room for improvement in the year ahead*). The other partners were the scientists – Julia from the Hypothalamus and the Professor from the Thalamus. No mention of Soul, of course, not that we would want to be one of ISS's business pals. I turned to the section on *The Way Ahead;* one of the aims over the next three years was to *Strengthen the influence of the ISS in all areas of decision-making.* Beneath that was a paragraph headed *Intimate Relations; intimate relations – particularly those with the opposite sex - are known to have caused Jessica emotional pain in the past. The ISS continues to promote a policy of cool detachment and non-engagement with all aspects of romantic liaison. The moratorium on dating is to be continued for the foreseeable future.* There then followed a list of 'forbidden activities' which included going clubbing, reading lonely hearts columns and joining dating websites. I felt the urge to scrawl *'No pain - No gain'* over the cover of the report, and indeed I might have done, had I not heard the sound of footsteps echoing on the parquet flooring. A tall man wearing a dark grey suit stood over me.

'The Major will see you now... follow me.'

7

He led me up three flights of stairs. The parquet floor had given way to a dark red carpet and we made no sound as we padded along the wood-panelled corridor.

'Go in,' he said.

The Major was standing and speaking on the phone, he turned to look at me as I entered and continued his conversation.

'... no... absolutely not... of course... I'm glad that's clear...'

I stood in the centre of the room, wondering what to do. I had expected a large man, an ex-army type with a straight back and a chest full of medals. This man was of medium height – only a bit taller than me – and thin. His hair, of which he had quite a lot, bushy like some mad professor's, was dark with streaks of early grey. He looked like someone who should be wearing a lab coat; he was, in fact, dressed in various shades of brown.

The room's three small lattice windows didn't allow in much daylight so the main source of illumination was from the anglepoise lamp on the Major's desk. On one wall was a large bookcase of leather-bound tomes which didn't look quite real. The other walls were panelled in a dark wood and it seemed that the Major might melt into them and disappear altogether. At last he finished his conversation:

'Ah, Colin ... come and sit over here.'

He gestured to a seat by a window and came and stood quite close to me, perching on the edge of the desk and folding his arms.

'What can I do for you?'

I cleared my throat.

'I've come to negotiate the release of one of Soul's members, Fola; she was put in the Oubliette this morning.'

'I see, how very intriguing.' His voice was cultured with a musical timbre. 'I'm sure your colleague is there for a good reason...'

'She made a joke and Marcia took it the wrong way. She really isn't any kind of threat. She's not dangerous...'

'This is not the time for jokes. I expect her punishment was proportionate. You said negotiate, I find it hard to imagine what you in Soul might have which would be of any use to me. Some joss sticks perhaps? Or maybe some prayer books?'

'I'm offering you some insurance,' I said. I let that sink in. It was important not to hurry this.

'Insurance?'

'We are in a code red emergency. Risk of death. Jessica could die. She nearly jumped in front of that train this morning. If she dies, you and everyone else in ISS dies.'

'I'm told the risk is currently about thirty per cent,' he said, 'and it will probably reduce further through the day as the chemical treatment kicks in.'

'That's not certain though is it? And it may even make Jessica feel worse.'

He shrugged.

'I'm sure everyone is pulling together to find a solution, we're doing what we can over here.'

I wanted to tell him that his Internal Security Services had a lot to answer for; the determination to keep all negative memories hidden away, the moratorium on relationships. He stared down at me with tired pale-grey eyes.

'You still haven't explained why you're here.'

'If the worst happens – if Jessica kills herself today – I may be able to offer you a way out.'

'A way out?'

'My colleague Alfred is an Old One. He spends a lot of time in meditation and prayer.' I tried to sound matter-of-fact, as if I was providing him with information for his next annual report. I was also being careful not to say anything which I knew to be false. Fola says that if the people who work in Soul are not truthful then we may as well all pack up and go home. 'It is generally believed that the Soul lives on after a human's death. I'm offering you an opportunity to join us... in return for releasing Fola.'

At first he had no idea what I was talking about but then the penny dropped and he gave a short, and not entirely genuine, laugh.

'And how exactly is that going to happen? Are you all going to close your eyes and hold hands and then find yourselves welcomed by St Peter outside the pearly gates?'

'I don't know what will happen. But you have to agree it is part of Jessica's ... er...cultural heritage. You remember... "*Now I lay me down to sleep, I pray the Lord my soul to keep, If I should die before I wake, I pray the Lord my soul to take.*" I felt that this wasn't the best poetic example that I could come up with and tried to think of something rather more profound.

'Jessica doesn't believe in life after death. It isn't one of the Certainties.'

There is a department deep in the Cerebellum that is the depository for Certainties. There are also outposts in both East and West Side; however, judging from that morning's meeting, Marcia was getting rid of the representative in Dominion House. We both knew that the list of Certainties has diminished over recent years. Rather than statements of political ideology or religious belief the list was now largely made up of superficial opinions like: *Tea is better than coffee first thing in the morning* and *Puffed sleeves are wrong for anyone over twelve years old.* I blame 'Looking Good in Front of Other People'. The influence of that team is so far-reaching that Jessica modifies her opinions depending on her audience. Jessica talking to her dying grandmother about life after death was very different to a discussion with some friends in the pub. I could have said all this to the Major, I could have pointed out that beliefs are complicated and that anyway, just because it wasn't a Certainty didn't mean that it might not actually happen.

'What's more to the point, I don't believe **you**, Colin. I know that you were in our Archives earlier on today. I know you tried to access some restricted memories and that you were denied access. You then went up to the Unloading Bay and made contact with the prisoner Fola by shouting down the ventilation shaft. I know that you were on your way back to Fornix along the Causeway when you turned round and decided to try out your preposterous proposal on me.'

He sighed and looked at me sadly, like a headmaster who was 'disappointed' by an unruly piece of behaviour from one of the year tens. 'I should probably send you down to the Oubliette to join your friend.'

I felt bile rising up from my stomach. Everything was slipping away, but I had one last card to play.

'I'll go back to Marcia then,' I said, 'and make the same offer to her. Marcia wanted to come in with us... in the event of Jessica's death. She came to Fola and me after the Executive meeting this morning. She wanted to know about Alfred's arrangements in case Jessica dies. Fola didn't give her the guarantees that she wanted.'

I stood up.

'You're right of course,' I continued, 'it may be a load of rubbish... Sunday school nonsense, but what have you got to lose? It's no skin off your nose if you let Fola go. But if Jessica dies today, you die too. I'm offering you the possibility of an alternative.'

The Major got up and looked out of the window at the boxes of Memories continuing their slow procession high up above the Causeway.

'I want to know what will happen, surely you must have some idea?' I shook my head.

'You must have carried out rehearsals, drills or whatever?'

'No, Alfred doesn't talk to us about it... he's very ... secretive.'

'How do I know you'd keep your side of the bargain?'

'I'm a member of Soul, I always keep my word. If it looks like Jessica is really going to commit suicide then you'd make your way to our office in the Thymus and then, whatever happens to us, you would be with us.'

'Just today? What happens when she dies sometime in the future?'

'I don't have the authority to promise anything beyond today. Our deal is that Fola goes free and if Jessica dies today you can join us in Soul for whatever happens next.'

The pause that followed seemed to last for ever. Eventually he said:

'I am about to call an emergency meeting for all staff, that will include the prison guards. That meeting will last twenty minutes. The code for the Oubliette key box is written on the inside cover of my diary which is over there on my desk.'

He continued to look out of the window as I hurried over to the desk and flipped open his diary. I didn't trust myself to remember the four digit number so took out my notebook and carefully wrote 1478.

'Hurry up for God's sake!' he said. 'You will padlock the gates after you. The guards don't count prisoners so no-one should realise that she has got out.'

'How do we get back to Fornix?'

'That's up to you, but not across the Causeway. My Whiteshirts are vigilant and your friend won't have the right papers to leave the island. You will have to pick a path across the marsh. And before you go... I want something in writing. Take a piece of paper from the printer and write the following: *I, Colin agree that in the event of Jessica's death, this day 19th November 2018, Major Grendon, Head of Internal Security Services is authorised to accompany Soul operatives* ...um, how shall we put this?'

'How about *accompany Soul operatives if there is any experience of the afterlife?*' I suggested.

'No, too vague... put *accompany Soul operatives to heaven.*'

I felt this was rather presumptuous on his part and appeared to indicate not only a sudden conversion to religious belief but also a certainty as to where Jessica's Soul would be heading. I wondered what Alfred, Fola and Grace would say if the Major turned up in our office with this bizarre piece of paper in my handwriting.

'Now put your signature at the bottom... and today's date.' He took the paper and, folding it carefully, secreted it in his inside breast pocket. 'I'm not entirely sure why I'm doing this but, as you say, I have nothing to lose.'

He went over to the desk and switched on the small microphone:

`‘Message to all ISS personnel, this is the Major speaking. All Fort personnel are required to attend an emergency Code Red meeting in the old banqueting hall immediately.’` He turned to me: ‘I suggest that you wait here for a few minutes. The Oubliette is in the basement, the back stairs are at the end of the corridor. You understand that you are on your own…. If you are caught then I will deny our arrangement. You understand?’

I nodded. I was in a state of shock that my plan had taken hold but I could still see problems ahead.

‘I don’t know a safe way across the marsh,’ I said, ‘and won’t we be seen by the guards on the Causeway?’

‘You’d best hide up somewhere until darkness… and the marsh isn’t as treacherous as people make out, just be careful.’ He collected up some papers from his desk and went to the door. ‘Remember, if you’re caught, you’re on your own.’

8

I waited until the sounds of doors slamming and people trudging up and down the wooden floors died down. The cable system linking the Fort with the Hippo Campus building stopped and the Memory boxes dangled motionless between the two buildings. I made my way along the corridor and down the stairs. All was quiet as I hurried down, flight after flight, until I reached the bottom. Here the ceiling was lower, the floor was grey concrete and paint was peeling off the sludge-green walls.

I stood still; in front of me was a wide corridor with doors leading off either side. The Major could have given me more help. Where was I to go now?

'Keep your hand on the plough, hold on.'

I willed my beating heart to calm down as I strained my ears. It was definitely Fola singing; it seemed to be coming from the far end of the corridor. As I walked further along the sound got louder:

'Hold on, hold on
Keep your hand on the plough, hold on.'

'Fola! Fola!'

I ran to the last door and opened it. The room was lit by a lone electric light bulb and smelt musty. At first, I could only make out a large wooden table and three chairs in front of a kitchenette area with a sink, a kettle and a microwave. On the table were a couple of mugs, half a packet of biscuits and some old *Hiya* magazines.

Then I noticed the circular grill set into the concrete floor. The grill was made of heavy iron work and was about four foot in diameter. It was made in two semi-circular halves which were locked together with a padlock on a chain.

'Fola!'

I knelt and peered down the shaft. It was about fifteen feet deep and I could just make out the top of Fola's head in the gloom.

'Colin, my dear Colin!' Fola's voice sounded hoarse but unmistakably hers. 'I'm coming up!'

There was a perpendicular metal ladder set into the wall of the shaft which Fola began to climb up steadily. I got my notebook out of my backpack and looked round for the key box.

'I'm going to get you out!' I shouted. The key box was above the chipped work-surface next to the microwave, I lined up the numbers: 1 – 4 – 7 – 8, there was a click and the door of the key box sprang open revealing a set of keys.

'I've got the key,' I shouted.

I ran back to the grill and tried to open the padlock. The first key didn't work so I tried the next one. Then I fumbled with them and they slipped out of my hand, falling through the grill and landing with a clink on the stone floor below.

'Damn! Damn! Damn!' I shouted, 'Fola, the keys!'

'Don't worry, I'll get them.'

Fola climbed back down the shaft and then disappeared.

'What are you doing? Hurry up.'

Nothing. For God's sake where was she? I thought I heard movement overhead and I ran back into the corridor and listened. Everything was quiet. I realised I was sweating; this was taking too long, we were going to get caught.

'I'm coming back up, I've got them.'

Moments later I saw Fola's hand appear through the grill clutching the keys. This time I was slow and careful as I unlocked the padlock and removed the chain. The two halves of the grill were on hinges and I pulled them back and set them down with a clang.

Fola was slowly emerging from the shaft. But in front of her was something else:

'Help me, Colin,' she said, 'pull her up.'

I bent down and grabbed hold of a small child, pulling her clear of the entrance of the Oubliette. The Child and I looked at each other. She looked about six years of age, pale with lank mousy brown hair; she smelt of stale sweat and urine. Meanwhile Fola was heaving herself up and off the ladder. She took hold of me and hugged me close.

In retrospect, I am not proud of what I said next. In mitigation I was scared, frightened that the Whiteshirts would appear at any moment, fearful for my own safety as well as Fola's. But that's just an excuse, mainly it was because I had a plan which seemed to be falling apart before my eyes. Things were going out of control.

9

'No, Fola,' I said pushing her away, 'this is no good, this is no good at all. She can't come with us.'

'She has to. I'm not leaving her here.'

I felt overwhelmed with exasperation and began pacing the room.

'We've no time for this... we've got to go now. We can't take her with us, that's not the agreement I made.'

'What's the matter with you? Have you lost your mind? She's just a child and I'm not leaving without her.' Fola spoke quietly.

I wanted to scream but I locked up the Oubliette and returned the keys to the safe.

'For God's sake...' I muttered, looking at both of them. The Child had picked up a copy of *Hiya* and was studying it closely. 'Come on then, we've got to get going.'

I hurried them along the corridor and up the stairs; I tried to work out how long we had before the Major's meeting was over. Five minutes? or maybe seven at the outside, and then there would be people milling about, returning to their offices. At least Fola and the Child were keeping up with me; running up the steps hand in hand, the Child still holding the magazine in her small tight fist. I kept them moving up and up until we reached the first floor. Then along the corridor and into the Unloading Bay. Once inside I closed the door; no sign of Pete, the cable machinery was still shut down and all was silent.

'This is our best bet,' I said. 'It looks dangerous but we'll be alright. It's our only chance of leaving this place quickly.'

They both stared at me blankly.

'Don't understand,' said Fola, still panting from the run up the stairs. 'What... what are we doing in here?'

She went over to the large open space in the middle of the far wall. The Child followed her and lent out of the opening. For a moment my heart stood still as I visualised her plummeting over the edge.

'Keep hold of her, for God's sake. She'll fall out.'

Fola looked up at the cables that were strung between the room that we were in and the building opposite. The Memory boxes hung down from the cable at regular intervals, swaying slightly in the breeze.

'What is your plan? Tell me please.'

'There must be an on switch here somewhere,' I said looking around. 'Look, here it is, when I pull down this lever the cable gets going and takes the boxes out and over to that building there. That's in Hippo Campus. Then look, look over there...' I pointed over to the Causeway. 'Do you see those pylons and the cables and the boxes going to and fro? That system takes boxes from the Hippo Campus and over to Fornix. It works like a cable car...'

'I'm not getting into one of those boxes.'

'It's the only way. We're on an island, surrounded by marshland. We can't just swan down the Causeway; there is a security post at the end.'

'There must be another way ...'

'The marsh is dangerous... there's quicksand in places. And anyway, we'd easily be seen unless we waited till it's dark. Come over here, all you have to do is get into one of these.'

I took her over to where a line of boxes were queuing to be shunted out over the void. The Child followed us, staring at me mutely, eyes like saucers. I pulled one of the boxes across the rollers and onto the adjacent inspection table. It was grey metal, rather like one of those old-fashioned baths that people on the Outside World use as a tub for their fig trees, only squarer and possibly smaller. I flipped open the plastic cover.

'Get in.'

'No way!'

'I know it's scary … but it's our only chance. If we stay here we'll get caught.'

'I won't fit in. I'm too fat.'

It would be tight but there was no choice; she had to get in.

'Of course you will. Imagine you're getting into a small bath. Just lie on your back with your knees up.'

'How do I know it will take my weight?'

I looked across at the cables dangling from the gantries and a new anxiety flooded through me. Fola probably weighed the same as both The Child and I together. Could the system cope with carrying her bulk? Again, no choice.

'I'm sure it will be fine, it all looks very sturdy. Come on, we've got to hurry up.'

I tried to help Fola up onto the table but meanwhile The Child was holding tight to her skirt. Fola got back down again and turned the Child to face her:

'I'm not going to leave you; Colin will put you in the next box. I'll see you on the other side.'

The Child began sucking on a strand of her hair.

Fola levered herself back up onto the table and managed to wedge her large frame into the box. The Child stretched across and helped to tuck the plastic cover over Fola's knees. I felt a pang of guilt for my previous brusqueness.

'What's your name?' I asked.

The Child gave a slight shake of the head as she stood back and surveyed me with wide-eyed seriousness.

'Your turn next,' I said.

It took all my muscle power to shove Fola's box off the inspection table and back onto the roller track. I looked round for The Child who was nowhere to be seen. Oh God, I thought, now where's she gone? Then I realised she was watching me from the box behind Fola's; she must have climbed up onto the rollers and got in the box by herself. Mute maybe, but not dumb.

'Keep your head down,' I shouted, 'put the plastic cover over yourself and stay put until I say so.'

I ran to the lever and turned on the mechanism. There was a grinding noise and then the large cog above my head began spinning. The cable delivered a new box onto the rollers from outside and all the boxes began their steady procession around the U of the track accompanied by an incessant clattering noise. There were a couple of boxes to go before Fola's would be picked up by the vertical arm and swept out of the opening. My plan was to climb into the box immediately behind The Child's but then I noticed that the *Hiya* magazine was lying on the floor at the far side of the room.

'Oh God...oh God,' I muttered, undecided whether to go back and get it. I couldn't leave it; there could be no explanation for it lying there in the middle of the floor so I sped across and picked it up.

Racing back, I could see Fola's box nearing the front of the queue. The vertical arm dropped down and clamped both ends of her box and then she was swung off the track and into open space. I clambered onto the rollers and flung the magazine into the bottom of the nearest box, hurling myself in after it and banging my elbow hard in the process. There were now two boxes between me and the Child but hers was already being whisked off the track so I couldn't risk getting any nearer. I lay down on my side and brought my knees up to my chin. The air smelled stale and dusty as I pulled the plastic cover over me but for a brief moment I felt safe and strangely comforted. Then the box juddered as the metal arms clasped either end and I felt a sudden lurch as it accelerated off the rollers.

Once I was in the air all was quiet save from the hum of the overhead cable. I breathed out and took stock. So far so good, we'd managed to leave the Fort. I remembered Jasmine, working on the other side. If she was the same person that I remembered from the Cerebellum she would definitely be an ally. I risked peeking out from under the cover and felt a blast of cold fresh air in my face. Over to my right I could see the Causeway and across to Fornix where the rows of factories and warehouses were receding into the distance. Up ahead of me the cable to the Hippo Campus building was supported by four pylons and I could

111

see that Fola was already between the first and second. The Child was behaving – nothing untoward from her box. Fola's box looked strange and I prayed that no-one was looking up at us from below. There was a clearly defined lump where her knees protruded above the top. It also seemed to me that her box hung lower than those on either side; the cable was definitely sagging, pulled earthwards by Fola's weight. *Oh God, please let it hold.*

In the middle of the Hippo Campus building was a square opening and the cable rose steeply between the third and fourth pylons before dipping down to its destination. Fola's box was making that ascent up to the final pylon, *nearly there!* I could feel the whole system trembling in complaint at the enormity of the task being asked of it. We were slowing down. *Shit, shit, shit! Come on, come on!*

Then everything stopped.

10

Jessica switched off her computer, packed her papers into her briefcase and put on her coat. She was pleased that she had chosen to wear the black wool instead of her old blue jacket that morning. Looking reasonably smart would be an advantage at a meeting where her default position was to feel insecure and inadequate. Philippa Markham was known not to suffer fools, gladly or otherwise. Her domain was on the third floor of Millennium House, a five-minute walk from Jessica's office. Jessica felt the fresh air would do her good and help her prepare for the meeting. She knew that Phillipa needed the performance of Children's Services to improve and she would not be happy with some of the data that Jessica had collected.

Why am I even going? she asked herself as she made her way down the stairs. None of this matters anymore, by the end of today it will all be over. It was as if she was on auto-pilot; finishing off the report, going to meetings and behaving to the world as though all was normal. Just get through today, she told herself, and then you can sleep for ever.

As she reached the bottom of the stairs everything went dark for a few seconds as a wave of dizziness flooded through her. She grabbed the banister and steadied herself, waiting for the reeling to subside and pressing her forehead against the cool metal. She remembered that she hadn't eaten anything since getting up that morning and wondered about buying a sandwich on route to Millennium House. She didn't feel hungry; in fact, she felt nauseous. But it would make sense to pick something up from the corner shop and she was in good time.

11

My box had come to a halt right next to the second pylon where it swayed gently over the rocks below. The only sounds were the breeze whistling through the gantry overhead and an ominous creaking from up ahead.

My heart was hammering.

If the cable snapped then we would all plunge to our deaths; the boxes would slide down onto the rocks and we would be smashed to smithereens. *Damn, damn, damn!* I wished that I had listened to Fola. She was right. The system wasn't built to carry her weight. It was a stupid idea which was going to get the three of us killed.

Start up again, please start up again!

The pylon was only about four feet away from me and for a brief moment I wondered whether I could make a lunge towards it and then climb down to the ground. No way would that work. I would probably fall to the rocks trying to fling myself out of the box. And anyway, what next? I wouldn't be able to get Fola out of her box and I couldn't just leave her hanging there.

Please God, please get it going!

The cable gave a shudder and the buzzing noise returned. We had started moving again. *Thank God!* Fola's box cleared the final pylon and a few seconds later it disappeared into the side of the building swiftly followed by the Child's. My box landed smoothly on to the rollers and then I felt a massive jolt as the next box cannoned into mine, propelling me forward so that my knees scraped against the metal side. The whirring of the machinery and the clattering of the boxes made it hard to think straight.

I peeked out from under the cover; the Hippo Campus building was light and airy after the gloom of the Fort. We had landed in one corner of a large open plan space that seemed to be a storage depot for memory boxes. I could see rows of shelving stretching up to the ceiling and over on the far side people going up and down the aisles ferrying boxes back and forth on luggage trolleys. There was Jasmine, I recognised her short, squat frame with her heavy dark plait hanging down her back. She was eyeing up the boxes as they shunted round the track. She had obviously noticed something strange about Fola's box and she leaned across and deftly took hold of it, dragging it onto the inspection table. There was no chance of us being undetected now and our only hope would be that she would be sympathetic to our plight. As I whipped off the plastic covering and clambered out of my box I could see Jasmine helping Fola out of hers.

'I'm going to be sick,' Fola said, and then, in a panic, 'the Child! The Child!'

The identical boxes were processing around the U of the track, queuing up to be launched back across to the Fort. Which one was she in? I ran along the line, flipping over the plastic covers.

All the boxes were empty. *Shit! That's my fault – telling her to stay put.* There was a grinding sound as the mechanism slowed to a halt.

Then I saw the Child's pale face looking out from the top of the box at the front of the queue. The vertical arm had already grabbed the sides of the container and lifted it off the end of the track. Her box was dangling over the edge of the building, suspended in space.

'Oh my God!' screamed Fola, running to the opening. 'Oh heavens, oh no!'

'Does it go in reverse?' I shouted to Jasmine.

'No, but no worries.'

I watched as she took off her leather belt. She looped it round the last roller on the track and held the ends in her left hand. She then leant her whole body out of the opening and stretched out her right arm up towards the Child.

'Come on,' said Jasmine gently, 'come to me.'

The Child looked down at the ground far below and shook her head.

'Come on, my dear,' said Fola, close to tears, 'just do as she says.'

The Child came to the edge of the box and put out her arms. In a blink of an eye Jasmine caught hold of her and deposited her safely on the ground. Immediately the Child ran to Fola, burying her head in Fola's capacious skirt. Fola stroked her head.

'You're okay now.'

'So Colin, long time no see, eh?' Jasmine gave me a thump on the back that propelled me forward a few steps.

'Any more?' she asked as she put her belt back on. Her muscled arms were covered in tattoos. A monochrome smorgasbord of snakes and skulls and writing I couldn't read. It was as if a graffiti artist had too much time on their hands.

'What?'

'Of you? Escape from Colditz, eh?' She grinned broadly, showing a flash of gold tooth. 'You're the first.'

'No, just the three of us.'

I suddenly felt exhausted and noticed I was shaking. I hugged Fola close for a few moments, the Child was still enveloped in her skirt.

'Oh … that was awful… when it stopped… I thought I would be stuck up there for ever.' Then she laughed, a hysterical laugh, but she was starting to look like the old Fola and the colour was returning to her cheeks.

'Thanks… thanks for saving the kid,' I said to Jasmine.

'Thought you were into poetry and contemplating your belly-button,' she said, folding her arms and looking at me intently. 'Didn't expect this kind of stunt from you.'

'Yeah well, it's a bit of a long story, it was the only way.' I was starting to feel a little bit puffed-up, like I really had just acted the hero.

'You were in the Oubliette?'

'No, these two were,' I nodded to Fola and the Child.

'We hear bad things … it's good they escaped. No-one's ever hitched a ride in my boxes before.' She grinned again and looked at Fola. 'I knew him when he was still in short trousers, but who are you?'

Fola went over to Jasmine and took her hand in both of hers.

'My name is Fola. I work with Colin in Soul.'

'And this?' She nodded towards the Child who had now left Fola's side and was wandering round touching things she shouldn't.

'She was in the Oubliette, she doesn't speak, I don't know her name.'

'Just a little child, that's terrible,' said Jasmine. 'There's some bad people over there.'

We all watched the Child who had now begun building a tower out of the metal memory canisters.

That reminded me:

'The magazine… I left a copy of *Hiya* inside my box.'

Jasmine shrugged.

'No worries.'

I liked Jasmine's laid-back attitude, I felt safe, but we needed to keep moving.

'We need to get across… back to Fornix. Can you help us?' I asked.

'Why not,' she grinned again. 'I don't much care for them over there. No-one here does.'

The phone on the wall began ringing:

'Talk of the devil..' she said, and then, down the phone: 'Pete? … I know … keeps stopping and starting … I'm switching it back on now … okay… Oh and Pete… I've put a *Hiya* in for you… no sorry, can't remember the box number…bye.' She returned the receiver to its holder.

'Idiot,' she said, switching the mechanism back on.

The familiar racket started up again and I took in some more of our surroundings. At strategic points throughout the room were lifts like dumb waiters which carried the boxes up and down between floors and over on the far right-hand side there was another cable system transporting boxes in and out of that side of the building. I guessed this was going to be our route off Hippo Island and wasn't sure how I was going to break it to Fola. Jasmine beat me to it.

'So across to Fornix eh? Get ready for another overhead trip.'

'What do you mean?' said Fola looking worried.

'If you want to get off Hippo Island fast you'll have to hitch a ride in another box,' said Jasmine bluntly.

'I'd think I'd prefer just to stay here for a while,' said Fola, 'just for a bit longer.'

I felt the same, but I needed to get back to Nathaniel and Felicity; let them know what I'd found out in the Archives. But did I dare risk Fola and the Child in more boxes?

'We must go,' I said. 'Is it safe enough, Jasmine? Will it hold our weight?'

'He means my weight,' said Fola.

'They're a bit bigger, the boxes that go across to Fornix, they're stronger, more memories, see? You'll be okay.'

The intercom crackled into life.

'Calling Spatial Memory Team. Millennium House Floor Plans to Uploading Bay. This is your Five-minute warning.'

'Ah... this could be your chance,' said Jasmine. 'Follow me.'

12

I was nervous about the next leg of our journey but I trusted my old friend with her broad shoulders and her heavy-metal tattoos. We attracted a few stares as we processed down one of the wider aisles, stopping at a glass booth set high up on stilts in the middle of the floor. I could see a man wearing headphones seated in front of a microphone rather like a commentator at a football match on the Outside World.

'Stay there,' said Jasmine as she bounded up the steps of the booth and knocked on the door. I watched the conversation between Jasmine and the man who now had his headphones round his neck. Jasmine was doing all the talking and occasionally he would glance on our direction and nod.

Fola was wheeling the Child round on one of the luggage trolleys while I focussed on the large RTM positioned next to the glass booth. Jessica appeared to be standing in the street eating a sandwich. Or at least, she was poking about in the sandwich, picking out and eating the pieces of cheese and tomato and avoiding the bread. How was that allowed to happen? I wondered. Surely the folk in Hypothalamus could make sure that Jessica was eating properly. Today of all days.

Jasmine's exchange ended with the man shrugging and them both smiling. He went back to his microphone:

'Millennium House floor plans to Uploading Bay — two minutes to departure.'

'Okay, quick-as-you-like.' Jasmine strode over to cable system on the right-side wall with the three of us in her wake. 'Here we go....'

There were three memory boxes lined up on the inspection table next to the rollers waiting to go. The first one was labelled *Ground and First Floor Millennium House.* Jasmine grabbed hold of the box and tipped the canisters of memories into an adjacent empty box on the floor. The contents of *Second and Third Floor Millennium House* and *Philippa Markham's Office* were also tipped into the same box.

'Right,' she said, 'here's what's happening... Jessica's got a meeting in Millennium House and she's on her way now. That means the Which Way? team will need these plans to get her to Ms M's office. This little lot will be fast-tracked all the way up to East Side. You just hop into those boxes and you'll be there in no time.'

I thought that we'd have a fight on our hands with Fola. But whether it was Jasmine's 'no-nonsense' attitude or the promise of being far away from Hippo Island I couldn't tell. All I knew was that I was very relieved when she helped the Child into the middle box and levered herself into the first one.

'East Side, you say?' Fola asked anxiously as Jasmine tucked her in, carefully adjusting the plastic cover over her knees.

'Right up to Pre-Frontal City – East Side; you'll know your way from there?'

I nodded and gave Jasmine a hug before climbing up into the third box.

'It's been good to see you,' I said, 'thanks a lot.'

She shrugged and gave her usual grin before adjusting the cover over me.

'Hold fast,' she said, and I felt her shove my box over onto the rollers.

This time our three boxes formed a convoy and soon we were out into the cold, fresh air, sailing high above the Causeway. The wind had got up and I could feel it tugging at the plastic cover and buffeting the side of my box. Jasmine was right about us being fast-tracked. Once we had cleared the Causeway we were channelled through some low sheds. There was a pause and some loud clicks and juddering as our boxes were pitched onto an open wagon. Now we were on some kind of underground railway system. We hurtled along in complete darkness for about twenty seconds; halfway along we passed another locomotive going in the opposite direction, hooting as it sped by. Then the train slowed down to a whine of brakes and smell of sulphur. My next sensation was of falling down a chute before our three boxes landed, in quick succession, onto the floor of the Which Way? Team's office.

13

I have often noticed that people who hold relatively minor, boring jobs are the ones who get most upset if their routine is disrupted in some way. The bloke on duty in Which Way? had a badge which said *Deputy Chief Navigational Officer*, as if Jessica was about to circumnavigate the globe, not simply find her way round an office block. He was not happy.

'What the hell?' he shouted as we shakily climbed out of the boxes. 'Where are my floor plans?'

I took this as a rhetorical question as we found a couple of office chairs and sat for a while to recover ourselves.

'We made it,' I said to Fola.

'Thank God,' she said drawing the Child close to sit on her lap. The three of us watched Mr Navigation pace up and down. Behind him was a bank of screens showing various shots of the street outside Millennium House. The RTM positioned over on one side showed Jessica was walking up and down a corridor inside the building.

'I won't be accountable for this,' he said as his phone rang. After several minutes of 'It's not my fault' and 'Beyond my control' he said, 'It's "Looking Good": they want to talk to you.'

Fola shook her head so I took the phone.

'Hello?' I said.

'Marjorie from "Looking Good,"' the woman announced with a considerable air of self-importance. 'Are you aware that you are the cause of Jessica being late to a Very Important Meeting ...'

And on she went. I watched as Fola smoothed down the Child's hair and spoke to her softly. The Child still didn't answer, but she looked like she was listening and was starting to look less pale and pinched. After a while I got bored with Marjorie's monologue and passed the phone back to Mr Navigation.

'Rested enough?' I asked Fola. 'Let's go.'

14

There was a sudden break in the cloud and a shaft of sunlight shone though the high window of the stair-well illuminating the grey lino floor. Jessica's watch said twenty-eight minutes past one. She had two minutes to get to her appointment. She had already been in the building for five minutes and had trudged along the lengthy second floor corridor. Now she was back on the first floor, staring at a notice-board which was trumpeting the benefits of joining the Union.

What the hell's wrong with me?

She had been in the Director's office half a dozen times and had never had trouble finding the office before. Now she simply could not remember the way.

I'm going mad.

At one end of the first floor was a large open plan office where the finance department was located. As it was lunchtime a number of the desks were empty. *Interesting that…. how they get a proper lunch break – not like social workers.* It pained her to do so, but she would have to ask someone. *They'll think I'm an idiot, and they'd be right.* She went up to the nearest occupied desk and coughed.

'Excuse me, could you tell me the way to Phillipa Markham's office?'

15

Nathaniel's office was quiet and peaceful. Josie Daydreaming had taken the Child away to get her cleaned up and Fola and I were seated next to each other on Nathaniel's large purple sofa. Fola had found a footrest, put her feet up and closed her eyes. She had lost her sky-blue turban somewhere along the way and her thick black curls seemed to relish their new-found freedom, forming an unruly afro which framed her face like a dark halo. I studied the pictures that covered the walls, focussing on the one of the woman reading a letter; I liked the way the light came in from the left and illuminated her blue smock. It felt calming. Nathaniel came in with two mugs of caffeine.

'Any news?' I asked, as he passed one to me.

'Not a lot happening.' He went over to his desk and peered at the RTM. 'Jessica's on her way to the meeting. We've been monitoring all Thoughts; looks like she's still planning on jumping.'

'What?' said Fola, opening her eyes, and I remembered that she had missed the whole business at the underground station. I told her what had happened.

'Good Lord...' said Fola. 'She wouldn't actually do it, would she? Take her own life?'

'Felt pretty close this morning,' said Nathaniel. 'You heard what the boffins said at Marcia's meeting, all that chemical stuff, she's never been this depressed before.'

'Oh God, what a day,' said Fola, her head in her hands. 'I think I'll go back to bed and pray it's all been a nightmare.'

'Yeah, but we're doing something about it,' said Nathaniel. 'At the moment we're trying to work out why she's in this state.'

'Then what?' said Fola.

'We'll work to get something into ActCon to make her change her mind. Anyway, we're getting together in five minutes. Fliss will be back by here by then. She's bringing Maxwell with her. I want to hear all about your adventures but I suggest we wait until they get here.'

I used the time to make a call down to Grace in Soul:

'Thank God,' she said when I told her that Fola was safe. 'When are you coming back? It's been weird on my own down here.'

'Don't know. It might be that we are needed up here a bit longer. Anyway, you're not on your own... Alfred's with you.'

'Yeah... but you wouldn't know it, he's been asleep in his room all morning. Let me know what you're up to.'

As I put the phone down I mused that no-one had asked me how Fola had got out of the Oubliette. I wasn't sure whether to feel relieved or slightly put out.

Felicity came bursting into the room with Maxwell in tow.

'This must be Fola. You rescued her. Bloody hell, Colin!' she said, wide-eyed with admiration.

'Ah, Felicity,' said Fola after they had been introduced. 'I can see the resemblance to your dear sister.'

'People call me Fliss.'

'But Felicity is such a lovely name, may I call you that?'

'Suppose so,' said Felicity with a shrug. It amused me how Fola invariably charmed people while getting her own way.

Maxwell gave me a nod and manoeuvred his large bulk into the already crowded room. Nathaniel gave up his chair to him and sat on the music stool while Felicity perched on the arm of the sofa.

'Right,' said Nathaniel, 'now we are all gathered... I want to hear from all of you, what do you have to tell me? Colin, let's start with you. What did you find out?'

I got my notebook out of my backpack and went through the scenes that I had watched in the Memory Archives. I relayed them in the order that I had viewed them, saving the one where Jessica poured the alcohol down the sink until last. When I had finished there was silence for a few moments.

'So,' said Maxwell, leaning forward, 'you never actually saw Jessica being hit?'

'No, I've told you that already. The actual hitting part had been made extra classified. There was no way that I was going to see those bits.'

'So, you don't know for absolute certainty that Jessica was hit... immediately after the bit that you saw?'

'Yes, actually I do,' I was starting to feel exasperated. What was with Maxwell? Why was he needling me? 'I do because we had already done a search on *Jessica being hit* and all these scenes came up. The librarian helped me. She showed me how to watch the earlier scene that wasn't classified... the one which immediately led up to the hitting part.'

I felt that Maxwell should be chastened by this, but instead he pulled a face, a face which said: 'So you say...'

'I'm satisfied,' said Nathaniel getting up and going over to a flip chart stand in the corner. The man seemed to be obsessed with recording things on large pieces of paper. 'It definitely fits in with the flashback this morning.'

He wrote:

JESSICA HIT BY ALCOHOLIC MOTHER. SEVERAL TIMES.

'That's physical abuse,' said Felicity, so he wrote that down too.

'It maybe explains the Child,' said Fola.

'What child?' said Felicity.

Fola told them about the Oubliette. She spoke slowly and deliberately. She told them about the metal grill and the ladder, about the different levels and the smells and the crying. She spoke about the people she had met down there.

'Should have freed them all, Colin. Can't stop thinking about them.'

Then she told them about the Child; about how she was mute and pale with a torn dress and bedraggled hair.

'We couldn't leave her there, it wouldn't have been right, so she came with us.'

'Where's she now?' asked Felicity.

'Josie's looking after her, giving her a bath.'

'Golly,' said Felicity, 'but who is she?'

'I've been thinking about that,' said Fola. 'I was put in the Oubliette this morning because I'd annoyed Marcia, but mostly it's Internal Security who imprisons undesirables there. It's people they think are a threat to Jessica's equilibrium, people who will upset the status quo.'

'How could a child do that?' said Felicity.

'It's probably what the Child represents,' said Nathaniel. 'Don't you agree, Fola?'

'Yes, I think that's it, we know that Jessica had a hard time when she was little.' She nodded towards Nathaniel's flipchart. 'Internal Security has tried to hide the feelings, way down in the Oubliette.'

We all sat quietly for a while. It was Maxwell who broke the silence:

'What I don't get is how you managed to escape.'

'Colin found the keys,' said Fola.

Maxwell frowned so I told them the whole story; all about my clever idea and how it had worked like a dream.

'Blimey,' said Maxwell.

'Why didn't you tell me before?' said Fola, she sat up straight and fixed her large brown eyes on mine.

'Well for one thing, you didn't ask,' I replied, suddenly defensive. 'I don't know how you thought we'd got away with it…. how did you imagine I'd got the keys? And where had the guards disappeared to?'

'But you told the Major he could get to heaven,' said Fola.

'No, I didn't. I was really careful about what I said. I only said he could come and join us… with whatever we were doing.'

'You must have given him that impression,' Fola pressed on. 'That wasn't honest.'

'Well you'd better go back and tell him,' I said petulantly. 'Tell him that you were let out on false pretences and that you'd like to go back inside.'

Fola pursed her lips.

'I think you did rather well. It was a clever idea and it worked,' said Maxwell. 'There's the small matter of a possible perverse incentive.'

'What do you mean?'

'Well,' said Maxwell, taking his time, 'you've told him ... Ah, no, let's rephrase that... you've suggested to the Major that if Jessica dies today he has an opportunity ... and only today mind... to get a free pass to heaven.'

'I never said that...'

'No but you *implied* that... You put the idea in his mind. So... it could be to his advantage for Jessica to kill herself today.'

It took me a moment to take in what he was saying and then I felt myself go hot and cold all over. I got up from the sofa.

'I've had enough of this, I need some air,' I muttered and I walked out of the room and down the stairs and right out of the building.

16

I stood for a moment on the steps of the Civic Centre, breathing deeply and willing myself to calm down. Across the road, forming the centre of the square, was a public garden surrounded by wrought-iron railings. I slipped inside the gate and sat down on one of the benches facing an expanse of grass and some unkempt herbaceous beds. The flowers were mostly over but there were a few roses still optimistically in bud and a bed of late season fading red chrysanthemums. Over on the far side were Josie and the Child. The Child was wearing a grown-up's pink jumper with a yellow scarf tied round her middle. At first I couldn't make out what she was doing – she seemed to be running backwards and forwards at random. Then I realised that she was trying to catch the leaves. Over in the far corner a group of tall lime trees were gently shedding their leaves over the garden.

The leaves unhooked themselves from trees
And started all abroad;

Very occasionally the Child would manage to catch one and she would run over to Josie and put it in her lap. The air smelled earthy and damp and when the sun came out I closed my eyes. Then I caught a whiff of sandalwood and opened them again.

'I thought I might find you here.'

'Hello Fola.' I moved along the bench to make room for her. 'I used to come in here sometimes when I worked round the corner.'

'It is very peaceful,' she said, 'and it looks like she's enjoying herself.'

We watched as the Child stopped collecting leaves and started climbing up one of the apple trees, getting quite high before Josie persuaded her to come down.

'She's quite feisty, isn't she?' I said. 'Perhaps we should give her a name.'

'Let's wait until she can speak to us, then she can tell us what it is.'

Fola turned to look at me. 'Sorry,' she said, 'I haven't said thank you.'

'No need.'

'It must have been really scary — seeing the Major. It was clever, in fact it was brilliant…'

'Not that clever,' I said, 'not if what Maxwell says is true, not if he now *wants* Jessica to die. Not clever at all.'

'Well, we don't know that,' said Fola, 'come back to the meeting. Felicity says she's found out something important. Says you need to hear it.'

I sighed. All I wanted to do was to catch a launch down to the Thymus, maybe have a game of Go with Alfred and pick up my usual life.

'Okay,' I said, 'but then let's get back to the office. I've had enough excitement for one day.'

PART THREE

AFTER NOON

1

'We've got a good story to tell,' Philippa Markham stared at Jessica intently, 'and I want to make sure that we tell it... loud and clear.'

Jessica had heard the Director of Children's Services say this before; it was one of her favourite sayings. Another one was: 'We've come a long way in the last ten months...' Philippa hadn't said that one yet; *She probably will in a minute,* thought Jessica as she studied the poster behind Philippa's head. It was a picture of the Great Wall of China, its sturdy crenellations snaking over the green hillside. Philippa had walked a chunk of the wall in the summer, for charity, and there had been a three-line-whip 'encouraging' the staff to sponsor her. Jessica had read somewhere that parts of this ancient wall had been rebuilt in the 1950s, and certainly the section in the photograph looked too well preserved to be the real thing.

She had been seven minutes late to the meeting.

'Thought you'd got lost...' Philippa had said with a touch of sarcasm.

And now she was on the back foot, having arrived out of breath at Philippa's office, full of apologies.

'I'd like us to take a look at the performance indicators on Child Protection,' said Philippa. 'These results are disappointing; wouldn't you agree?'

Jessica had a suspicion about what was coming next. *I don't want to be here. I don't want to be here at all.*

2

I followed Fola back up the stairs to Nathaniel's office and sat down on the sofa. I caught a smirk on Maxwell's face but was determined to ignore it.

'Ah, Colin,' said Nathaniel, raking his hand through his hair, 'I have just been saying…. I've known Major Grendon for many years. Not sure he'd want to swap the certainty of this life with the uncertainty of death, even if there was some kind of promise of an afterlife. I don't think you need to worry.'

'There you are… it's all going to be okay,' said Fola squeezing my arm.

'I wouldn't put it quite like that,' said Felicity briskly. 'We're in a Code Red emergency and there are suicidal Thoughts ricocheting round in ActCon. Jessica still might do it on the way home.'

'It doesn't really make sense,' said Fola. 'How did the first Thought to kill herself get into ActCon… do we know who took it in there?'

'Good question,' said Felicity. 'Max, what did you find out?'

'Nothing.'

'Nothing?'

'Nothing, zero, zilch, nada.'

'Did you go up there?' said Felicity testily, 'did you talk to your mate?'

'Yep. I talked to him and the Looking Good lot who are always outside ActCon. Then I interviewed Will from our office and got him to tell me everything that he saw around ActCon this morning. They all say the same; there was nothing unusual, they didn't see anything, hear anything... nothing at all.'

'That's strange,' said Nathaniel, 'you'd think that someone would have seen something.'

'Oh well. Let me tell you what I've been doing,' said Felicity, suddenly animated. 'After the brain-storming exercise this morning I had a real sense that we were missing something. Like there was an elephant in the room that no-one was mentioning.'

'Okay,' said Nathaniel, 'and what might that be?'

'The Old Ones.'

'What?' said Nathaniel. 'You're not serious!'

'Deadly serious, we hardly ever talk about them but they're spread all over the Body. When they first settled here they brought all that genetic stuff with them...'

'Genetics?' said Nathaniel. 'You're not going down that road ....'

'It's a factor,' interrupted Felicity, 'and we can't ignore it. I've been over to the Social Work Library down in the Temporal Lobe. There's a whole section on depression and suicidal thoughts. Jessica studied all this when she did her training.'

She went over to the flip-chart, rustled over a fresh sheet and began writing fast.

'Look,' she said, taking hold of a red pen, 'it's really very simple: all I'm saying is that there is an extra component that we hadn't thought about. We know that Jessica's got a whole pile of *stressors*... that's the stuff that came up in the brainstorming. Now we can add the physical abuse as a young child under *early life events*. And look... *availability of means*...that means the opportunity for her to kill herself. So that's jumping in front of a tube train in her case. But we'd forgotten the genetics bit. That means the influence of an Old One makes Jessica predisposed towards feeling depressed... that's just the way she is.'

With that, Felicity looked round the room triumphantly and sat down. No-one said a word. Not even Maxwell who usually had something to say about everything.

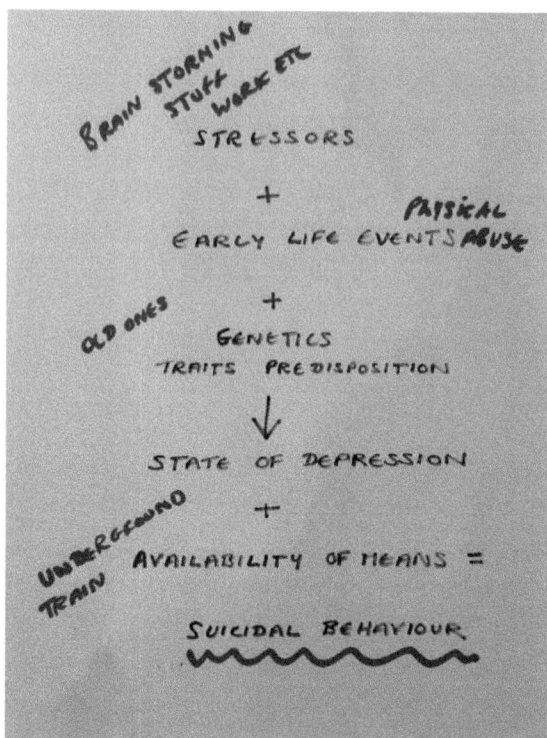

BRAIN STORMING
STUFF
WORK ETC

STRESSORS

+

EARLY LIFE EVENTS   PHYSICAL ABUSE

OLD ONES

+

GENETICS
TRAITS   PREDISPOSITION

↓

STATE OF DEPRESSION

UNDERGROUND
TRAIN

+

AVAILABILITY OF MEANS =

SUICIDAL BEHAVIOUR

It was Nathaniel who spoke first. 'We've gone about as far as we can with this.' He stood up and began collecting up the papers off his desk. 'You can all carry on here if you want, but as far as I'm concerned, this meeting's over.'

Felicity stood up too; she looked so slim and slight next to Nathaniel; like a whippet next to an old English sheepdog.

'Doesn't this even deserve a discussion? It's got to be one of the reasons why Jessica's in this state…'

'I'm not interested in hearing about traits and predispositions,' he said glancing at the flip-chart. 'And neither is anyone else.' Then he turned to the sofa. 'You did well, both of you, bringing the Child out of the Oubliette. Now, we're going to have to work out what to do with her. Come on Fola, we'll go and talk to Josie.'

Fola heaved herself off the sofa and followed Nathaniel out of the room. As she reached the door, she turned back.

'He's right,' she sounded weary, 'we're the ones who've caused this mess… we can't blame it on the Old Ones. It's us who are responsible, no-one else.'

3

'That went well,' said Maxwell.

'Shut up, Max,' said Felicity.

'He seemed very upset,' I said.

Maxwell shrugged. He was still sitting in Nathaniel's chair and didn't look like he was going to give it up in a hurry.

''Twas ever thus,' he said, and then to Felicity: 'You knew he would be. I don't understand why you wanted to bring up the 'G' word. You know it's verboten.'

'I brought it up,' said Felicity, 'because it happens to be true.'

Maxwell snorted. 'That's as maybe… but on-one wants to hear it.'

'Well they should,' said Felicity pacing the room. 'Trouble is they like to persuade themselves they're in complete control, Marcia and Nathaniel, they're both the same. And even Fola thinks that way. They think they call all the shots. They don't want to accept that the Old Ones carry on influencing anything. But maybe they do. There's probably an Old One out there with a death wish, someone who wants to persuade Jessica to kill herself.'

I didn't know what to think. I felt confused. I couldn't believe that any of this was caused by one of the Old Ones. As Felicity had said, they were all around us. Most of the departments had them, usually in an advisory role; Soul had Alfred, so old that he was an Ancient and the kindest person in the world.

All us Newbies were raised on the hillsides of the Cerebellum and the Old Ones had looked after us when we were small, cared for us in kindergarten and taught us in school. I tried to remember my Biohistory; I knew that when Jessica began, in her mother's body, she was entirely populated by Old Ones and Ancients who had come across from her mother and father. They hadn't come empty handed, those early settlers. They had brought with them everything that Jessica needed to get going in the world. It is true that some of the Old Ones had all sorts of odd quirks – carried down from Jessica's ancestors – but it was hard to believe that any of them wanted her to kill herself.

'I agree with Fola, we shouldn't turn on the Old Ones,' I said. 'And even if it is true… and Jessica has some kind of tendency to be depressed… there's nothing we can do about it.'

'Maybe…but isn't it better to know what we're up against?'

As Maxwell gave another of his shrugs Fola suddenly came back into the room:

'Something's up… Sean from your office has just rung. Says you're to look at the RTM.'

Maxwell swivelled the RTM's screen round so we could all see it, and turned up the volume.

'Where is she?' I asked.

'Philippa Markham's office,' said Felicity sitting down on the music stool.

'Who's that?'

'God, Col, don't you know anything? Only most important person in the world of work.'

The RTM showed that Jessica was sitting down in a bright and airy room. On the other side of the desk was an older woman with interesting hair which was pulled back towards the nape of her neck. I liked the way the dark brown hair gave way to silvery-grey streaks around her temples. Jessica was intermittently glancing across to the woman's eyes which were a surprising shade of blue. I wanted to see what was outside the window to the left, but whenever Jessica wasn't looking at the woman, her eyes were focussed on the introductory page of the report in front of her.

'We've come a long way in the last ten months,' the woman was saying, *'and we need to make sure that our figures reflect the improvements we've made.'*

Jessica wasn't saying anything.

Here we go... We heard Jessica's Thought loud and clear. The woman was continuing:

'I want to take another look at the figures for children who have had Child Protection plans for more than two years.'

'What does that mean?' I asked.

'Ssh ... tell you later,' said Felicity.

'You've got to remember what's behind these indicators. The government wants to know that children don't keep on suffering from the same set of abusive experiences. So I want you to go through the cases that fall foul of that indicator ...'

'I don't understand... what does she want Jessica to do?'

'If you'd just shut up, we'd find out,' Felicity said sharply.

'Wants her to cook the books,' said Maxwell. 'We thought this might happen. The results aren't good enough.'

'...I want you take a second look at the data. The figures as they stand are not acceptable. It would be entirely reasonable to exclude some of the data where there are particular special circumstances....'

Jessica made some sort of noise.

'Did she just say 'okay'?' said Fola. 'Turn the volume up some more.'

The sound of rustling paper was all we heard as Jessica shuffled the pages of her report.

'No, I don't think she did... or if she did it was so softly that Philippa wouldn't have heard it.' Felicity began pulling on her red jacket. 'We're going to have to get back. Sean will want to call a meeting; we'll need to decide how to respond. We're done here anyway.'

'I was just getting comfy,' said Maxwell getting up, 'but duty calls, I suppose... it's an interesting dilemma, although I can't help but feel there are more important issues at stake. Like whether any of us are going to exist in a few hours' time.'

'Life should go on as normal,' said Felicity. 'Jessica's facing a problem and that's what we're here for.'

'One of us will have to go too,' said Fola looking at me.

'What?' I said. 'What for? It's got nothing to do with us. This is work stuff.'

'It's got everything to do with us, if what you say is true.' She turned to Maxwell. 'If Jessica is being asked to do something dishonest, then it is a Moral Question.'

'We've not had one of those for ages,' I said, suddenly interested. 'Not since Jessica found that wallet outside Boots.'

'Surely not,' said Felicity. 'This is a work-related instruction… morality doesn't come in to it.'

'Think you'll find it does, and Sean will agree with me. Under the protocol a member of Soul must be present if a Moral Question is being discussed. You'll have to go with them, Colin.'

I frowned.

'Me? Why me? Can't you go, or Grace?'

'Not me, I can't go,' said Fola. 'I'm still supposed to be in the Oubliette; and Grace shouldn't leave Alfred on his own.'

'But I won't know what to say.'

'You will when you get there, all you have to do is to hold fast to what is right.'

'Come on then, both of you,' said Felicity. 'I'll explain it all to you, Col, on the way.'

4

I had no desire to return to Dominion Tower after my experience of the morning. It was a place where, if you upset Marcia, you could end up in the Oubliette. However, I was getting accustomed to first class travel on the CorpCal. I would miss this, I thought, as I sat back in the spacious seat and hit the 'recline' button. I decided I would speak to Fola when everything blew over. Get her to agree that members of Soul should always travel first class.

Meanwhile Felicity talked at me non-stop. She explained, as we strode from the Civic Centre to the station, about the myriad performance indicators by which all Children's Services throughout the land were judged. As we lined up to go through Security she told me in great detail about how every Local Authority is judged by way of an annual Performance Assessment. Maxwell had enough and went off to sit with a friend he'd spotted. As we fastened our seatbelts, she explained how Jessica's Social Services Department had gone from 'Pretty Bad' two years ago to 'Not Good Enough,' last year.

'This year we're on course for a 'Quite Reasonable, All Things Considered.'

I closed my eyes. I didn't enjoy the sensation of accelerating and at the same time dropping down the near vertical shaft of the CorpCal. Felicity carried on talking:

'The whole point about these indicators is to show Continuous Improvement.'

'But supposing there hasn't been?'

'Hasn't been what?'

'Suppose there hasn't been continuous improvement... Suppose things have stayed the same ... or got slightly worse. What happens then?'

'Well obviously we'd stay where we were with 'Not Good Enough.' Or even go back down to 'Pretty Bad.''

'Like in 'Snakes and Ladders?''

We had reached the bottom of the ravine and were now hurtling along on the flat.

'No, not really,' she sounded tetchy; 'it's all very well for you down in Soul, with nothing to do all day. But we've been working really hard on this... for weeks.'

Felicity turned to look out of the window; there was nothing to look at except the grey walls of the tunnel speeding past.

'Okay... sorry...but you still haven't told me what Philippa is asking Jessica to do.' My stomach lurched as we started the sharp climb up to West Side.

'It's about those children who are on child protection plans, I guess even you know what they are.'

I nodded. I remembered that much from when Jessica was a front-line social worker. Most of her caseload had been children who had those special plans; sets of tasks that, in theory, were for all the professionals, including teachers and health visitors, to carry out, but in practice always seemed to land on Jessica's to-do list. The plans usually had stuff for the parents to do, or not do. Not get drunk, not fight with each other, that kind of thing. If things didn't improve then social workers went to the next level: Seeking Legal Advice.

'She wants her to look at the figures for the kids who've had CP plans longer than two years.'

'What exactly does 'look at the figures' mean?'

'Review them... check them out.'

'...and..?'

'I don't know...Philippa said something about what's behind the indicators... didn't she? But we didn't catch what she said ... because you were rabbiting on at the time.'

We had started to slow down and Felicity began gathering up her things. We seemed destined to argue whenever we were on the CorpCal.

'We are now approaching Pre-Frontal City West Side. Please ensure that you have all your belongings with you. Customers are reminded that we are currently in a Code Red Emergency. Please be vigilant and keep your belongings with you at all times.'

At Dominion Tower, Felicity insisted that I get a new security pass, even though I was still wearing the old one. It was only six hours earlier that Fola and I had been at the reception desk but it seemed an age ago. I remembered to say 'Thymus, Residual Projects' rather than 'Soul' and the blonde receptionist printed my new ID badge without a murmur.

'I often walk up,' asserted Felicity as we waited for the lift, 'but we're in a hurry today.'

Maxwell said nothing but raised his eyebrows.

We arrived at the twenty-first floor and I followed them as they adeptly negotiated the maze of office furniture that surrounded Problem Solving.

'Ah good,' said Sean when he saw us, 'excellent timing. I've booked Committee Room One for the meeting. Now that you're here we can round everyone up. I'd like you to come, Fliss, and Will as he understands the indicators like no-one else. Col, I take it that you're representing Soul?'

Everyone in Problem Solving was referred to by one-syllable names: Max, Fliss, Will, Biz, Baz, Boz. They were such hard-working beavers that no one had time to get their tongues round a multi-syllable moniker.

'That's right... but...'

'Excellent, well let's get up there.'

'What about me?' Maxwell was sitting on a nearby desk. 'Can I come?'

'Do you have anything to contribute?'

'Nothing to declare but my genius.'

Felicity rolled her eyes but Sean smiled and said, 'Come on then... but I don't want you upsetting folk.'

'Moi?' said Maxwell, 'as if I would.'

'Jacket….?'

'Oh God, do I have to?'

'For upstairs? Yes, we're wearing ours,' said Sean nodding towards William. We hung around while Maxwell found a red blazer that looked too small for him. I was glad that we didn't have a uniform in Soul; the others except, of course, for Felicity, looked like a group of delinquent schoolboys who were hitting the local cafés during the lunch-break. We followed Sean, single file, climbing the back stairs and up to the twenty-third floor.

5

Committee Room One had been tidied since the early morning collision. The broken glass had been swept away and the pictures that had fallen off the wall were neatly stacked in the corner. I spotted the track-suited woman from East Side's brainstorming exercise so I took the empty chair next to her.

'Hello again,' she said, 'didn't see you on the CorpCal just now.'

'No, I was with them,' I nodded towards Felicity and Maxwell. 'They got me a pass for first class.'

'Oh bully-for-you. I'm Shona, by the way.'

'Colin,' I said. 'Are you representing Nathaniel?'

'Yes, you?'

'Soul ...' but I didn't get a chance to say anything more as Sean, who was seated at the head of the table, was asking everyone to introduce themselves. Problem Solving had come mob-handed with Sean, Maxwell, Felicity and William. Marjorie from Looking Good in Front of Other People sat on the opposite side and next to her was a woman with short cropped grey hair and very blue eyes. She was an Old One and she introduced herself as Jane from the Department of Certainty. Maxwell and this woman seemed to know one another, he gave her a big grin while she nodded in return.

Sean told us that the purpose of the meeting was to decide 'yes' or 'no' to Philippa Markham's request and then come up with an agreed Thought or sequence of Thoughts for ActCon. He asked William to take us through the indicators and explain the changes Philippa was wanting Jessica to make.

William got up and stood next to the flip chart. At least it was not a Powerpoint presentation. He was just about to begin when the door opened and Marcia came into the room followed by a tall man. Sean looked surprised and began standing up.

'Don't mind us,' said Marcia, 'just carry on as if we weren't here… we're just observing.'

I sunk down further in my seat. This was the same grey-suited man who had taken me up to Major Grendon's office in Amygdala Fort.

'Who's that?' Shona muttered.

'The bloke with Marcia? Internal Security.'

William began again, nervous this time and talking much too fast. He had a nasal sing-song voice which seemed designed to render the listener comatose. He went to the flipchart and began writing sequences of numbers that he called denominators and numerators which made no sense to me. I had a strong sense of déjà-vu from the morning meeting and began to watch the RTM above William's head. Jessica had returned to her office and was making a mug of tea. Perhaps she will bang her head again, I thought, as she pressed the teabag against the side of the mug. This time she managed to get the teabag in the bin without dropping it. She leant against the sideboard and rubbed the front of her head.

William stopped talking numbers.

'There are too many children who have had child protection plans for more than two years so that takes the department into 'Not Good Enough' on the Government's performance scales.'

Felicity gave a sudden intake of breath. 'What exactly is Philippa suggesting, and will it help?' she asked.

'All that she is asking Jessica to do is to look at the individual cases. There could be good reasons why a child has had a plan for more than two years; maybe it is a new set of circumstances.'

'Like what?' asked Marcia. 'Give me an example.'

'We've done some work on this already,' said Sean. 'We know that there are some children who started off with one problem and the family

147

get help with that; and then a new problem arises. Like a new boyfriend on the scene who turns out to be violent.'

'So what you're saying is that it would be good practice for those children to stay having a child protection plan? What's the problem? Why doesn't Jessica just explain all that in the report?'

Marcia directed this to Sean but it was Maxwell who cleared his throat.

'The problem,' he said slowly, 'is that the UK Government is not that interested in the explanations. They're really only interested in the figures. That's why Philippa wants Jessica to take those cases out of the statistics altogether... to exclude them from the data. That's right, isn't it, Will?'

William nodded and began talking about denominators and numerators again. On the RTM Jessica was back at her desk and looking out of the window. I thought about the Child and what I had seen in the Memory Archives. The dozen scenes that I had viewed which spanned most of Jessica's childhood: her mother swaying around the room, her red angry face too close to Jessica's, the feeling of fear and then the hitting. It was time for me to say something.

'Can I ask a question?' It was Jane who spoke before I was able to open my mouth. 'I heard Philippa say something about what's behind the indicators. What values are we talking about here?'

'Government objective,' said William, 'reducing the incidents of repeated harm to children. That's what this indicator relates to.'

'That's clear then,' said Jane. 'I think we would all agree that it is a Certainty that children shouldn't carry on having a horrible time...'

'That's not the point...' muttered Felicity.

'And is it a Certainty that Jessica should always be completely honest?' asked Marcia.

'No, you know it isn't, Marcia, we've been down this road before.' Jane sat, perfectly still and straight-backed, and met Marcia's gaze. 'If the outcome is a greater good, then dishonesty may be permissible. There is no 'greater good' in this situation.'

Marcia snorted.

'That's just your opinion,' she said airily. 'Actually, why are you here? Shouldn't you be packing up? You need to be out of Dominion House and back to the Cerebellum by the end of the day, we agreed that this morning. I'm sure you've got more important things to be doing. There's no need for you to stay.'

Maxwell looked like he was about to say something but Jane caught his eye and shook her head. She left her seat, walked to the door and turned back to face the meeting:

'There will repercussions,' she said, 'if Jessica doesn't do the right thing.'

'Is that a threat?' asked the Internal Security man quietly.

'Of course not,' Jane looked pained, 'merely an observation, based on past experience.' And with that she left the room.

No-one said anything. A few people shifted in their seats, looking uncomfortable. Marcia shrugged.

'Ever the drama queen,' she said, and then, turning to me, added, 'Maybe Soul has a view about honesty?'

I felt myself redden. I didn't want to get involved in this discussion.

'Yes, do tell us about Soul's line on total honesty,' said Maxwell with a sneer.

I cleared my throat.

'Being honest in all our dealings is something that we always …strive for in Soul,' I said, without enthusiasm.

'What will happen,' said Marjorie, ignoring what I had just said, 'if Jessica doesn't go along with what Philippa wants?'

'Excellent question,' said Marcia.

'Well, we don't know,' replied Sean. 'Best guess is that she gets irritated with Jessica and then asks someone else to change the figures.'

'Could she be sacked?'

'Not openly, no… but Philippa would probably move her on to somewhere that she didn't want to be.'

For a fleeting moment I had a vision of Jessica being hauled off to the Oubliette. Then I remembered that things like that didn't happen in the Outside World, at least, not in South London.

'We ought to wind this up…' continued Sean.

'Can I say something?' I said. 'I think we should just remember the children … those girls and boys… who live in families where they are carrying on being scared and unhappy… and abused. We should think about them for a moment.'

'Of course we *care* about them,' said Felicity, 'but what you're saying makes no logical sense… this is about data; our decision this afternoon will not affect them one way or another.'

There was silence for a moment as everyone looked at me expectantly.

'I guess it's about making sure we count them properly,' I said, 'making sure that they have a voice… making sure that they are heard.'

'Well said,' said Shona quietly.

'Okay,' said Sean, 'let's go round the table and get everyone's views. A 'yes' means that Jessica should do what Philippa asks and 'no' obviously means no.'

There were Yeses from Marjorie and also from William and Felicity. Shona and I both said No.

'Maxwell?' said Sean.

'No.'

'What?' said Felicity, her voice sharp with surprise.

'No,' he repeated. 'Once people start mucking about with the data to suit their own ends the whole system is fu-… I mean the whole system breaks down.'

There was a pause while everyone looked at Sean.

'That means we are three Yeses and three Nos. Looks like I have the deciding vote. I can see both sides of the argument …' He reddened as he glanced in Marcia's direction, 'but on balance I'm a Yes.'

Marcia smiled at everyone.

'Thank you, Sean, and thank you too William, most illuminating. I think you've come to the right decision. We are still in a Code Red. All Thoughts into ActCon must continue to be work-related this afternoon. Jessica will comply with what her manager is asking her to do. I'm authorising Problem Solving to do the necessary work on the data. Sean, I'll leave you to compose the Thoughts for ActCon.'

With that she and the IS man left the room.

'Good result,' said Felicity. Maxwell made a face at her.

'Right,' said Sean, 'I've got some ideas for the Thoughts and who should say them. William, will you put them on the Flipchart for me?

There then followed a discussion, mostly between Maxwell and Felicity, agreeing the exact wording. After a number of crossings-out the Thoughts were written up as follows:

WILLIAM: BETTER GET ON AND DO WHAT SHE WANTS.

MAXWELL: BUT IT'S NOT RIGHT TO FIDDLE WITH THE DATA.

FELICITY: IT WON'T MAKE ANY DIFFERENCE TO THE CHILDREN, IT'S ONLY STATISTICS.

COLIN: BUT IT'S NOT BEING HONEST.

I didn't like my Thought, and, in retrospect, I wish that I'd said something at the time.

MARJORIE: BUT IT IS WHAT PHILIPPA WANTS ME TO DO, AND SHE IS MY BOSS, AFTER ALL.

FELICITY: GIVE HER THE FIGURES AND SHE CAN DO WHAT SHE LIKES WITH THEM.

WILLIAM: BETTER GET ON AND DO WHAT SHE WANTS.

EVERYONE: BETTER GET ON AND DO WHAT SHE WANTS.

Sean made us practice the sequence twice. The second time round I tried to add a bit of emphasis to my Thought: 'It's *not* being *honest*.'

Sean frowned. 'Colin, once you're in ActCon you must just speak normally, no drama, is that clear?' I nodded.

'Okay, let's get up there.'

6

One of Marcia's most controversial decisions, when she took over as Chief Executive of West Side, was to move the Seat of Active Consciousness to the top of Dominion Tower. It used to be in the centre of a public park, opposite the Tower, easily accessible to everyone. Then Marcia arranged for it to be dismantled, stone by stone, and rebuilt right on top of the roof of West Side's headquarters. She then bulldozed the park to make way for the new Financial Services Building.

There are still several other sites, sprinkled around West and East side and open to the public, but these have been downgraded to Receiving Booths. You go in to one of these and record your Thought which then gets relayed to the top floor of Dominion Tower. Then one of the ActCon Control Officers listens to it and decides whether the Thought is allowed to be heard. In my experience it is usually rejected, but then again, I don't work for Problem Solving or Looking Good in Front of Other People.

Marcia's argument was that as most of Jessica's 'key cognitive processes' took place in Dominion Tower it made sense for ActCon to be on the roof of the building. She also said that Dominion Tower, being the tallest office in either West or East side, was ideally placed to house the requisite communication antennae. She would boast that information could be relayed from the top of the tower to anywhere in the whole of Jessica in a fraction of a second. It was laid down by statute that the general public had to have access to ActCon. Marcia got over that by installing a lift on the outside of the tower which went straight up to the roof. Needless to say, if you worked in Dominion Tower you could take the lift to the 25th floor and then walk up the internal staircase; slipping into ActCon with your Thoughts without any hassle.

'Glad to see you were on the side of the angels just now,' I said to Maxwell, as he slowly made his way up the stairs. Felicity had gone on ahead, it didn't look like she was speaking to either of us.

'Angels don't come in to it,' he gasped, wheezing, 'There's no point in having a performance assessment framework if people feel they can fiddle the data.'

'I suppose,' I began, as we stopped on the landing for a moment to let him catch his breath. 'What I don't get is why we all have to traipse up here…. now we've made the decision, can't you lot just get on with it. Why does it have to go through ActCon?'

'Protocol,' he said. 'It's a decision on a Moral Question. It has to be broadcast on the RTM so that all the departments are 'singing from the same hymn sheet' as they say.'

'Come on you two, hurry up!' Sean called down to us.

We climbed up past the twenty-fifth floor, where the ActCon Control Officers were busy rejecting Thoughts, and straight up onto the roof. It is usually windy up on the top of the tower, and I pulled up the hood of my anorak. The last time that I had been up there had been several months earlier. I had gone with Fola and we had been allowed in with *It would be good to join a choir*. The trouble was that we were let down by Looking Good in front of Other People who decided, at the last minute, that they didn't want to support us. And then no-one from Making Music bothered to pitch up either so it was just the two of us. We got the Thought into ActCon but it didn't lead to anything. Fola said not to be downhearted. She said we should try again but with a much more specific Thought next time like: *Go to the library and ask about local choirs*.

The place always reminds me of the top of a multi-storey car-park in the Outside World, a car-park, that is, with a jewel-like piece of architecture set in the middle of it. A circular polished-limestone building with a gold-domed roof, ActCon would be not be out of place on the brow of a hill of some English country estate or on an isle in a Venetian Lagoon.

Next to ActCon stands the Communication Centre immediately recognisable by its receivers and antennae. This ironwork structure has a hinged arm which overarches the dome of ActCon and at the end of this arm is a round saucer, like a satellite dish. It looks like one of those old-fashioned hair dryers you see in hairdressers in the Outside World. There is a circular hole at the top of the dome and the receiver-dish collects Thoughts from ActCon and relays them onto the huge screen which sits next to the Communication Centre. This screen forms the Real Time Monitor which is relayed throughout Jessica's brain and the rest of her body. All Thoughts which go through ActCon, even those which don't result in Actions, are relayed on the RTM along with everything that Jessica is seeing or hearing.

Internal Security Services had a permanent hut up on the roof and that day they were searching everyone as they got out of the lift, waving their submachine guns round in an alarming manner. As we queued up to be frisked by a Whiteshirt I looked to see who else was up there. I noticed that Looking Good in Front of Other People still had their permanent booth positioned right outside ActCon so that they could lobby everyone on their way to say a Thought. There was also a new booth which I had not seen before. It was clean, bright and well-lit. The blue, red, yellow and green letters over the stand spelled out the word Google.

'What the heck's that doing there?' I said to Maxwell.

He shrugged.

'Some deal struck by Marcia. Apparently, it's cost efficient. No need use energy on an internal search when Jessica can just Google the info she needs to retrieve.'

I looked over at the two clean-cut young people standing in front of the Google logo.

'Where have they come from?'

'Been seconded from Library Services in the Temporal Lobe.'

'Really?'

'Marcia's talking about cutting Library Services and relying on Google instead.'

The only other presence up on the roof was Leaf. His tent was pitched over on the far side so that he could see both the ways up to the roof. For the past two years Leaf has kept a one-man demonstration in favour of Jessica becoming vegan. His tent is surrounded by placards saying things like *Say No to Animal Products* and *Meat is Murder*. A while ago he came down to Soul to try to get us to support his 'Good to become Vegan' Thought. We said we'd be willing to support a 'No to Eating Mammals' Thought but he said that was inconsistent and it should be all or nothing. The guards don't let him get into ActCon so he spends his time lobbying everyone who comes up onto the roof. Last time he wanted our Thought to be 'How about join a choir and become vegan at the same time'. Like that was going to work. I feel sorry for him really.

Once we had cleared security Marjorie wandered off to chat to her chums in the Looking Good booth. Leaf came bounding up to us, his ginger dreadlocks framing his face and with his usual earnest expression. He thrust a leaflet into my hand: *Veganism: the moral choice*. Looked quite interesting, I thought.

'Piss off, Leaf,' said Maxwell.

I caught sight of a flash of blue housecoat next to the Google booth. Annie was there with her trolley, giving out drinks. The wind was bitingly cold and although I don't usually take caffeine, I quite fancied a shot of something warming. But I had no time to approach her as Sean was calling us together.

'Okay everyone, gather round…' He paused 'I shall stay outside. You know your script, once you've said the Thoughts come straight back out. I can always send you back in if we need to.'

Sean opened ActCon's heavy wooden door and we filed in.

7

It took me a moment to adjust to the dim space. The hole at the top of the roof lets in minimal light, while the only windows are high up, set just under the lip of the dome. I like the simplicity of ActCon; the walls are painted white and there is a circle of columns forming a perimeter of the central space. Once Thoughts are said out loud they are flashed up around the walls and then picked up by the receiver dish overhead. The marble floor has a six-pointed star at the centre and the five of us formed a circle around the star.

'Should we hold hands?' asked Marjorie.

'Definitely not,' said Maxwell. 'Go on, Will.'

'Better get on and do what she wants,' said William.

'But it's not right to fiddle with the data.'

'It won't make any difference to the children, it's only statistics.' Felicity said her line slowly as if trying to convince an unbeliever.

There was a pause, it was my turn. They all looked at me.

Looking back, what do I remember? There was the almost silence, the only sound was the rasping breathing of Maxwell to my left. Then, for a moment, the sun came out and the cool walls and pale columns shimmered in the bright sunlight. Would she really do it, kill herself? Would all this disappear to nothing?

Jessica needed help.

'Not honest,' Felicity whispered.

I remembered a catch-phrase from an old quiz programme:

'Phone a friend,' I blurted out. 'Yes, phone a friend, ring Giulia.'

'No!' said Felicity. The others were staring at me wide-eyed.

'Yes, phone!' said Marjorie, 'Ring Giulia, see what she says.'

Maxwell grinned and shrugged.

'Why not,' he said, 'ring Giulia now.'

He looked Marjorie and me and the three of us chorused:

'Ring Giulia now!'

The door opened and Sean yanked hold of my backpack, dragging me outside. The others followed.

'What the fuck! What the hell do you think you're doing?'

The enormous RTM screen was flashing RING GIULIA NOW.

'Bloody hell! Marcia's going to hit the roof, you're going to be for it.'

My mouth had gone dry and I couldn't speak.

'And you!' Sean turned to Maxwell. 'Don't know why you're smiling; that was completely against protocol.'

Maxwell shrugged. 'Yeah, but it was a good idea, wasn't it?'

Sean shook his head as we all gazed at the RTM. Jessica was reaching for her phone. Good, I thought.

'You two had better scarper… lie low for a while.'

'What about Marjorie?' said Maxwell.

We looked over to the Looking Good booth where Marjorie was explaining what had happened to her colleagues.

'She can probably take care of herself,' said Sean, 'but you two should leave now.'

As Maxwell and I hurried over to the lift I caught sight of one of the Whiteshirts speaking into a phone. He looked over towards us the lift doors closed and Maxwell pressed the 'descend' button. I held my breath all the way down and didn't let it out again until the doors opened and we were on the pavement at the side of Dominion House.

8

Jessica took a sip of lukewarm tea. It had started to rain as she walked back from Centenary House, a fine, soft drizzle, and her wool coat gave off a musty smell as it hung damply on the back of her office door. She had switched her computer on and opened up the latest version of her report. She had then looked out of the window for a while before going to the kitchen and making a mug of tea.

I don't know what to do.

She scrolled down the report up and reread the section on child protection. She knew that she'd have to make a decision; one way or the other. *Better get on and do what she wants ... but it's not right to fiddle with the data. It won't make any difference to the children, it's only statistics.*

Jessica put her head on her hands and closed her eyes. Then the idea flashed across her mind: *Phone a friend, ring Giulia, see what she says.* A sense of relief came over her as she found her phone and dialled Giulia's work number.

'Giulia William's phone.'

'Is Giulia there?'

''Fraid not, who's calling?'

'It's Jessica, Jessica Drummond.'

'Hi Jessica. Mel here. No Giulia. She's in court, all day. You could try her mobile but I guess she probably won't have it switched on.'

'Okay, thanks anyway.'

'Shall I give her a message?'

'No, don't bother.' Jessica put the phone down. *Damn, damn, damn.* She sighed and rubbed her fists into her eyes. She felt like crying but no tears came. She hadn't cried properly for a long time; it seemed her tear-ducts were empty. *Oh well, better get on and do what she wants.*

9

'I'm not running anywhere.' Maxwell caught up with me, panting. We weren't actually running but I had led us, walking fast, down a side street and then around a couple more corners. I had no idea where we were: my aim was to get clear of Dominion Tower.

'Do you know where you're going?' he said. I ignored him and kept on walking.

'Stop!' he shouted after me, 'for God's sake. I've got a stitch.'

I walked back. He was bent over, hands on his knees.

'You're supposed to touch your toes,' I said.

He gave me a withering look.

'Have you got a plan,' he said, catching his breath, 'or are you just wandering about?'

'Going back to Soul,' I said, and then, not because I wanted him to join me but because it felt like the polite thing to say: 'You can come with me if you like.'

'Where are you again?'

'Thymus.'

'What, Thymus as in Chest?'

'Yep.'

'Blimey. It's years since I've been outside Jessica's head. Could do, I suppose. But first I need a drink. There's a little place I know round here.'

He set off back the way we had come and then down a narrow side-street.

'Here we are. This'll do us.'

We were outside a row of gloomy warehouses. There was a half open door with The Blue Lion picked out in gold over the lintel. Inside the place had styled itself as a typical English pub from the Outside World with tobacco stained walls and small dark wood tables with plush red chairs. It was almost empty save from a couple of Old Ones, a man and a woman, nursing their drinks in the far corner.

'Any endorphins, Frank?' Maxwell asked the bartender, an elderly gaunt man who seemed to be all angles.

Frank grunted. 'Endos are in short supply …but I can probably find you something.'

'I'll have an endo-caff; better make it lite on the endo.'

Maxwell looked at me. I don't usually go to bars and I'd never had any endorphins before. I don't do drugs. But then it had not been a usual sort of day, not by a long stretch. In fact, it had been a nightmare of a day.

'Come on, Col.'

Perhaps I should try something different. Experiment for once.

'I'll have the same, can I have an extra lite one please? That's lite on endo and on the caffeine.'

The bartender raised an eyebrow at Maxwell and poured two half glasses of water adding a measure of brown liquid to one glass and half a measure to the other. He then reached under the counter for a small bottle of colourless liquid and, using a pipette, he dropped two drops into Maxwell's glass and one into mine.

'Gnat's piss,' said Maxwell, eyeing up my glass.

'What are you doing here anyway, Max?' Frank said, as he topped my glass up with more water. 'Shouldn't you be saving the world?'

'We're working on it,' muttered Maxwell.

'Looks like it,' he said, handing Maxwell his glass. 'Do you think she might really do it?'

'What, jump?'

'Yeah, jump… kill herself and all of us too. End it all.'

'Probably not,' said Maxwell calmly, sipping his drink. 'The scientists down in Thalamus are sorting out the chemical side...'

Frank snorted.

'Good luck with that,' he said sourly. 'There's not much endo around and serotonin's even worse. My usual supplier's clean out of it....'

'...And you can't move for Whiteshirts outside ActCon,' continued Maxwell. 'I can't see anyone getting another suicidal Thought in there.'

'Yeah, but how did it get in in the first place? You're in Problem Solving, what are you guys doing about it?'

'As I said, we're working on it.'

On the wall, above the pool table, was a Real Time Monitor. The view was of a calculator; Jessica was doing sums.

'What's been happening?' asked Maxwell nodding his head towards the RTM.

Frank shrugged.

'Dunno... boring stuff... more report.'

'Did she phone?' I asked. 'Did she ring Giulia?'

'Yeah, but she wasn't in.'

'Shit!' I said as we made our way over to a corner table. I sat down and took a sip of the endo-caff. I'm not a huge caffeine drinker and I could immediately feel a boost of energy and a new sense of alertness. Then the endo kicked in and a sensation like warm treacle flowed through my body. Maxwell gulped his drink down and smacked his lips.

'That's more like it,' he said.

'Do you think there're looking for us?'

He shrugged and then abruptly stood up.

'I'll ring Sean,' he said, 'get the low-down.'

He went back to the bar and spoke to Frank who passed him a phone. Nothing much was happening on the RTM so I took in the rest of my surroundings. The place was really quite cosy; the faded yellow walls were bathed in a soft golden light from a number of small wall-lamps. Next to the bar was a large blackboard with chalked-up columns and a lot of writing. Maxwell was still talking on the phone so I went over to study it.

There was a list of biscuits with names next to them, followed by numbers. Some of the names I recognised; Maxwell was there next to *Chocolate Digestives*; then I spotted Nicholas, Marcia's PA, by *Hobnobs* and further down there was Felicity next to *Orange Club*.

'Biscuit Lotto,' Frank came and stood next to me, 'I've got Plain Hobnobs but they've been rubbish this season.'

'How does it work?'

'Every time Jessica buys biscuits you get a point if she chooses yours, and then every three months we see who's the current champion. Some of them, the likes of him…' he jerked his head towards Maxwell, 'and Nicholas, have a side bet going on. Max's Chocolate Digestives are on good form. They've pushed Nicholas's Chocolate Hobnobs into second place.'

'It's not random though, is it?' I was feeling for the person who had Fig Rolls, way down at the bottom of the list. I couldn't remember the last time Jessica bought a packet of those.

'It's usually between the top four or five. No-one's been able to work out the exact formula for the choice. Sometimes we're all taken by surprise. You can join if you like. No-one's got Garibaldi.'

I suspected that *Garibaldi* would have about as much success as *Fig Rolls* but I was feeling carefree and bold so I said yes and watched as my name was added to the list of players. As I went back to my seat I reflected on the predictability of Jessica's actions. If no-one could accurately second-guess what biscuits she would buy how would we know whether or not she would jump in front of a train?

I put this to Maxwell as he eased himself into his seat. He had a second glass of brown liquid.

'Just caffeine, need to stay awake. The interesting thing about biscuits,' he continued, 'is that the ActCon Thought is usually just 'buy biscuits'. The choosing bit is *almost* automatic. I have actually written a paper on it. I'll send it to you if you like.'

'Don't bother.'

'Now jumping under a train… That's a very different choice. Can't be done under automatic. A Thought to commit suicide would have to go through ActCon and then be broadcast on the RTM.'

I didn't like the way Maxwell said 'commit suicide' in the same tone as 'buy biscuits.'

'Anyway,' I was keen to change the subject, 'why were you so long? Did you speak to Sean?'

'Yeah, and then Fliss wanted to speak to me.'

'So, what did he say?'

'All hunky-dory mate, they're a bit narked that you went off-piste. Not supposed to happen with a prepared Thought. But they had to admit that phoning Giulia was a good idea. Not just for the work business, but generally, could have cheered her up a bit. Pity she wasn't there. Want another drink?'

I shook my head. Maxwell was slurping down his second glass with relish. His plump cheeks were taking on a rosy glow and I wondered whether it really was just caffeine he was drinking.

'We're not in trouble then?'

'Well, you are. You're the one that started it all off, you deliberately sabotaged a Thought. Sure you won't have another? There's time, it's not like we're going anywhere.' He got up rather unsteadily and made his way back towards the bar with me following.

'I'll have another endo – better make it extra-lite.'

The pleasant warm feeling was starting to wear off.

'Doesn't come extra-lite, it's one drop or two. Come on Col, are you a man or a mouse?'

He said 'mouse' rather too loudly with his face up close to mine and then threw his head back and laughed. I was suddenly reminded of the archive footage I'd seen of Jessica's mum lurching round the room after too many vodkas.

'Okay, but don't you think you've had enough?'

'Make it two endo-lites and have one yourself, my good man.'

'You know I don't touch the stuff,' said Frank as he mixed the drinks.

'So what exactly did Sean say about me?' I asked Maxwell. I could hear that my voice sounded plaintive.

'You're not exactly Mr Popular, and you should stay away from Dominion Tower for a while.' Maxwell handed me my drink and we went back to the corner table. 'But they're not scouring PF City for you.'

We sat quietly as I sipped the endo-lite. The warm feeling wasn't as pronounced as it was with my first glass but welcome all the same. Maybe I could just stay here, I thought to myself, until it is all over. And if it doesn't work out, there are worse places to spend one's last few hours. After all that I've been through, I deserve a bit peace and quiet... Max is alright ...and this endo drink is really quite pleasant ... everything is going to be okay.

10

Jessica glanced at her watch; it was ten past three. *Come on...* she told herself, *you're running out of time.* She had her note-book in front of her with a hand-written list of children who had been on a child protection plan for more than two years. She looked up each family on the computer system. Mostly it was the usual suspects: drugs and alcohol, mental illness and domestic violence. The stories made depressing reading and they weren't even about the children. It wasn't Kaleigh or Jade or Jordan who were centre stage in these accounts, it was their parents. The chronologies of missed appointments and broken agreements; of neighbourhood fights and police call-outs. The drama, and there was plenty of that, invariably cast mum and boyfriend in the leading roles. The children had walk-on parts with very few lines but they would always be watching from the wings; an audience for the car-crash of their parents' lives.

She had worked out the maths. If she took just five children out of the list it would swing the statistics. It would mean that the performance target would be met and Philippa would be happy. She experienced a twinge of unease as the arguments circulated in her brain: *It's not right ... it's not right to fiddle with the data.* And then: *it really won't make any difference to the children, it's only statistics.* There were a couple of families which could meet Philippa's criteria, new bad things happening instead of the old bad things simply repeating. One family had three children and the other two... *It could work. Better get on and do what she wants.*

11

The door of the bar was suddenly flung open.

'For God's sake you two....'

Felicity grabbed a chair and sat down in front of us.

'How much has he had?' she said, nodding towards Maxwell, and before I could answer continued: 'And you, Colin. Didn't put you down as a dope-head.'

'Felicity! Joy and rapture!' said Maxwell, then turning to me: 'Did I mention she was on her way?'

'Hi Fliss, I've got Garibaldi.'

'You both need to sober up, there's work to be done.' She went over to the bar and ordered some more drinks. I finished up my endo-lite quickly as I half expected Felicity to confiscate it. She returned with three steaming mugs.

'Glucose water with thiamine for you two,' as she plonked the mugs down on the table.

'What are you drinking?' asked Maxwell looking hopefully at Felicity's mug.

'Caffeine. Drink up, I need your help.'

'Thought you'd be still cross with us,' I said, 'we sabotaged a Thought....'

'You sabotaged it, not me. I just went along for the ride,' said Maxwell. He took a sip of drink and screwed up his face. 'This is horrible stuff.'

'That was very irresponsible,' said Felicity. 'You just can't do that with pre-agreed Thoughts.'

She then started a philosophical lecture about Reason and Thought which I only half listened to. I watched her small mouth and firm, set chin. She was altogether too 'pointy' I decided, not like her sister Grace. I missed Grace, she was softer and sensitive and not inclined to lecturing people. Once Felicity had finished her tirade she sat back and looked at us both.

'Have you sobered up yet? You're not going to be much use to me all doped up.'

'Just get on with it,' said Maxwell, picking up a beermat and flicking it against the edge of the table.

'Remember what I saying in Nathaniel's office, about genetics and the Old Ones?'

'Your thing about an Old One having a death wish and wanting Jessica to die?'

'Let's work on the hypothesis that it's true and that it was an Old One who put the thought of jumping in front of the train into ActCon this morning. We need to find out who that is and stop them from doing it again.'

I shook my head; it still didn't seem likely to me.

'Come on you two, I need your help.'

There was a pause as Max and I sipped our disgusting drinks. Eventually Max said, 'Each of the Old Ones is aligned to one of Jessica's ancestors. Maybe one of her ancestors killed themselves…'

'And now the Old One is trying to repeat the pattern,' said Felicity.

'But why would they?' I said.

'Dunno,' Maxwell shrugged, 'that's just the way genetics works… the Old Ones bring good stuff but also the crap from their past lives. The sins of the fathers are visited upon the children, even to the third and fourth generation.'

'The Memory Archives!' said Felicity. 'They could tell us.'

'Possibly…'conceded Maxwell, 'but only if Jessica has been told the information. The Archives only keep Jessica's lifetime experiences;

you'd be banking on someone telling her or else her overhearing that great granddad or whoever killed himself. It's a bit of a long-shot.'

'Come on, let's go down there and do a search' said Felicity. She was already starting to put on her jacket.

'No way,' I said, 'I've seen enough of Amygdala Fort for one day. And anyway, it won't work. You won't be able to do a search on anything related to suicide; there's an embargo going on because of the Emergency. You'd need special security clearance from Nathaniel and Marcia.'

'You won't get that,' said Maxwell.

'Couldn't we just try a search anyway?'

'No, you're not listening, there's a security embargo. All that happens is that the screen will say Access Denied.'

'God, you're both so defeatist.' Felicity began banging her foot against the table-leg. I tried to think of something helpful to suggest.

'Can't the Whiteshirts stop all Old Ones from getting into ActCon? They could stop them getting out of the lift on the roof of Dominion House.'

'Yeah, but what reason would you give?' said Maxwell. 'Surely not, "We suspect that one of you, out of all the thousands of Old Ones, is really a terrorist and is trying to get a suicidal thought into ActCon".'

'Very discriminatory,' agreed Felicity.

'But just for the rest of the day…' I said.

'Except it wouldn't be just for today, would it? said Maxwell. 'How would we know that they wouldn't try again tomorrow, or next week?'

'That's why we need to know who they are and find them.'

'Well you suggest something,' I said to Maxwell.

'I need another drink,' declared Maxwell. 'A caffeine this time.'

'I'll get you a lite,' said Felicity getting up. 'Col.'

I was starting to feel hot and headachy. I was tempted by the idea of more caffeine but I shook my head; I knew that Felicity wouldn't approve and I felt the need to be in her good books. While she was at the bar we sat in silence and I examined the wall in front of me. The woodchip wall-paper had been painted the colour of dried spaghetti; the paper was coming away at the join and a slender shard hung loose. The place wasn't all that cosy. There was an oppressive chemical smell and I could hear the couple in the corner. The man was swearing and carrying on.

'She's doing it then,' Maxwell nodded towards the RTM, 'she's going to fiddle the figures.'

The RTM displayed Jessica's latest Thought:

Better get on and do what she wants.

I remembered Jane's 'there will be repercussions.' The mood bar at the bottom of the RTM screen was showing 'very low'. I felt sweaty and chilly at the same time. It's our fault, I thought, we should have tried harder. We should have stopped this.

12

Felicity returned with Maxwell's drink while he sat flicking the beer mat.

'Can you stop doing that? I'm trying to think.'

There was a sudden commotion from the corner as the man scraped back his chair and lurched towards us.

'Leave it, Hughie,' shouted the woman.

'Just going to talk to 'em,' said the man. The next thing we knew he was standing over us. I could smell stale sweat and his sour chemical breath.

'Shame,' he said, swaying slightly, 'bleedin' shame.'

'I'm sorry, but I don't know what you're talking about,' said Felicity in a hoity-toity voice. I looked down at my drink and hoped he'd go away.

'You feeling it too, Frank?' shouted the woman.

Frank had been drying some glasses. He flicked the tea-towel onto his shoulder.

'What, shame?' he said, coming over. 'Yes Ada, I'm feeling it.' He tilted his head toward the RTM. 'She's doing something wrong isn't she?'

I remembered that Old Ones have a kind of sixth sense. They always pick up if Jessica's doing something that they think is morally wrong; they experience a kind of physical discomfort. They feel shame.

'She's not actually doing anything wrong,' said Felicity, 'she's obeying a management instruction.'

'Of course, the two are not incompatible...' muttered Maxwell.

'It's shame, Felicity,' said Frank, 'it's like my ears are burning. If us Old Ones are feeling it, then she's doing something wrong.'

'Sure is,' said the man, 'end of argument. You've fucked up.'

'Steady, Hughie,' said Frank.

'We let you lot get on with it,' continued the man, 'you Newbies, but you're fucking everything up.'

We didn't say anything. The man looked like he was running out of steam, his face was red and blotchy and his eyes were glazing over. He stood over us, still swaying back and forth, his arms loose by his side. The woman, Ada, sensing that the confrontation was in danger of winding down, stood up and came towards us. She was tall with white hair swept back in a bun. She had large dimpled arms which she folded in front of her.

'He's right,' she said, 'and look what you're doing to the Outside World, global warming and melting the icecaps ... and poisoning the seas with all them plastic bags...'

'Hardly our fault,' muttered Maxwell.

'You're screwing up Jessica's life as well,' she said, 'there's no balance. East Side should be able to keep the West in check. Now it's all Marcia and her cronies in Dominion Tower.'

'It's true,' said Frank. 'You're supposed to be in Problem Solving... but you can't see what's in front of your noses. It's all work, work, work, and not real work – pretend work – and getting more money.'

'There's no living,' agreed the woman. 'We had it hard... but we knew how to live. There was singing of an evening and someone playing the fiddle...'

'...and laughing,' said Hughie, who seemed to have come back to life. 'Jessica doesn't laugh no more.'

I felt I needed some air. I mouthed to Felicity that we should go but she ignored me.

'She does laugh,' she said, 'just not very often, she hasn't got much to laugh at. And she has to work to pay the mortgage, and if she didn't have a mortgage she'd have to pay rent... so she has to work.'

'I've no problem with work… but it should be work that she's proud of doing… not this.'

Frank nodded towards the RTM. We could see that Jessica had just deleted a sentence in the report and slowly typing an alternative.

'See?' said Ada, 'Not sure what she's doing, but it's definitely wrong. Writing down lies or some such…'

'Not lies exactly…' murmured Maxwell.

'Don't know why we're bothering, Frank… we'll probably all be dead by the end of the day.'

'Look, we're trying our best, alright?' Felicity was angry now, she had got up and was facing the woman.

'Oh yeah?' Ada took a step closer to Felicity. 'How's that helping then? Making us feel shame, getting her to do something wrong. Just when she wants to kill herself. It'll be your fault if she dies.'

'That's rubbish,' said Felicity raising her voice, 'it's not our fault at all. Actually, it's one of you, it's an Old One. You're to blame, not us.'

'Fliss…' warned Maxwell, placing his hand on her arm.

'What d'you mean, you silly little bitch!'

'You,' shouted Felicity, taking no notice of Maxwell, 'I mean you…an Old One is putting suicidal thoughts into ActCon. One of your lot…'

But before she could finish her sentence Felicity was felled by the woman. Maxwell said afterwards that Ada had aimed a right hook but I think it was more of a shove to the shoulder. Felicity, who was probably half her weight, fell backwards. I saw it all in slow motion. She caught her head on the edge of the table as she went down. I heard the crack. Felicity lay on the floor, eyes shut, her arms splayed out and her leg buckled beneath her. She looked, to all the world, like she was dead.

13

Humans tend to feel responsible; it is their curse. The infantile ego-centric view of the world seeps into adulthood, claiming agency, shouldering the blame. The first farmer stared out at the inundated plain and thought: *I caused this flood; I made the gods angry.* He set about placating the gods; the first fruits of the harvest, a spring lamb, even a tiny infant left on the bare mountainside. Later, the church declared that men and women are to blame from the get-go; they don't even have to do anything to deserve the wrath of God as original sin permeates the soul like the letters in a stick of Blackpool Rock.

Jessica did not cause the death of her grandmother, she frequently reminded herself of that fact. Nevertheless, she was haunted by 'if only' thoughts: *if only I had spoken to the doctor, if only I had moved Nan's bed downstairs ...* When she was feeling strong Jessica dismissed these thoughts as a piece of self-indulgent madness, but she could not guard against their intrusion several times a day. They stalked her and waited for their chance to strike; the hiatus between sleep and wakefulness, the idle moment waiting for the kettle to boil, the mid-afternoon lull alone in her office. And now, as she took her calculator out of her desk drawer: *if only I had gone up to stay with her, been there when she collapsed, she might still be alive.*

14

Maxwell got out of his chair at lightning speed and crouched over Felicity. Ada was whimpering softly.

'Oh God… Oh no, didn't mean to hurt her. Oh God. She'll be alright, won't she?'

Felicity opened her eyes. 'Ow, ow, ow.'

'Oh God, I'm sorry, didn't mean to hurt you, but you shouldn't have said those things…'

Frank took her by the arm and ushered both her and Hughie out of the pub.

'Just stay down there, for a mo,' said Maxwell, examining Felicity's head. 'Doesn't look like any skin is broken, no blood. You need to improve your blocking technique if you're going to start doing fisticuffs.'

'I'm okay,' said Felicity, slowly getting up off the floor, 'stop fussing.'

Frank came over with a glass of clear liquid.

'Drink it up,' he said, as she eyed it suspiciously. 'A drop of endo with some glucose, help the pain.'

He drew up a chair and sat down at our table, his eyes looked tired with wrinkles in the corners.

'What was all that about?' he said. 'An Old One putting a suicidal thought into ActCon?'

'Fliss has got this theory…' said Maxwell. He nodded at her. 'You'd better explain.'

Felicity leant forward. She looked a lot paler than usual and she spoke softly.

'I've been doing some research and it looks like there could be a genetic component'

'She means you,' interrupted Maxwell cheerfully.

Felicity frowned.

'Of course, I don't mean you specifically, Frank, but do you think it's possible? What do you remember about your past lives?'

'Heavens above,' he raised his eyebrows, 'you don't pull any punches, do you?'

'It could be important ... important to the situation.'

'For starters it's not past *lives,* most of us have only really been in one life properly and, as you know, we're not supposed to talk about it.'

'When was yours?' asked Maxwell.

'Oh... about ten generations back... it's getting to be a bit hazy to be honest. I remember fighting which was horrible and then we used to run an ale-house. I suppose that's why I'm working here.'

'Do you remember anyone in the family killing themselves?'

Frank screwed up his eyes.

'No,' he said.

'Are you sure?' said Felicity.

'Pretty certain, there wasn't much of that sort of thing about back then. You were just trying to survive.'

'But what about later lives?' said Maxwell. 'You must have had more lives as an Old One?'

'A few I guess, but often I've been dormant. But we don't really remember all our reincarnations as Old Ones. It's the first life that you remember, everything's fresh ... Like for you three.'

The door of the pub opened and in staggered Hughie with his pugilistic friend in tow. Frank sighed. 'Better go and sort them out,' he said, as he made his way back to the bar.

I thought how strange it all was. We had been used to the Old Ones all our lives and generally took them for granted. We knew better than to ask them about their past experiences, it simply wasn't spoken about. I wondered whether I would ever volunteer to be an early settler in a

New Life. What kind of Old One would I be, and what would I take with me from this life? No point in thinking about it though, the only way I could volunteer would be if Jessica got pregnant, and that wasn't going to happen anytime soon.

'It's hopeless,' said Maxwell. 'I've just worked out the number of Jessica's ancestors, and only as far back as Frank's time, they run into hundreds. We can't possibly interview all of them.'

Felicity then turned to me: 'You're very quiet.'

'There's something wrong,' I said.

'Wrong?'

'Yes, wrong with your theory. It doesn't make sense.'

'Go on,' said Maxwell, 'enlighten us.'

'If I wanted to volunteer for New Life it would be when Jessica's pregnant. Yes?'

Maxwell nodded. 'We're lucky Jessica's not a bloke; they'd be calling up for volunteers the whole ruddy time,' he said darkly.

'Well then,' I said, 'you can't volunteer *after* you're dead.'

'Of course,' said Felicity quietly.

'That means,' I said, ignoring Felicity, 'suicide isn't a thing like having red hair or being a musical genius that can be passed on from one generation to the next. It's no use you searching for an Old One who killed themselves in a past life. You won't find any. All the Old Ones must have volunteered at some point to be an early settler. They couldn't possibly do that after their Host Person has died.'

'Blimey!' said Maxwell. 'We should have worked that one out, Fliss!'

'But there *is* a genetic component,' said Felicity. 'The stuff I read was quite clear about that.'

'Yeah, but you're over-simplifying,' said Maxwell. 'Col's right, there's no way that actually killing yourself could be passed down through the generations. The nearest thing you could say is that maybe a *tendency* to have suicidal thoughts could have a genetic component. So maybe you're looking for someone who *wanted* to kill themselves in their past life. Perhaps they tried and didn't succeed.'

'Oh God,' said Felicity 'so we're back to square one.'

'Bandits at twelve o'clock,' announced Maxwell quietly.

'Shit,' said Felicity, as Ada strode towards us.

15

'Came to apologise,' said Ada, as Maxwell stood up to block her path to Felicity. 'Shouldn't have hit you, sorry,' she sniffed and sat down at our table, 'but I just see red sometimes. Always been like it. Can't help it. Frank's told me your idea, you're looking for an Old One who wants to kill themselves.'

'More specifically,' said Maxwell, 'an Old One who *tried* to kill themselves in their past life. Know anyone like that?'

'Nope.'

Felicity sighed.

'We thought about consulting the archives ...'

'Won't do you any good,' Ada folded her arms across her large bust. 'The archives only have a shallow kind of truth, it's just stuff that's happened to Jessica. You need deep truth, solid truth. The truth that carries on from one generation to the next. You need the Cerebellum for that.'

Maxwell nodded.

'Of course,' he said. 'The Department of Certainty.'

'That's your name for it. For you lot everything's department of this and department of that. It's just what it is. And it's just *who* it is. Hathor's the one you need to see. She would know. Whether she would say would be another matter...'

'Why wouldn't she?' said Felicity. 'She'd want to live, wouldn't she?'

Ada shrugged.

Hathor. I remembered the tales we were told when we growing up in the kindergarten of the Cerebellum. Stories of the great sage Hathor, one of the oldest of the Ancients. How she and a small group of females lived deep in the centre of the Cerebellum, never travelling to other parts of the brain – let alone the rest of the body. Hathor, so the story went, knew everything that had gone on before and all the things that happened in the present. If we misbehaved us young Newbies would be told, 'Hathor's Eye is on you, she knows what you've been up to.'

I always imagined a very old woman with one enormous all-seeing eye who knew my darkest secrets. But as we grew up we dismissed those tales as fairy stories. I hadn't thought about her for years.

Ada continued.

'She doesn't concern herself with your world,' she said. 'She doesn't care about what happens in PF City, who's in power and who's out of favour. But she knows what's gone on before; she has knowledge of the Old Ones. If someone's trying to persuade Jessica to kill herself, Hathor will know all about it.'

'We should go then,' said Felicity. 'Go now. Could you take us?'

'Hold your horses,' said Ada. 'You need someone older than me, you need an Ancient to show you the way.'

Felicity slumped back in her chair.

'Does it have to be an Ancient? Can't we just ask the way when we get there?'

Ada shook her head. 'That's not how it's done.'

She stood up.

'I'll leave you three to it, that's all the help that I can give, I'm afraid. And sorry about your thump, you alright now?'

'Yeah, yeah,' said Felicity, only half listening, 'it's okay. An Ancient, who do we know?'

'There's our Alfred, in Soul…' I said dubiously.

'Ring him!' demanded Felicity imperiously. 'Ring him now.'

Alfred hadn't stepped outside the Thymus for months so I wasn't hopeful that he would fall in with Felicity's plans. But I went over to the bar and used Frank's phone to ring Grace and explain her sister's request. She went off to talk with Alfred, leaving me at the end of the phone studying Frank's rows of bottles of coloured liquid. Eventually she returned.

'He says yes, but we'll come up by blood and meet you at Medulla Central.'

'Okay, whereabouts?'

'Better be over by the quayside – meet us there, give us about fifteen minutes, I need time to get him ready.'

'We're on,' I said as I returned to our table. 'He's agreed, they're going to meet us at Medulla Central.'

'Good,' said Felicity, 'let's go. You coming, Max?'

'I'll come,' he said, 'I've always wanted to meet Hathor. Have I got time for a quick bevy before we go?'

Felicity shook her head as she pulled on her jacket. She hustled us out of the bar and set off down the street with us in her wake.

16

Medulla Central was more crowded than ever. It seemed everyone was on the move, trying to connect up with family and friends. There was an atmosphere of fear and tension as people scanned the crowds for a familiar face. We passed couples embracing, holding one another tightly, as if their love was enough to keep Jessica safe. As we approached the quayside, we were met with a throng of people who had just come off one of the boats. Some were bearing placards: 'SAVE US ALL', 'WE WANT TO LIVE!' Once they had dispersed, I spotted my work colleagues. Alfred was in a wheelchair with a tartan blanket over his knees and a yellow plaid scarf wound round his neck like a geriatric Rupert Bear. Grace waved and wheeled him over, then punched me lightly on the arm.

'Good to see you in one piece,' she said, and then, turning to her sister, added, 'Hello Felicity, alright?'

'Yeah, not bad… considering this day could be our last.'

Grace shook her head.

'It's hard to believe… Everyone's very scared. On the boat, we've been talking to a bunch of folk who'd come up from the Spleen. They said they can't sit around and wait for the end. They said they're going to demonstrate outside Dominion Tower.'

'It's the terrible twins!' Maxwell lumbered up towards us, out of breath.

'We're not twins,' said Felicity. 'I'm a year older than her…'

'... but not wiser,' said Grace with a grin.

'I've heard a lot about you,' said Felicity, as she was introduced to Alfred. 'Honoured to meet you sir.' Grace and I exchanged glances. It was good to see Grace again. I felt lighter inside.

'Fola not coming with us?'

'No Alfred, she's working with Nathaniel, over on East Side. I'll explain on the way,' I said.

'Right folks,' said Felicity, taking charge, 'we need to find the launch for the Cerebellum.'

Along the quayside the launches were lined up like teeth on a comb. Their destinations were chalked on small boards in front of each boat and they had names like Pelvis Express and Stomach Tornado. Mostly they seemed to be going in the wrong direction; down the wide vertebral river. Further along the bank we came across several boats going to the Cerebellum.

'Which one?' Felicity asked Alfred. Each of the motor launches was advertising a different route.

Alfred was sunk down in his wheelchair, blinking. Eventually he said, 'Does that one go via the Pica River? We should take that one.'

We trooped on board, Grace and I supporting Alfred as he tottered across the gang plank and down the steep steps into the bowels of the boat. All the seats faced forward towards a large RTM screen where Jessica appeared to be staring at her computer again. The wheelchair was stowed next to Alfred who immediately wrapped the blanket round himself and fell asleep. Maxwell sat next him and closed his eyes while the sisters and I went back up top. There were no outside seats. The launch resembled an oblong metal cigar case with a slender running board all the way round it.

'Let's sit up there,' said Felicity.

'It doesn't look very safe,' I murmured, as Felicity and Grace hauled themselves on to the roof.

The engines coughed and then thrummed into life, spewing out a dark cloud of fumes. The smooth flat roof held a number of fixings with pieces of rope threaded through them and I seized one of these with both hands, in case we hit some rough waters.

'We're going up a cerebral artery,' shouted Felicity, laughing. 'We're not being pumped round the heart.'

As we left the crowds and bustle of Medulla Central, the buildings became fewer, replaced by fields and trees. We gained speed and the air smelled fresher and the wind tugged at our clothing and hair. Felicity and Grace were chatting and laughing in front of me but I couldn't make out what they were saying. I thought about our quest; Ada had seemed certain that Hathor would know who we were looking for, but how long was it all going to take? It could just be one of Sean's FWOTs. At least Alfred and Grace were on board, which made three of us from Soul, outnumbering Felicity and Maxwell from Problem Solving. That led me to Fola. Had the Child started to talk yet? I regretted that I hadn't had time to speak to her, to let her know what we were doing. Without her, Soul was not complete.

PART FOUR

DUSK

1

The big fear that haunts every social worker is a death on her caseload. Baby M was three months old when she died of Sudden Infant Death Syndrome. She had been born to parents who had been in care themselves and who, in the past, had intermittently used crack cocaine to numb the tediousness of always being short of everything. She was on a Child Protection Plan because she was considered to be 'at risk of harm'. So, even though things were getting better, even though her young parents hadn't gone near the drug for the past six months, her death was understood in the context of failure. Her bedding and bottles were collected up for forensic analysis and her grieving parents were interviewed, separately, by two members of the Police Child Protection Team.

Search hard enough and you'll find something amiss. Something that wasn't quite perfect. Baby M's bedding was not as clean as it might have been. Dad had been smoking, always on the balcony, he said, but weren't those fag-ends in the sitting room? Enough to convey, so very subtly, a message that these parents were not quite fit for purpose. They had squandered their gift. The forensic paediatric pathologist ruled out foul play and put forward the cause as an 'unexplained death'; nevertheless, the stench of blame clung to this family. Internalised by the couple into a nagging self-doubt and guilt. The knowledge that whatever they did they would fall short and mess it up.

Blame can be contagious. Internal procedures meant that there was an immediate lock down of the family's computer records. Then followed a scrutiny of the work that Jessica had done with the couple and their child. As a social worker, Jessica was both conscientious and imaginative. But search hard enough and you'll find something amiss. Not a lot to find: a home visit postponed (Jessica was in court on another case that day). A delay in recording a meeting with the health visitor.

Then a memo from the head of department went out to all social workers reminding them to do everything on time, but not explaining how to achieve this when there was too much work to cram into the working day. Everyone was kind and understanding, but Jessica was left with a sense of being complicit in failure.

She alternated between feeling numb with sorrow for the couple and furious at the way that they had been treated. She stopped doing the comedy gigs. It was possible to find the funny side in most scenarios but not this one. Her routine had a whole section based around social work. She had carefully filleted the golden comic moments from her job and reassembled them into a riff about a Troubled Family called the MacKenzies. The MacKenzies always came out on top and it was the naïve social worker who was the real butt of the gags. But after the baby's death there were no more jokes to be found. Jessica packed up her scripts and put them in the bottom of the wardrobe.

Once it was all over, she needed a break from the sharp end of social work. The post in Performance & Information Management came up, poacher turned gamekeeper were the snide comments, and at first it seemed like a holiday. No more evening visits, no more spending the weekend writing court reports. But she missed her families and the cut and thrust of the front line. She also suspected that much of what she did during her working day was pointless. Or possibly worse than pointless. She was now part of a performance management system designed to make everyone feel that, like the baby's parents, they needed to improve and were simply not quite good enough.

2

The journey made me think back to my early days on the hillsides of the Cerebellum. Us Newbies were allocated, six to a house, to a couple of Old-Ones. We had Hannah and Rosie, kind and idiosyncratic, who looked after us just as parents in the Outside World should nurture their offspring. Hannah always talked about the virtues of physical exercise and made us run up and down the hills whenever the weather was fine. Rosie encouraged us to enter the world of the written word. She had a friend up in East Side who made sure that the young Jessica was always reading. Rosie would then get us to imagine ourselves into the narrative – what would it be like to be Roald Dahl's Matilda or Judy Blume's Margaret? It was Rosie who got me my first posting in Creative Thoughts.

I thought about my five old school-mates and wondered what had become of them. Maybe something science-related, wearing white coats somewhere in the Hypothalamus or Pituitary. Or maybe opting for an easy life, on a barge going up and down the lymph system. There was Jasmine, of course, lugging around her boxes in the Hippo Campus, a woman of few words but abundant strength. Someone whose muscle power and determination could get you out of any kind of trouble. Then I remembered that if we did not find Hathor, and get her to help us, this could be the last day for Jasmine, and for us too.

'You alright?' Grace turned round and shouted above the sound of the engine.

'Yeah, okay.' I held tight to the fixings.

'A bit blowy,' she said, 'but it's a great view.'

I was unfamiliar with this region of the Cerebellum; the terrain seemed a lot flatter than in the north where we all grew up. The river meandered through a field of tall reeds and the late afternoon sun caught their feathery fronds, turning them pale copper and gold. I was glad to be in the fresh air away from the wretched RTM below and all the pressures on Jessica. I would have been happy to stay there longer but the boat began to slow down as the river narrowed. Up ahead I could see some low wooden buildings with ramshackle jetties poking out into the water.

Maxwell appeared from the deck below.

'We've got to change boats here apparently, better come back down.'

Downstairs I was surprised to see Alfred up and out of his seat, holding on to a headrest and looked alert.

'This is where the Pica River divides,' he said. 'We'll need a smaller boat to take us further.'

The five of us worked our way along the thin wooden plank leading to the jetty. Maxwell and Grace managed to haul the folded wheelchair up between them, Maxwell cursing all the while, under his breath. Then we watched as the launch made a three-point turn and set off, back the way we had come. We were standing on a simple wooden pier that jutted out into the river. There was no sign of life from the collection of dilapidated huts. I felt uneasy, it was as if we had been abandoned.

'Now what?' said Felicity.

Alfred nodded his head towards the quayside. I could just make out a figure lying prone on a wooden bench, a straw hat covering their face. Alfred took Maxwell's arm. 'Come with me,' he said.

Alfred appeared to have adopted Maxwell as his best friend. They were a surprising pairing, I thought, as I watched them walk in front of us arm-in-arm; Maxwell, towering over Alfred, comfortable to slow his pace to the old man's shuffling gait. He prodded the dormant figure, who stood up, shaking a mass of chestnut corkscrew curls. After a few moments' conversation Maxwell beckoned us over.

'This is Maya; apparently, she's been expecting us,' Maxwell raised an eyebrow.

'How did she ?...' started Felicity.

'Follow me,' interrupted Maya, 'my boat's over there. You can leave that thing,' she pointed to the wheelchair, 'on the quayside. It won't be any use where you're going.'

Maya's boat was long and narrow and it bobbed up and down like a discarded seed pod in a stream. Maxwell sat in the front and then there was just about room for the rest of us to sit in twos side-by-side with the unsmiling Maya at the rear, presiding over the outboard engine. The river lapped close to the gunnels and I noticed there were no life jackets or anything else that would be useful if we capsized.

Alfred sat next to me, his plaid blanket tucked round his knees, looking serenely untroubled.

'Is this a good idea?' I asked him in a whisper. 'There's surely too many of us.'

'Maya knows what she's doing,' he said, 'all shall be well.'

We set off up the meandering river and Felicity turned around and called to Maya over the noise of the outboard.

'Excuse me, is there an RTM on board?'

Maya gave a small snort.

'Does it look like it?'

'Thought you might have a hand-held.'

'Nope.'

'How long till we reach...till we reach our destination?'

'Not long.'

Felicity pursed her lips and was about to say something further but Grace shook her head. So instead she prodded Maxwell.

'Max', she said, 'there's no RTM in the boat.'

'So?'

'But how will we know? ... Know what's going on?'

'I'm sure we'll get by.'

I understood Felicity's concern; there is always an RTM, unless you're in the Oubliette. I've never been anywhere without being able to glance up at the monitor and check out Jessica's thoughts or what she is looking at. I felt isolated and vulnerable and cut off from the rest of the body. Also, without access to an RTM I had no idea what the Outside World Time was. There's a programme that constantly runs from ActCon which tells Jessica to check her watch – usually around every twenty minutes. Nearly everyone I know uses Outside World Time rather than Internal Time. The exception being Alfred: he always says that the Great Circadian Clock in the hypothalamus has been sufficient for thousands of years and is good enough for him.

I was frustrated at how long this escapade was taking. We only had about an hour before Jessica would finish work and be ready to take the tube back home again. Just an hour to stop any more suicidal thoughts from getting into ActCon. Yet here we were, in the depths of the Cerebellum, far, far away from ActCon and probably wasting valuable time.

I guessed that Felicity was feeling the same; her shoulders were hunched with tension. Every so often she would mutter to Grace, 'How much further do you think?' and 'Surely we must be there soon?' To which Grace responded with a shrug and a shake of her head.

Meanwhile the terrain was changing; the vegetation had thickened, the reeds replaced by tall trees with curious misshapen trunks. As the river narrowed their branches met over our heads, cutting out the sunlight. Maya switched off the engine and reached for a paddle tucked beneath where we were sitting. It took a while to adjust to the quiet; the only sound being the gentle rustling of the leaves in the breeze and the soft lapping of the wake washing against the bank. We sidled round the bends in the river and I think we all began to feel a sense of calm. There was a hypnotic rhythm to Maya's paddling, first to the right, then to the left, guiding our small boat beneath the green dappled light.

Then, up ahead, the river broadened into a small lake and we could make out a collection of wooden huts on stilts over on the far side and a tall column of smoke curling out of the roof of the middle hut. Maya gave three low whistles and a figure descended the ladder of one of the huts and ran towards us along the jetty, waving enthusiastically. I recognised her as Jane, the Old One who had been sent out of Marcia's meeting that afternoon.

'Welcome! Welcome!' she beamed, as Maya threw her a rope. She looked more relaxed than when I had last seen her. 'Hathor is expecting you.'

Maxwell stood up and nearly capsized the boat as he lunged towards the jetty. Maya swore but Jane laughed as she grabbed Maxwell's arm and hauled him onto dry land. The rest of us followed, Alfred seeming remarkably agile as he stepped off the boat and onto the jetty.

'So this is it,' said Maxwell looking around, 'this is where the certain and absolute Truths are kept. Is there a storeroom or library or something?'

Jane frowned.

'Just how many do you think there are?'

Maxwell shrugged.

'Dunno…but…'

Alfred, sensing Maxwell's confusion and disappointment took him by the arm.

'Certainties are few in number, very few,' he said. 'There's no need to keep records, Hathor knows them. Come and meet her.'

3

I shared Maxwell's disappointment. I expected more than this. I had imagined somewhere impregnable, like Amygdala Fort, or beautiful, like the Seat of Active Consciousness. I, too, wanted a vault where the ancient texts were kept. Or maybe just one manuscript, but something at least which listed those absolute certainties that had been passed down through the generations. Those unchanging tenets of belief which would act as a moral framework, as compass points to guide Jessica through a life of uncertainty and shifting values. But here we were standing in an empty clearing, surrounded by mud huts. It was all just too basic, too simple, too nothing.

We were led to the central hut and up a ladder to a veranda. Mia flopped down on a low bench while Jane called through a heavy red curtain into the room beyond.

'They're here,' she turned back and smiled.

A tiny elderly woman emerged from behind the curtain. She wore a shiny robe of blue and silver, which reminded me of fish-scales, and a turquoise amulet round her neck. Perched precariously on the top of her head sat a tall headdress with a pair of horns surrounding a bright orange disk. Wispy white hair framed her wrinkled face and her bright brown eyes looked intently at each of us in turn. Sighting Alfred she went over and took both his hands in hers:

'Alfred.'

Her voice was horse and little more than a whisper.

'My dear!' was his response.

'The Child! You didn't bring the Child.'

'I know of no child,' said Alfred.

'She means the child from the Oubliette,' said Felicity. 'Colin rescued her.'

'You should have brought her to me,' said Hathor.

'She's with Fola. Fola's looking after her.' I said.

Hathor turned to me.

'So you are Colin,' she said, 'Colin from Soul.'

She shuffled towards me and, to my surprise, took hold of my arms above the elbow. I felt the ferocity of her grip as she pulled me down so that my face was almost level with hers. She smelled of wood smoke and coconut oil.

'You tried your best... you showed spirit.'

I didn't know what she meant so I didn't say anything.

'Jessica made a bad choice, we all felt it here,' Hathor continued, 'but you tried to stop that Thought. It was good that you tried. And the Child, the Child is free... from that place ... you did well.'

She turned and slowly walked back to the curtain.

'Come,' she said, 'tell me about the Child.'

Then she slipped back behind the curtain and was gone. We looked at one another wondering what to do next.

'Go,' said Jane, 'she wants you to go in, not all of you. Just him.' She gestured at me.

All I saw at first was a lively fire burning in a stone grate in the centre of the room. Then, as I got used to the dim light, I noticed the rugs on the floor and densely patterned tapestries and bright silk hangings on every wall. The designs were of flowers and trees, and creatures of air, land and water, picked out in rainbow colours and silver and gold thread. Everything shimmered in the firelight.

Hathor sat on a low stool and gestured to me to sit on the rug at her feet.

'Now Colin, tell me about the Child.'

I began nervously, telling her about Fola and the oubliette but she shook her head with impatience.

'You don't listen…the Child.'

So I told her everything that I could think of, how she was dirty and smelly but seemed quick and lively even though she hadn't said a word. I finished off with how Josie had cleaned her up and how I had watched her catching leaves in the park.

Hathor smiled at that bit.

'More wood,' she shouted.

Jane came in and fed the fire. The flames leapt high as they consumed the dried branches. Then she threw on some larger logs and the fire settled down, crackling and hissing as the logs turned from black to orange. The heat was intense and Hathor's face glowed red in the reflected light. Jane slipped back into the shadows.

Old Ones love a flame. A candle will do, but a real fire is one hundred times better. Jessica doesn't often get to see a fire these days. She has a gas fire in the flat which just isn't the same. Giulia has a real fire and whenever Jessica visits in winter a call goes up and all the Old Ones stop what they are doing. A command goes to Vision and Jessica simply stares at the fire. Nothing else happens for several minutes, nothing in or out of ActCon, no Thoughts, no Decisions. Some folk, in their various departments, just get on with stuff and take no notice. But I always follow the Old Ones and watch the RTM. If you stare right into the fire you enter another world; a city where the orange and red walls melt into caverns of white light, a place where, very slowly, everything turns to dust.

I don't know how long I sat staring into the fire, mesmerised. Hathor called for herbs to be burned and a strong sweet smell pervaded the hut. I was aware of feeling heavy and very relaxed. I didn't want to move, just to stay where I was. If Jessica were to kill herself I felt that I was in the right place. I would be safe here, deep in the Cerebellum. It was tempting just to sit and do nothing.

'Hathor,' I said, thinking that I should approach the issue slant-wise, 'what is your story.'

She looked down at me with an amused expression.

'I came out of the dry lands with my people and we discovered the sea.' She spoke slowly and softly and I had to concentrate hard to catch

195

her words. 'We travelled with the flame and it was my task to keep it alive. I never let the flame die.'

'And what did you know?' I pressed her.

'I knew all things,' she said. 'I knew about Certainty. That what you want to know isn't it? I knew how to feed the flame. I knew how to smell water and how to find the best herbs. All these things were good to know but they were not the same as Truth.'

'Which was…?'

Hathor smiled and shook her head.

'You know…' she said. 'Alfred knows… the only Certain Truth is that we are all one and the same. We are made of the same dust as the water and the herbs. You think of truth as something to search for and find; and knowledge as something to collect and keep. Truth is what you feel, and not what you know. Every day I feel it; it is wonder and astonishment. It is wonder that there is anything at all, it is wonder that there is a Jessica, it is astonishment that there is an Outside World. We are all dust and to dust we will return.'

At that she stood up and tottered towards the fire. For an awful moment I thought that she was going to topple right into it, but she took a stick and manoeuvred a log so that it was more central to the heart of the fire. I watched as the yellow and white flames cradled the wood, making it splutter and spit.

'Take the Child into ActCon,' Hathor said, 'let her speak… her voice should be heard in every part of the Body.'

'We can try to do that, but we can't really make her speak if she doesn't want to.' I decided to plunge on: 'We have come to see you because of what happened today. There are bad Thoughts getting into ActCon, Thoughts telling Jessica to kill herself.'

'So I heard,' she shrugged and slowly walked back to her seat.

'We are living in hard times. East Side and West Side have never been so far apart. West holds power tightly; East is in disarray and Internal Security clamps down on all that is good.'

'These things must be played out,' said Hathor. 'We have seen this before, things come around in a circle.'

'That's true,' I said, 'but now it seems that Jessica is not able to get out of her depression. She is paralysed by it and by the divisions within her. She wants to kill herself.'

'She should not die today; her time is not right. Not while the Child is still to speak. But it is for others to act. You are all agents in the world, not me. My work is to cherish the flame.'

'That flame will be snuffed out, extinguished entirely if Jessica kills herself. We think that there's an Old One who put the suicidal thought into ActCon this morning. You have knowledge of all the generations that have gone before. Who amongst the Old Ones would want Jessica to die?'

'Many have suffered sorrow along their path.'

'We think that it could be someone who tried to kill themselves in a past life but failed, and now they are trying to repeat the past. Please, just think of who it might be.' I knew that I was starting to sound desperate but I was afraid that Hathor was going to clam up completely.

'More herbs,' said Hathor, sitting stock-still with her eyes closed. Jane came forward again and threw bunches of greenery onto the fire, and the leaves fizzled and collapsed in on themselves giving off a sweet pungent aroma. Glancing over at Hathor, I wondered whether she had fallen asleep but at last she began speaking softly, this time with a sense of urgency.

'Darkness and a chill wind, a bitter chill wind, coming up eastwards from the sea.'

Then suddenly I was there.

It wasn't that I saw it all on the RTM, I was *actually* there. I wasn't sitting on the floor of Hathor's hut anymore; it was dark and damp-cold and I was walking along a stone pavement. There was soot in the air and the smell of rotting vegetation coming up from beneath me. I was on a bridge across a wide river. I was wearing a long skirt that was making a swishing noise with every step. The only other sounds were the clip-clopping of horses' hooves as a carriage rumbled past and the wind rattling the glass in the gas-lamp overhead.

Get to the middle.

A man lurched towards me out of the mist.

'Looking for business?'

I shook my head and moved on quickly. A heavy shawl was round my head and I pulled it tighter across my chest. By now I had overshot the middle of the bridge, I glanced back and saw that the man had reached the far end so I turned around and doubled back towards the centre.

Wait, not yet, too many people.

A couple, arm in arm, were walking towards me. I stood by the iron railings and pretended to study the view down river. The couple passed by. But then came the sound of another carriage, a horse and cart this time, moving so slowly, almost at walking pace.

At last it passed me. I glanced up and down, there was no-one else around. Next to where the lamppost joined the railing was a stone side strut. I stepped up onto it and looked down. The river was far below, flowing silently with barely a ripple. As far as I could see there was nothing to break my fall.

I held up my skirt with one hand and reached up and grabbed the lamppost with the other. I heaved myself up onto the metal rail so that I was half-sitting on it and swung my legs over. I gripped the rail tightly; it was ice-cold. Below me was inky black water stinking of decay and death.

You can do it, just end it. Let go, just do it now… jump.

The wind plucked at my shawl, sweeping it off my head.

Lord have mercy…

I jumped.

The shock was indescribable; unbelievably cold. I tasted the bitter water in my mouth and then felt a burning, choking sensation as it went up my nose. Then nothing.

I was back, sitting on the wooden floor of the hut. I was shaking and still had the bitter taste of the river in my mouth.

Hathor made a low groaning sound and opened her eyes.

'Water,' she said, 'I need water.'

Jane came forward with metal beaker, Hathor took a gulp, rinsed out her mouth and spat it back into the beaker.

'Terrible, terrible,' she murmured, 'she was only a child... just fifteen years old. So afraid. Jumped off the bridge when she found out she that was pregnant. So alone, so afraid.'

'Did she drown?'

'They saw her jump and dragged her out of the water. Poor little one, so cold... couldn't stop shivering.'

'She lived?'

'Yes, she lived.'

'But who was she?'

'She lived, and so did the baby, she was strong, even the poison water of the foul river didn't kill her. Four generations back; Jessica's great great grandmother. She went on to have four children and one of those was Jessica's great grandmother.'

'Her name, Hathor, what was her name?'

Hathor closed her eyes.

'She was Jessica's great great grandmother. One hundred and thirty years ago she tried to end her life. Annie, her name was.'

'Annie,' I repeated. At first the name meant nothing, then I remembered the woman with the trolley.

'The caffeine lady?'

'Take care, she is desperate. She will not give up easily. Now I am very tired; you can go now, you have what you need to end this. But remember the Child, she must speak. She must be heard.'

With that Hathor waved a hand and closed her eyes. I was dismissed.

4

'We should have thought of her before,' said Felicity. 'An Old One with easy access to everywhere, not noticed as she sneaks about.'

'It's hard to believe. Not Annie, she's always seems cheerful,' said Nathaniel.

'Yeah well, looks like that's a bit of a front.'

Felicity, Maxwell and I were back in Nathaniel's office on East Side. Nathaniel was perched on the piano stool having, once more, offered the swivel chair to Maxwell. I sat back on the purple sofa next to Felicity and closed my eyes, relieved that it was all over. The journey back to Pre-Frontal City had been swift and uneventful; like we were part of a video being played backwards, as we glided back the way we had come. Maxwell barely spoke to me in Maya's boat; he was peeved that I had had the private audience with Hathor and not him. But once we were on the launch he couldn't contain his curiosity and questioned me closely on everything Hathor had said. When I told him the part about Truth, he nodded.

'What I always thought,' he said.

Once we were back in Medulla Central Station we said goodbye to Alfred and Grace. Alfred needed a rest so they caught the Lymph paddle-steamer back down to Soul. At the station, Felicity put a call through to Dominion Tower and updated Sean with all that Hathor had told us. A warrant had been put out for Annie's arrest; she would not be able to get back into ActCon. The threat level was down to a Code Orange. We were safe.

'It's a bit odd, don't you think,' continued Felicity, 'that no-one saw her. You asked around, didn't you?' She looked at Maxwell.

'Yep,' he said, performing a 360 degree spin on Nathaniel's chair, 'they all said there was nothing unusual. I guess they were so used to seeing her with her trolley that she sort of merged into the background. Hiding in plain sight.'

He stopped spinning and sat still for a moment.

'Also,' he continued, 'you know she carries stuff on her trolley.'

'What d'you mean "stuff",' Felicity spoke sharply.

'You know, this and that.'

'What are you saying, that she gave them some drugs?' Felicity said 'drugs' in a schoolmarm way. For her, anyone caught using deserved an instant detention.

'A bit of dope and serotonin…'

'It's true,' I said, 'she offered me something this morning, even though we'd never met before.'

'You should have reported her,' said Felicity. Maxwell rolled his eyes.

'All I'm saying is that maybe she slipped something into the caffeine while she was up there. Something to make the 'Looking Good' folk up there feel a bit woozy. I dunno … I guess it's possible.'

'What will happen to Annie…when they find her?' I asked.

'Oubliette, I should imagine,' said Nathaniel. 'She can't be left to wander about and get back into ActCon with her suicidal thoughts. She's dangerous.'

I remembered Hathor's hut and how it felt being Annie; the stink of the water, the choking sensation as she nearly drowned. Hathor's words: *poor little one, so cold, couldn't stop shivering.* She needed help but wasn't going to get it in the Oubliette.

'Anyway,' said Nathaniel, aware that the mood had turned downbeat, 'you've all done very well. This should be the end of these negative thoughts. And even I have had a reprieve,' he smiled. 'Marcia has decided that it was Annie who caused this morning's bump on the head so she has rescinded the warrant for my arrest. I'm a free man.'

'Has she got any evidence… that it was Annie?' said Felicity screwing up her eyes.

'Marcia doesn't need evidence, she decides what's true and what isn't,' said Maxwell.

'The other bit of good news,' said Nathaniel, 'is that Jessica has finished the Performance Report and has emailed it off.'

'Thank God for that,' said Felicity.

'And did she fiddle the numbers?' asked Maxwell.

'Kind of … I think so. I wasn't really paying attention. Left it to your lot in Problem Solving. It's done now, anyway.'

Nathaniel was blasé about Jessica changing the statistics. He seemed happy to put the responsibility over to West Side and ignore the moral issues completely. It was left to Jane from Certainty and, I guessed, me from Soul to kick up a fuss, and no-one cared anymore what either of our departments thought.

Maxwell and Felicity were bickering about the statistics and whether Jessica had a choice about obeying orders. The RTM on Nathaniel's desk showed that Jessica was still in her office reading case-notes on the computer. She glanced up at the clock on the wall which showed that Outside World Time was 5:15 pm. Jessica's working day was supposed to finish at 5:30 but she rarely left the office before six and sometimes it was after seven. Surely this was an opportunity to go home early, just for once. I went over to the RTM and turned up the volume so that I could hear as well as see what Jessica was reading:

Home Visit: Helen (Mum) and Chloe seen. Wondered if Helen drinking as appeared flushed but no smell of alcohol. Rubbish still in front garden. Discussed police referral re dispute with neighbour (see documents). Helen denied being abusive. Kitchen quite messy with piles of dirty dishes in sink. Chloe's bed now has bedding but bedroom still looks bare. Discussed place available detox and rehab at Clare House. Saw Chloe on her own. Says things are okay and continues to be guarded. She's looking forward to school starting again next week …

The words 'Heightened emotional response' appeared at the base of the RTM picture. With it the sound of depression increased. The static interference, which had continued all day, began to drown out the sound of Jessica's reading. I turned up the volume on the RTM.

'What's going on?' said Felicity.

I swung the RTM round so everyone could see it and increased the volume some more. Jessica was flicking through various screens:

Ah, here we are.

Jessica had downloaded something titled Report for Review Child Protection Conference. She scrolled to the back page.

Summary and Recommendation

Chloe who is 6 years of age has had a Child Protection Plan for three months. She also had a previous CP Plan when she was between 3 and 4 years old. Chloe's mother Helen has had problematic alcohol use since she was a teenager. Helen underwent successful rehab two years ago but in the past six months has begun drinking again. Recently she has been drinking on a daily basis (mostly strong lager but spirits if she can afford it).

'Why's she reading this stuff?' said Maxwell. 'She could just go home.'

Everyone ignored him and concentrated on the screen.

When Helen is sober she is a good mother to Chloe and meets all her physical and emotional needs. When she has been drinking Helen will often fall asleep on the sofa and Chloe is left to her own devices. Chloe is very loyal to her mother and is guarded when talking to me. She has told her nan that she has found Helen's bottles of vodka and poured the contents down the sink...

There was pause as Jessica closed her eyes for a moment.

...that she has found Helen's bottles of vodka and poured the contents down the sink. She clearly wants her mother to stop drinking.

I felt the floor shaking beneath my feet as one of Nathaniel's piles of books toppled over. The RTM was totally black. Jessica's eyes were closed. An alarm call came out of the monitor, a shrill piping sound of five short blasts followed by a longer blast: beep, beep, beep, beep, beep, beeeeeep. The sequence then repeated.

'Oh God no,' said Maxwell getting out of the chair and crouching down onto his knees.

The mood band appeared at the bottom of the screen, it read: DANGER NAUSEA.

By now we had all left our seats and were on the carpet with our hands over our heads. The floor was undulating in waves and books were hurtling out of Nathaniel's bookcase as the whole room pitched and rolled. The desk-lamp fell over with a clang. I sneaked a look up at the RTM and saw that Jessica was running along the corridor and into the ladies. The next view was of a toilet bowl. Pine disinfectant overlaying a musky urine smell. It was stained brown beneath the water level and there were two small shit-marks below the rim. Beep, beep, beep, beep, beep, beeeeeep.

The next thing that we heard was a terrible retching which welled up from the depths of Stomach and then the splash as Jessica's vomit hit the toilet bowl.

5

Sick is like pain. No-one working in Jessica can escape it when it happens. Some say it's much worse; at least with pain, you can get on with something else while it lasts. But with Sick it's impossible. They used to run sick drills when we were Newbies in the Cerebellum: the five short beeps followed by one long one. Then it would be down on the floor, keep away from windows, hold on to something. We had plenty of the real thing as well; there was a time, when Jessica was a child, that she seemed to be throwing up every other week. Other children's parties, a journey in the back seat of the car, any kind of troubling news would activate the Nausea Alarm and we would have to take up our positions.

The CorpCal actually stops during Sick; if you have the misfortune of trying to get from West to East when the alarm goes you're stuck, stationary, in the dark tunnel, sometimes for as long as half an hour. The most unsettling thing is the way the floor moves up and down, as if you are on a boat. The temperature rises and everyone feels hot and sweaty.

The alarm went into recovery mode. This is a sequence of slightly quieter beeps with no longer one. We are trained to remain down on the floor during recovery mode as another bout of Sick often follows. Jessica had flushed the toilet and was now on the cold tiles of the floor; sitting with her back against the wall. She had unrolled a wodge of toilet paper and was wiping her brow with it.

Oh God.

The Regulators in Hypothalamus began putting Thoughts into ActCon, trying to establish the cause of Jessica vomiting.

Must have been the sandwich, it tasted a bit odd.

The alarm stopped, the floor had stopped moving and we slowly got up. I helped Nathaniel to put the books back on the shelves.

'It's obviously what she was reading,' I said.

'What?' said Felicity.

'Not the sandwich, not that at all. She was reading about that child, Chloe, throwing her mum's drink down the sink. That's what did it.'

I reminded them about the recordings that I'd seen in the Memory Archives inside Amygdala Fort. Was it only that morning? The bit where the five-year old Jessica climbed up on the chair that she had placed next to the kitchen sink and carefully poured her mother's two bottles of spirits down the plug-hole. I couldn't tell them exactly what happened next; all I knew for sure was that Mum had come in and caught her. And, of course, that she'd been hit round the head and maybe more but, as I explained, I hadn't seen that bit.

'Blimey,' said Maxwell, 'grim. You should let them know, tell the Regulators that you think it was psychosomatic.'

Maxwell and Felicity began bickering over the meaning of 'psychosomatic' while the RTM showed that Jessica was now outside the toilet cubicle and splashing her face with cold water.

Mirror!

The word flashed up on the RTM with the usual ping sound. A lock of hair lay damply across one eye, the left hand came up and pushed it back. The face looked pale and clammy; the eyes red and swollen. Jessica went back into the toilet and got some more toilet paper with which to blow her nose. That done, she threw the paper into the pan and flushed the toilet again. She came back to the mirror and put her right hand up to her forehead. *Hot!* She gripped the edge of the sink and closed her eyes. *I wish I were dead.* At the bottom of the screen were the words *Current Mood = very low, depression high.*

I sat back down on the sofa feeling dejected and worn out. Everything that we had tried to do seemed to be thwarted. Jessica could have phoned Giulia and heard a friendly voice, but that hadn't happened. We now knew who had been putting suicidal thoughts into ActCon but what difference did it make? There was still a Thought circulating around ActCon from this morning. We were no further forward.

Nathaniel was slumped in the sofa next to me, staring at the floor while Maxwell sat chewing his fingers. It was only Felicity who seemed to have any energy left; she was pacing backwards and forwards, and kicked Maxwell on the shin.

'Ow, what was that for?'

'Come on Max… think! Where are we?'

'Nowhere,' he said, and then after a pause: 'You were right, we've got the hereditary bit with Annie, we've got the current circumstances – this bloody job, we've got the unresolved trauma – nasty horrible childhood. Yeah we've got all the ingredients, just like you said, satisfied?'

'What about the Child?' I said.

'Hasn't she got a bloody name yet?' said Maxwell testily.

'Hathor said we should take the Child into ActCon. Maybe we should just do what she says.'

'Can't authorise that,' said Nathaniel. 'Far too risky and not fair on the kid, and anyway – she's still not speaking.'

I knew that he was right. It seemed very unlikely that the idea would come to anything other than harm.

On the RTM Jessica had left the toilet and had walked back to her desk. She began looking at the case-notes again, reading snippets of information:

When Helen is drunk she can be aggressive, there is a worry that she could be emotionally or even physically abusive towards Chloe …

She closed her eyes.

Not the tube – the bridge ….I'll go to the bridge.

'Oh fuck,' said Maxwell.

'You're right, Colin,' said Felicity, 'we are running out of options. We must take the Child to ActCon.'

'Okay,' Nathaniel sighed, 'go and talk to Fola and Josie, see what they say – they're in the Art Room.'

6

The Art Room is situated at the back of the Civic Centre – it's a long low extension with windows on all sides. The place is full of arty-crafty stuff with one whole side devoted to pottery; there's sacks of different coloured clays and a potter's wheel, as well as a shelf of bottles of glazes and slips. The only thing that is missing are the ovens for firing the pots. That's because things rarely get finished in the Art Room. It is not a place for producing work but for trying out different ideas and concepts. A place for design and planning. All the pottery equipment was put in when Jessica joined an evening class, years ago. A layer of dust now covered the whole of that side.

Opposite the pottery paraphernalia were rolls of material; cottons and silks, a sewing machine and a tailor's dummy. Spread out on a wide table were a pair of striped blue curtains. I remembered these, they were to be for Jessica's bedroom and they nearly got made for real. But then Problem Solving decided it as too much work and Jessica went to John Lewis instead.

The only part of the room in everyday use was the bit nearest the door where there was a large table with sheets of paper and coloured felt-tip pens. This is where Josie and the Child were sitting. At least Josie was sitting – the Child was kneeling on a stool concentrating on a drawing of what looked like a dagger. She was busy putting small crosses along the blade. Josie looked up from the daffodil she was drawing and smiled:

'Hello, looking for Fola? She's getting us some drinks. We're doodling.'

I nodded. I could see that the walls of this part of the room were covered with the familiar designs of Jessica's favourite doodles. A simple flower with rounded petals, an eye with a staring pupil but mostly box-like grids, netting with heavily shaded diamond patterns and jagged edges.

'Do you do these?' I asked.

'I'm mainly flowers,' said Josie, 'Eric does the abstract stuff.'

'I like the flowers… the other stuff gets a bit tedious.'

'Yeah, well. It's usually Eric's work that gets chosen.'

The Child looked up at me and frowned, chewing the end of her pen. She had changed out of Josie's jumper and was now wearing what looked like red pyjamas.

'You look very smart,' I said.

'Fola ran them up over there,' Josie nodded over toward the needlework area, 'she did them really quickly, they're good, aren't they?'

I nodded and the Child continued to frown at me, still chewing.

I have such limited experience of talking with children that I felt quite uncomfortable. I peered over her shoulder at her picture.

'A dagger,' I said, 'that's nice.' And then, as the Child continued to stare at me, sucking at a wisp of her hair, I added, 'You're good at drawing.'

Fola came into the room with a tray of soda.

'Colin! More adventures?'

'A few, I need to talk to you… in private.'

The Child had got down from the stool and was waving her picture in front of Fola's face.

'That looks sharp and pointy.'

The Child nodded.

'Good for cutting,' added Fola.

The Child nodded again and got back up onto the stool. She then made a stabbing motion with the pen, putting black dots over the whole piece of paper. There was something rather unsettling about her forcefulness.

'Can we go somewhere?' I said.

We crossed the corridor into the kitchen area.

'Like a drink?' asked Fola.

I nodded and she poured me a soda. The sweet fizziness made my mouth tingle and gave me a small boost of energy. I glanced up at the RTM positioned over the sink and saw that Jessica was logging off her computer. This was getting ready to go home mode. Time was running out.

I sat down on one of the kitchen chairs and told Fola about our journey to the Cerebellum and my meeting with Hathor. I told her Annie's story and how she was most likely the source of the morning's suicidal thoughts.

'But it's not over,' I said. 'Now there's thoughts about jumping off a bridge.'

'Can't they just make sure that Annie doesn't get into ActCon?'

'They're supposed to be doing that, but either she's back inside or else she's got an accomplice.'

There was silence for a while as we mulled this over.

'Could just be the Thought from this morning, still echoing around.'

I shook my head.

'It doesn't make sense. The Thought just now was specifically about the bridge – that's a new idea and would have needed a new Thought.'

'You've tried your best; there's nothing else that you can do.' Fola sounded resigned as she turned back towards the sink and began rinsing out our cups.

'There might be something.' My heart was thumping; I knew this was going to be difficult. I told her about Hathor's interest in the Child and her insistence that she be taken into ActCon. 'I think I get it, Fola, Jessica's experiences when she was little have been hidden, deep down. Hathor said that the Child must be heard, heard throughout Jessica, so that means getting into consciousness, into ActCon.'

Fola turned to face me, the corners of her mouth had gone down and her eyes were bright.

'No! you can't do that.'

'Hathor was very clear, she said we had to do it.'

210

'Maybe one day, but not *now*, Colin. What are you thinking? You said yourself the place will be swarming with Whiteshirts. We'll get picked up straight away and that will be me and the Child sent back to the Oubliette. Do you want that?'

'You don't have to come,' I said feebly.

'Do you think I'd let you take her without me? Anyway, in case you hadn't noticed… she doesn't speak, so there's no point. She's not ready. You can't *make* her speak. It's not good to force her. She needs time.'

Fola was putting the cups back in the cupboard with a clatter and a banging of the cupboard doors. She turned back to face me with her arms folded and begun another tirade of how impossible the idea was and how thoughtless I was to even suggest it.

Meanwhile Jessica was looking out of the window. Sounds of slamming car doors and revving engines as people left for home. Dusk was settling in, no sunset, just the slow draining away of light from the sky. Jessica put her head in her hands. The screen went blank. Her eyes were shut.

'Look,' I said to Fola, pointing up at the RTM, 'she's in a hopeless state.'

The screen remained blank but then we heard a Thought, but not just a Thought… Jessica was speaking… This was Out Loud:

'Will do it …Vauxhall Bridge…jump, then it will all be over.'

211

7

The immediate problem was how to get the Child over to West Side without drawing attention to ourselves. It is rare for children to be seen outside the Cerebellum so taking her on the CorpCal would be dangerous, particularly with all the Whiteshirts about. Questions would be asked and it was likely that she would be sent over to the Cerebellum, or worse scenario, back to the depths of Amygdala Fort. The second problem was Fola. She was, of course, insistent on coming but she hadn't set foot on West Side since escaping from the Oubliette and she was such a familiar figure it was likely that someone in Dominion Tower would spot her and, again, ask questions.

We left the Child with Josie and went back up to Nathaniel's office.

'She agreed!' I said as we entered the room.

'Against my better judgement,' said Fola.

'Good,' said Felicity, 'we thought he'd win you round.'

'I don't know why you thought that,' said Fola huffily, 'it is a reckless idea, dangerous for the Child. She's still fragile, psychologically. We don't know what your experiment will do to her.'

I thought back to our escape from Amygdala Fort in the memory boxes, how scary it had been. She had survived that alright.

'She's tougher than you think,' I said. 'Anyway, how are we going to get back up to Dominion Tower?'

'Ah,' said Nathaniel, 'we've been working on that.'

We gathered round Nathaniel's desk while he unrolled a large map.

'This shows all the routes out of East Side,' he said. 'You don't want to be using the CorpCal or even the CNS, but there's a back route down to the Pineal Gland that I'd recommend. Should be pretty quiet. From there you can take another of the pathways back up to West Side; it ends up close to Dominion Tower.'

'How long's that going to take?' I said. Jessica had packed up her bag and was doing up the buttons of her black coat.

'It's a branch line of the NS, it'll be quick.'

'Yeah, but then what?'

There was silence as Nathaniel rolled up his map and cack-handedly tried to squeeze it back into its cardboard tube. The RTM gave a ping and Nicholas's face appeared.

`Attention all personnel. I have a broadcast message for you from the Chief Executive. Please listen carefully.`

Then Marcia's face filled the screen, looking grave but also, I noticed, rather well made up, her lipstick well-co-ordinated with the ruby beads round her neck.

`In view of recent Thoughts we have returned to a Code Red level of emergency. I am asking all workers to remain calm and carry out their normal business as usual, remaining vigilant at all times…`

'God,' said Nathaniel, 'she thinks she's the Queen.'

`…however,` continued Marcia, `I have put in place restrictions on access to ActCon. No-one is allowed in the vicinity of ActCon which includes the roof of Dominion Tower without a permit. I have also instituted a moratorium on travel. All personnel to remain in their specific units.` Her voice then became lower in pitch. `We are facing challenging times ahead, but I have confidence that we will all pull together and overcome the trials that face us.`

'Oh shit,' said Maxwell, and then to Nathaniel, 'Can't you give a counter command or something.'

Nathaniel shook his head.

'I've got no authority on West Side, it's up to Marica.'

Felicity was doing her usual pacing back and forth when she suddenly stopped dead.

'It worked before …' she said slowly, looking at Fola. 'What have you got, that Marcia wants?'

We stared at her.

'Let me rephrase that…'

'Get on with it,' interrupted Maxwell.

'What does Marcia *think* you have, Fola?'

'A ticket!'

'What?' said Maxwell.

'For the Heavenly Airplane!' and Fola laughed one of her deep belly laughs that I hadn't heard since early that morning.

'Of course!' I said.

The others decided that it would have to be me to speak to Marcia and get her to agree our safe passage up to ActCon. As Nathaniel passed his phone to me we could see on the RTM that Jessica was leaving the building.

'We've not got long,' he said.

The words 'Colin from Soul' and 'personal matter' got me put through to Marcia in seconds.

'Colin,' she said, 'what can I do for you?' Her voice had the intimate, chummy quality that she usual reserved for her assistant, Nicholas.

I went into my spiel as rehearsed by the others. Don't lay it on too thick. Don't promise anything, be vague.

There was a pause at the end of the line once I had finished my speech. When Marcia spoke, she was positively purring:

'I quite understand, you want permission to travel?'

'That's right.'

'And access to the top of Dominion Tower? To ActCon?'

'Yes please.'

'What are you planning?'

I paused. How was I going to sound convincing?

'Erm, not easy to explain over the phone, but Soul personnel should be near ActCon if there's a danger of … danger of things ending.'

I screwed up my face. It sounded weak to me but the others were nodding in encouragement.

'Taking CorpCal?'

'Er no, we're coming up on one of the back routes, we'll use the outside lift to come up to ActCon, can you ask security to let us through?'

'That's not a problem Colin, so that'll be all of you from Soul? Alfred, Fola and, who's the other one?'

'That's Grace, but…'

'Yes of course, Grace. As you know, we're doing everything we can, to prevent a disaster, but it is very wise of Alfred to take precautions, to be ready for all eventualities. May I ask, do you know, what contingency has he prepared?'

'Can't really say, at this point,' I answered truthfully.

'Quite understand,' came the reply. 'Be assured of my support when the time comes. I'll make sure that members of Soul are cleared through security. See you in a while.' And with that she put the phone down.

'That was weird, either she knows you've escaped, Fola, or she's forgotten all about sending you to the Oubliette. She's expecting four of us and especially Alfred.'

'Makes sense,' said Nathanial. 'She's only going to believe in an escape module of some kind if you're all there together.'

'Wonder what she thinks will happen,' mused Maxwell, 'that perhaps that Alfred will mutter some incantation and away you'll fly, like angels with wings. Sounds rather fun, can I come?'

'Shut up Max,' said Felicity briskly, 'that stuff's all just fantasy,' and then, to me: 'You'd better phone Alfred and Grace, tell them to meet us in the Pineal Gland.'

'Alfred may say he's not coming,' said Fola. 'He'll be tired, he's already travelled a lot for one day.'

But Alfred didn't hesitate when I telephoned down to Soul and Grace explained the plan to him.

'He says we should follow the commands of Hathor,' said Grace, 'and he wants to be there when it happens. He also says that he'd like to see Maxwell again.'

'Maxwell?'

'That's what he said. We'll come up by Blood and meet you on the main lobby.'

'Looks like you're coming after all,' I said to Maxwell as I put the phone down.

'Yippee!'

215

'If he's going, I'm coming too,' said Felicity.

'That's too many,' I said, but secretly I was relieved. I felt that there might safety in numbers.

'We'll be the Magnificent Seven,' said Maxwell, 'and I'll be Steve McQueen… at least he survives until the credits.'

Maxwell's words hung in the air as Fola went off to get the Child and I felt very uneasy. We were obeying Hathor's command but this was a half-baked plan, short on details, and where the outcome could be very bad indeed. We seemed to have blagged a way of getting to the roof of Dominion Tower. But then what? The truth of it was: we had no idea what we were doing.

8

I had never been to the Pineal Gland or, as it is affectionately termed –
the Pine Cone, before. This is despite my putting it forward to my
colleagues as a possible alternative site for Soul. It has a lot going for it.
Nice and central and, most importantly, unlike so many other places in
that region, there is only one of it. So, no confusion as to whether you're
East or West Side. Good transport links too; well served by Blood and
the Nervous System. I was hoping to have the opportunity to take a bit
of a look round. Maybe raise the idea of a move with Alfred. I was in a
state of denial. Still unable to grasp that all of us, Soul, the Pine Cone,
East and West Sides were all about to be completely annihilated. Unable
to grasp that we had less than half-an-hour to stop the calamity.

The building was smaller than I had imagined. Only four stories high,
it sits like a short fat pine cone made of glass and steel. What's strange
about it is that it has rows of struts going all round the circular building;
each set of struts supports a solar panel facing up towards the sky. On a
sunny day the place must look like a Christmas decoration but when we
got there the sun had already set so the only reflections were of the dark
night sky.

The reception area was cheerful, though; brightly lit with a number of
display boards advertising the virtue of a good night's rest. There was a
central counter complete with a vase of flowers and someone sitting at
a desk behind, working on a computer. Above the counter and next to
the RTM was a 24-hour Circadian Clock which currently had its only

hand pointing to 'Dusk to Dark.' I have met purists on East Side who refuse to use 'Outside World Time' and only use Circadian time. They say things like, 'We will start the meeting a little past noon,' or 'My appointment is just after sunset.' It's pretty annoying because it's so vague, and also because it is usually accompanied by a lecture on the Tyranny of Outside World Time.

Felicity and Fola sat down on one of the sofas in the waiting area, the Child sandwiched between them. Felicity, still wearing her red jacket, looked neat and efficient; whereas Fola's dark hair blazed outward, like an aura. The Child squirmed between them, itching to go off to explore, but Fola kept a firm grip on her shoulders.

'Just stay put for a moment, we'll be going soon,' she said.

Maxwell and I went up to the reception desk. I was hoping to find out whether there was any spare space upstairs but before I could open my mouth Maxwell coughed to attract the attention of the woman behind the counter.

'Yes?' she said.

'Just calling in,' said Maxwell, 'on the off-chance, wondering whether you had any melly available.'

The receptionist raised her eyebrows.

'For your own use?'

'Problems sleeping,' said Maxwell.

'I can let you have five tabs, wait there,' and she went off into a back room.

'What's that?' I asked.

'Melly, melatonin, they make it upstairs, worth getting hold of. Could come in handy.'

I didn't have a chance to raise the possibility of Soul relocating to the Pine Cone as Grace and Alfred arrived and everyone was getting ready to leave. Maxwell pocketed his tablets while Fola introduced Alfred and Grace to the Child. Steadying himself with his stick Alfred bobbed down to her level.

'It is good to meet you,' he said, 'you have been a strong one, you have shown great fortitude. But we will help you to take off your armour. We will help you to become weak.'

The Child looked at him wide-eyed and alarmed, holding tight to Fola's hand.

As we left the reception area I turned back to look at the RTM. The view was of a South London street. There was an impression of brightly lit shopfronts and traffic crawling by but Jessica had her head down. No thoughts were being relayed but it seemed to me that the low noise of her depression was getting louder.

9

It is dark as Jessica strides past her usual underground station and heads towards the river. A soft drizzle is falling and droplets of water gather on her fringe and trickle down her forehead. Somewhere, in her bag, she has a small umbrella, but she does not stop to find it. She is oblivious of the rain.

Her journey home is often a time of reviewing the day. Counting the positives and negatives, trying to pinpoint exactly what has been achieved during the previous eight hours of work. If Jessica carries out that exercise now, what would her verdict be? She has finished the Performance Report and sent it off. But that relief would be tempered with a feeling of unease. The figures are not right, they are not truthful. And she has been sick. Throwing up at work for the first time ever.

But Jessica does not think these things. She has no thoughts at all. She does not notice the leaves underfoot turning to a brown slippery sludge. She does not hear the wailing ambulance siren in the distance, nor catch sight of the white plastic bag caught in the nearby railings, fluttering as a white flag. There is only the dark grey pavement and the twin shadows, now appearing, now receding as she passes under the sodium street lights. And a noise, painful, like radio interference, that's located somewhere in her brain.

10

The street outside Dominion Tower was empty but there were signs that a demonstration had been and gone. Discarded leaflets wafted along the pavement, caught by the breeze, and there was a load of the 'Save Jessica' placards piled up under a lamppost. Felicity and I left the others round a corner, a block away, while we strolled past the front of the building which was mostly in darkness, many of the departments having closed down for the evening. I tried to appear nonchalant but my heart was beating so loudly that I felt it could be heard inside the building. There were four armed guards outside the main entrance and then, as we skirted the building and looked down the side alley we could see two more outside the ActCon lift. We reported back to the others.

'We can't all go,' I said. 'Marcia has only given clearance for four members of Soul... not seven of us.'

'That obviously doesn't work,' said Maxwell scornfully, 'unless you propose to leave Grace behind and pretend that the Child is working in Soul.'

'I'm with Alfred,' said Grace. 'I'm not staying behind.'

There then followed a discussion which developed into a bout of bickering as to who would go and who would stay. I would have been happy to have stayed behind, while everyone else seemed determined to play the hero. Only Alfred and the Child kept out of the discussion. He had taken her a little way away from the rest of us and was showing her the upturned crane from the morning's collision with the cupboard door. It was obvious that no-one was going to give way and the argument petered out.

'I've an idea,' said Maxwell. 'Come on.'

We followed him to the corner and then watched as he set off down the alley to the ActCon lift. The guards bristled as he approached them and then seemed to relax as he engaged them in a discussion. I could see him pass something over to the two men who pocketed what they had been given. Maxwell then waved us over.

'Right,' he said in the guards' hearing, 'these two gentlemen have been given clearance for Soul personnel to go up to ActCon. There's been an oversight though,' he looked at the guards sternly as if it was their fault, 'clearance should say seven, and not four. Any old road, these fine fellows have agreed for us all to go up in the lift and sort it out once we get to the top.'

One of the guards pressed the call button and we waited in silence for the lift to descend. Fola kept the Child close to her so that she was nearly invisible amongst the folds of her skirt. I glanced at the guards furtively; they wore army fatigues and carried sub-machine guns. One of them was chewing gum. At last the lift arrived, the metal door slid open, and we piled in. Maxwell got in last having muttered a few words to one of the guards. Almost half the lift space was taken up by Fola's majestic bulk and Maxwell's large stomach so the rest of us had to squash together to accommodate them. I winked at the Child who almost gave me a smile in return.

'Was it the melatonin?' I whispered to Maxwell as the lift door clanged shut.

He shrugged.

'Soldiers always have a use for melly. Strange though, I was expecting Whiteshirts, not the army.'

The lift slowly ascended. We stood in silence avoiding eye contact. Felicity was biting her lower lip and there were beads of perspiration breaking out on Maxwell's forehead. The lift juddered to a stop and nothing happened. I was starting to fear that it had broken down, leaving us stranded for ever, packed like pilchards in a tin. Then there was a whoosh and a clang and the lift door slid open, letting in a blast of cold night air.

I braced myself for more guards with sub-machine guns, but there was no-one there. We spilled out of the lift and I strained to peer through the fine drizzle. The place was deserted. ActCon sat in the middle of the flat roof-top, all lights blazing, like a pleasure boat floating on a dark lake. There was a heavy-duty chain wound around the handles of the double doors secured by a large padlock. On the far side of the roof the huge Real Time Monitor screen showed dark puddles on grey pavements as Jessica weaved her way through dawdling pedestrians. No Thoughts. Just the sound of an ambulance siren in the distance.

A sharp clang sounded behind us as the lift door snapped shut followed by a whine as the lift returned to the ground floor.

'What's going on?' muttered Felicity. 'Where is everybody?'

To our right the Security post stood empty as did the Google booth. I walked over to the Looking Good stand, also abandoned. One of the chairs had been tipped over and a glossy magazine lay on the floor, its pages fluttering in the wind. A short distance away, nearer to the door of ActCon, was a caff trolley: thermos flasks lined up on the upper level, and the shelves of mugs below.

'Oh God, is that Annie's?' said Felicity.

'Looks like it,' said Maxwell, opening one of the flasks, 'still hot.'

I looked around, no sign of Annie. A dusky pink felt hat lay discarded on the ground. Maxwell bent down to pick it up.

'It's Leaf's.'

There was a sound of laughter coming from the other side of the receptor mast. Maxwell walked over to Leaf's tent and then beckoned us over.

'Keep the Child away.'

Fola and Alfred kept the Child between them while the rest of us went around to the other side of the mast. Outside Leaf's tent was a small pile of machine guns. Maxwell opened the flap and we peered in. The small tent was full of people. Leaf sat, crossed legged in the middle, while either side of him were four soldiers in various stages of relaxation. One of them seemed to be asleep while the other three sat back against Leaf's cushions with cards in front of them. In the centre was one of Annie's flasks and five mugs.

'Hello,' said Leaf, 'no guns allowed in here, this is a peace tent.'

'Hi Grace,' said one of the soldiers with a grin, 'we're playing Chase the Lady.'

'Sebastian?' Grace stared at him in surprise. 'What are you doing?'

'I just said… we're playing Chase the Lady.'

She shook her head.

'Let's get him out of here,' she said to me. We took an arm each and half dragged him out of the tent. Felicity fetched one of Looking Good's chairs while Maxwell gave him some water from Annie's trolley. I could see that he had T Cell Company embroidered over the breast pocket of his army fatigues. This had to be one of Grace's running buddies from the Thymus.

'Sebastian!' she said, shaking him by the shoulder. 'Sebastian, look at me. What's happened? Where's Annie?'

'I do like you, Grace,' the soldier looked at her fondly. 'I really, really do…'

'This smells like ordinary caffeine,' said Maxwell, passing Grace a mug of liquid. 'Try this.'

The soldier took some long draughts of caffeine. Meanwhile above our heads the RTM beamed out shots of cars and busses. Jessica was waiting at a pedestrian crossing, appearing not to notice the spray that splashed her shoes every time a vehicle thundered past. Over the lines of traffic, I could make out the weird architecture of Vauxhall Bus Station.

'Tell us what's happened.'

'Orders to take over from the Whiteshirts…done that… secure ActCon … done that …no-one inside … no-one in or out. Clear the roof of personnel … all gone except for the hippy… he won't budge…'

He paused and screwed up his face as if trying to remember something.

'Then what?'

'Now he says he'll go, but that he's cold and needs a hot toddy first. … I'm cold too… we're all cold. We'll just have a bit…' his voice trailed off and he looked sheepish. Maxwell went back into the tent and came out with the flask.

'Not sure what it is, smells like some kind of Serotonin.'

'Did you see Annie?' asked Felicity, standing over him.

The soldier looked up at her, uncomprehending.

'The Old One, with the trolley.'

He shook his head.

'You're certain ActCon was empty… when you locked it up?'

'Yes Ma'am.'

At that point, two things happened at once: I caught sight of a shiver of movement high up on the receptor mast and simultaneously there was a whoosh and a clang as the lift door opened and a group of Whiteshirts poured out. Two of them ran towards us, training their guns at us.

'Hands behind your heads!'

'What?… for God's sake …' muttered Maxwell.

'Stand there!' shouted one of the Whiteshirts, pointing to the base of the RTM. We did as we were told and lined up like defeated soldiers from a war movie, Grace supporting her soldier friend while Alfred, Fola and the Child were pushed over towards us. Another guard peered inside Leaf's tent.

'Over here, Major.'

Major Grendon stepped forward and looked inside the tent.

'Bloody shambles,' he said coolly. 'Get them out of there. They should be court-martialled for this. And don't let this lot out of your sight. Especially that child.'

11

Major Grendon took out a mobile phone and began talking while pacing back and forth.

'… came up here to see for myself…it's chaos… they're a complete shower… pissed as newts … you had no authority, Marcia … you didn't consult … didn't need a neutral force … IS are now back in control. If there's fall-out from this, it is your responsibility.'

He snapped the phone shut.

'The gang's all here, I see,' he said, surveying us all, 'with a few hangers on. And this,' he said, bending down in front of the Child, 'this, is an escapee from the Oubliette.'

The Child flinched back and pressed herself closer to Fola.

'Are you completely insane?' He turned to me. 'Bringing her up here? She's a danger to us all…'

'…she's just a frightened little girl,' interrupted Fola.

'This child,' continued the Major, 'is the embodiment of fear and pain. And you want to let her loose near ActCon? Today of all days?'

The Child hid her face in Fola's skirt.

'But maybe that is exactly what you want, is it Colin? Maybe you want to hasten Jessica's departure from this weary life? Well, I hope you have remembered our agreement; I certainly have.'

'And what agreement would that be?' Marcia's sharp voice cut through the night air.

Marcia was flushed and out of breath. She must have been running up the internal stairs. She looked from the Major to me and then back again.

'What agreement?'

The Major went into the attack immediately.

'I'm surprised that you have the gall to show your face here. Your ill-thought-out decision to bring in the squaddies has left ActCon undefended. Look at them.' He gestured towards the sorry band of soldiers who were struggling to remain vertical. 'They're a complete disgrace.'

'I'll remind you,' said Marica coldly, 'that we are not in Amygdala Fort. This is Pre-Frontal City, this is *my* jurisdiction. I can defend Dominion Tower the way I choose.'

'Except that you haven't defended up here, have you? You've always needed me, Marcia. My Whiteshirts have kept you in power. You'd be nothing without my help.'

'Ha, that's what you tell yourself is it? Maybe that arrangement suited us in the past. But that's now changed. I'm ordering you to leave now.'

You had to hand it to Marcia. Her voice was clear and unwavering and, although she was outnumbered by the Major's Whiteshirts, she projected power and authority over him.

For a moment the Major blinked, then he gave a kind of hollow laugh. 'You and whose army?'

Meanwhile Felicity had stepped away from the bottom of the RTM and had turned to look up at the large screen behind us.

'Look!' she shouted.

We all turned to watch the screen. Jessica had crossed the road; the bridge lay directly in front of her. She glanced up to her right and we could see the towering glass and stone of the MI6 building. The rows of rectangular windows reminded me of the ones at the top of Amygdala Fort. Further round, the sheets of black glass seemed to suck up all the light, reflecting nothing. Jessica shivered and looked down at the pavement.

Nearly there…

The Thought was faint but we all heard it.

'There's someone inside!' said Maxwell, turning to the soldier, Sebastian. 'I thought you said you'd cleared ActCon.'

'We did,' said the soldier, 'it was empty.'

'...*then it's all over.*'

'For God sake!' said the Major tersely, 'we need to get in there. Unlock those doors. Keep that child away. In fact, get her away from here. Take her back to the fort.'

One of the guards stepped forward and grabbed the Child's arm.

'No!' shouted Fola, kicking him in the shins. There was a scuffle and the guard swore, holding his wrist.

'Little bugger bit me!'

The Child had wriggled free and ran over to the mast.

'After her!' shouted the Major.

The Child heaved herself up onto one of the horizontal metal struts and began climbing upwards. She ran along the diagonal bars and pulled herself up onto the ledge above. She was agile as a cat; and soon her small red figure was halfway up.

'Come back,' called Fola stepping up onto the base of the mast, 'get down, it's dangerous. Don't chase her!' One of the guards was following the Child, climbing slowly up the girders. 'She'll fall.'

Not here, further on.

Jessica had now reached the bridge proper. She walked slowly with the rust-red railings to her right. There was a metal box-like structure interrupting the line of railings with a life buoy attached. She stopped and leaned over the side. It was colder here and she gave another involuntary shiver.

'Get those doors open! What's the delay?' barked the Major.

One of the guards emerged from the tent, holding a set of keys.

'Got them!' he said, running to the padlocked doors.

Meanwhile, the Child had the reached the top of the mast; the guard was gaining on her.

'Oh God, she'll fall!' Fola ran to the Major. 'Order him down, what if she jumps!'

The Major took no notice. Everyone was transfixed on the RTM now showing black water, thick and inky and laced with grey scum.

Get to the middle.

Then a view of the pavement as Jessica, head down, walked slowly towards the centre of the bridge.

'Where's Alfred?' the Major's red face was close to mine. I looked about but couldn't see him.

'In the tent?'

He flung open the flap of the tent. Alfred was sitting on one of Leaf's cushions with his eyes closed.

'Leave him,' I said.

'We have a deal,' muttered the Major tersely, 'don't forget.' And then, louder, to one of guards: 'Keep your eye on him, them too,' nodding to Fola and Grace who were holding on to each other, staring up above their heads. The Child seemed to have disappeared. Then I spotted a flash of red; she was crawling along the horizontal arm, away from the main body of the mast and towards the suspended receiver dish. She was now above the top of ActCon, too high to hear Fola calling, urging her to go back.

'You'll stick with me,' said the Major, grabbing me by the arm.

The guard swore as he fumbled with the keys.

At last the doors were open and four of the guards ran inside, their guns cocked and ready.

Seconds later they were back out again.

'All clear, sir.'

Then, as if taunting the Major, a Thought echoed inside ActCon:
Stop here.

Jessica had reached the middle of the bridge. Another metal box-like structure interrupted the railings, standing about head height and carrying another lifebuoy.

There, in the corner, next to that side strut, there's a step-up there. Wait, not yet, too many people.

The rain was coming down heavily now. Jessica looked from side-to-side. There were two figures walking swiftly towards her from opposite directions. Umbrellas up. She leant against the rail.

Hold on, wait.

'It makes no sense,' said Felicity. 'Where's it coming from?'

'We need a counter Thought,' said Maxwell. 'Come on!'

He grabbed hold of Felicity and me and pulled us inside ActCon. Marcia, the Major and a couple of the guards followed us in.

'Okay,' said Maxwell, 'repeat after me: no, don't do it.'

'No, don't do it!'

'Louder!'

No, don't do it!

Our voices were strong and the sound reverberated round the inside of the building. There was a pause and then:

You have to ... there's no point in carrying on.

'Look!' said Felicity, pointing up at the round hole at the top of the dome, 'Look up there!'

There was Annie, on the receiver dish above ActCon. She must have been lying flat on top of the saucer. Her head was just visible, poking out from the side, looking down at us. One of the guards took aim.

'I have a shot, sir.'

'No, shatter the receiver and we're all done for.'

My heart was pounding. Round the white walls of the building flickered the scenes of what Jessica could see: two figures, almost passing her; and then the sight of black water far below.

Hold on, in a moment.

'Let me try,' said Felicity. 'We can work this out,' she yelled up at Annie. 'You don't have to die!'

It's too late. I'm too tired.

'Everyone!' urged Felicity. 'Think about your father, your friends!'

Your father, your friends!

They're better off without you, came the reply. *Now! There's no-one around. It's quiet. Step up, get up onto the bar...metal feels icy cold. Heave up, hold on to the side strut, don't look down.*

Jessica hauled herself up so that she was half-sitting on the rail, still holding firm to the side strut. She swung her legs round to face the river.

'Don't do it!' I shouted.

Don't do it! everyone repeated.

You can do it. End it. Let go. Do it now. Jump.

The walls of ActCon went blank – Jessica had shut her eyes. A pause.

Annie turned her head back for a moment.

'Get back!' she said.

Get back. Get back. echoed round the building.

Then a scream. A child's scream high and piercing.

The Child dangled from the rim of the receiver dish. She clung to the edge, her little legs flailing uselessly.

'Help me!'

The Child's words reverberated round the walls of ActCon.

Help me!

Full of pain and pleading.

Help me, help me, help me!

Then, the walls came to life as images flickered and took hold. There is Mum, blotchy face and bloodshot eyes. Shouting, swearing. Now's she asleep on the floor, she won't wake up. Now a fight with next door. Two policemen. She's holding me too tight. She's being taken away. Angry again. Hitting dad. Stop!

'I've got you, you're alright,' Annie edged over toward the Child and grabbed her arms with both hands.

You're alright.

The scenes kept coming: Shouting and crashing about. Throwing stuff, the books are flying. She's broken the lamp. Pieces on the floor. Pick them up. Careful they're sharp. Asleep on the sofa. Won't move. Wake up, wake up. A bottle in the laundry basket. A bottle behind the CDs. Pour down the sink. Watch it swirl round and round. Down the plug hole. Round and round. She's coming! She's raised her hand. BANG on the head. And another BANG on the head. And another.

The sound of each hit was like a terrific peel of thunder. It shook me to the very core of my being and I dropped down on my knees. Then gradually the images cleared and were replaced by the view of the pavement. Jessica had swung her legs back and was standing on firm ground.

'Help!' shouted Annie. *Help, Help, Help* came the echo. 'I can't hold her much longer.'

Another set of arms appeared over the edge of the receiver. The guard pulled the Child clear of the edge and both he and Annie disappeared from our sight.

Then a new sound. It began quietly, like a breeze ruffling the tops of trees; then it broke like a wave. Running water, first a babbling tarn and then stronger, the noise filling the air, like a sudden shower in the depth of night. Water hitting the parched ground; the long-awaited deluge at the end of the dry-season. The rains heralding cleansing and release.

Jessica was crying.

12

It was so long since I had heard Crying that I had forgotten its powers. Everyone appeared to relax. I got up slowly from my knees and helped Maxwell to his feet. The sound of rushing water was now a roar – blocking out all other thoughts. All the screens were dark; Jessica had her eyes closed. The Major pulled himself upright, supporting himself against one of the pillars.

'Dreadful,' he said, 'those hits, just a small child.'

'It's okay now,' I said. 'Jessica's safe, we're safe.'

Tears were falling down the Major's cheeks.

'I did it for the best, keeping it all restricted. It was always to keep her safe.'

I would have liked to have argued. To prove to him that he was wrong, terribly wrong, but I didn't have the energy. We made our way outside onto the roof. The Whiteshirts were taking off their guns and making them into a pile. Fola was at the base of the mast, helping the Child jump down.

'I nearly fell,' said the Child, 'but that lady held on to me.'

She pointed up at Annie, who, with the guard, was slowly picking her way down the mast.

Fola hugged her close and then dropped down to her level.

'I'm so happy to hear your lovely voice. So,' she said, looking into the Child's eyes, 'what shall I call you?'

There was a pause as the Child hopped from one foot to the other.

'Jessie,' she said, 'my name's Jessie.'

'Okay, Jessie it is.'

I glanced over to the Major. Surely he was not still thinking of sending her back down to the Oubliette? But then a voice came over the RTM.

'You a'right, miss?'

Jessica opened her eyes and searched for a hanky to blow her nose. The voice came again.

'You a'right?'

It belonged to a tall, lanky man of about forty. He was rough-shaven with long greasy hair and wore a check donkey jacket that seemed too small for him. His trousers had some dubious stains and he held a black bin-bag over his head to protect himself from the rain. There was a smell of stale beer.

'You're gettin' very wet.'

Jessica sniffed and nodded, she had found the hanky and blew her nose.

'It's okay,' she said.

'Walk you to the station,' said the man. So off they set, back towards Vauxhall Station. The man opened the bin-bag some more so that it kept them both dry. The rain was falling in sheets and bouncing off the pavement in front of them. It was lovely the way the car headlamps made the sprays of water tremble and dance. Jessica had no thoughts at all; ActCon still stood empty. Maxwell and Felicity glanced at one another and then slipped back inside.

'Just get home,' we heard them say in unison.

Just get home echoed the Thought.

By now Annie and the guard had climbed down from the mast. The guard gripped her by the shoulder but she did not look like she was about to make a run for it. Her small frame was bent over and she had her head in her hands.

'Couldn't hold her…' she said, 'thought she was going to fall. I'm sorry.'

I wondered whether she was sorry for nearly dropping Jessie or for trying to kill us all.

'Take her away,' said the Major.

'The Oubliette?' asked the guard.

The major paused and looked over towards Marcia.

'The Oubliette,' she said, 'for observation. If she calms down you can put her to work in the archives.'

'No, no, not me,' said Jessie, darting behind Fola.

'No, not you,' said Fola, 'you're staying with us. Isn't she?'

The Major shrugged.

'Looks like the damage has been done.'

Hardly damage, I thought, in fact the opposite of damage; repair and restoration. The Major seemed to have recovered from his earlier show of emotion and was now dismissing what he had just witnessed.

'How dare you say that!' Fola stepped forward and drew herself up to her full height so that she looked down on him. 'You allowed that child be imprisoned in the Oubliette. She was there for years with no-one to care for her, no-one to love her. You were wrong, terribly wrong. You did a bad thing and Jessica suffered because of it. And now you don't have the courage to admit what you did.'

'I did what I believed was right in the circumstances.' He was back to his usual smooth manner. 'You can take her with you, but be careful as she tells her story: not all at once.'

The Whiteshirts picked up their guns and shook hands with the soldiers. Annie was led down the stairs, Marcia and the Major following.

The man's voice came over the RTM again:

'Here you are,' he said. *'You gonna be okay now?'*

'Yes... thanks,' said Jessica.

'Spare a couple of quid? Get meself a sandwich.'

Jessica rummaged for her purse and gave him a five-pound note.

'Thanks miss, look after yerself.'

And he set off at a pace, crouched under the bin-bag.

Just get home. There's a tin of soup in the cupboard, came the Thought.

Alfred had emerged from the tent and was standing next to me staring up at the screen. He looked worn out even though he had missed all the drama. He linked his arm in mine.

'You all did well,' he said. 'I was getting a bit worried there for a moment.'

13

It was a relief to be back in the Thymus. Everything was the same as it had been when Fola and I left early that morning. We invited everyone down to Soul for a celebration, even Leaf and Grace's soldier friend, Sebastian. Leaf had found a bottle of amber liquid in the bottom of Annie's trolley and was pouring shots into china cups which Felicity was handing round. Fola was showing Jessie the pictures around her desk while Grace and Sebastian were deep in conversation.

'Where's Maxwell?' asked Alfred.

'He's coming in a minute,' said Felicity. 'Some friend of his has come up with some results he was after, so he's gone to pick them up.'

There was a ping-pong sound on the RTM and Marcia's face appeared.

This is a public announcement for all departments: I am very pleased to be able to inform you that the danger level has now reduced to a normal state and that the risk of self-harm has now abated. I was able to oversee the operation personally and the source of the suicidal thoughts has been apprehended by our special forces of T Cell company. Appreciation is also due to members of the West Side Problem Solving team and to the Residual Projects Team (formerly known as Soul).

'We get a mention, at last,' I muttered.

'Sort of,' said Fola. 'Residual Projects, my arse.'

Jessie looked wide eyed up at Fola and giggled.

Marcia continued.

I am also able to inform you that we have decided to build closer links across our two great hemispheres and I shall be meeting with Nathaniel from East Side for talks on the way forward. Meanwhile I am proposing an Early Night so that all day-time units can get some well-earned rest after the day's exhausting events.

'She really is a piece of work,' said Fola. 'She's dropped the Major and his cronies as allies and is now looking to curry favour back with Nathaniel.'

'Yeah, maybe, but it's probably for the best. Ah, here he is,' said Felicity as Maxwell burst through the door.

'Blimey, you're not easy to find. Had to ask one of those soldier johnnies. I hope there's some of that left,' he said, indicating towards Leaf's bottle.

Once he had a drink in his hand Maxwell plonked himself down in Fola's chair.

'Interesting information,' he announced airily. 'This stuff is really rather good, by-the-way, a kind of dopamine liquor.'

'Get on with it,' interrupted Felicity.

'You may remember, well at least Col and Fliss may remember, that Problem Solving was tasked some time ago, was it really only this morning? to find out how Jessica got the bang on the head. How she hit the cupboard door? Considered by Marcia as a possible terrorist act of sabotage, and very possibly the catalyst for the day's events.'

'Accident surely?' said Leaf.

'Ah well, Freud says that there is no such thing as an accident...'

'Oh for God's sake,' interrupted Felicity loudly. I wondered if she'd had a bit too much of Leaf's brew.

'Wasn't it Annie?' asked Grace.

'Nope,' continued Maxwell, 'the thing is, I have a mate in the Motor Cortex and she let me look at the incoming data at around the time of the bang on the head.'

'And?' said Felicity.

'And, with her help I was able to trace the source of the 'drop teabag' command.'

He paused theatrically.

'Which was?' said Felicity, irritated now.

237

'Here!'

'What?' said Fola.

'Here, Hut 23 of the Thymus. Soul or Residual Projects or whatever you are.'

'Golly,' said Felicity, staring at Alfred and then Grace and then back to Alfred again.

'Don't look at me,' said Grace, 'I had nothing to do with it.'

I remembered that Alfred's Go opponent was in the Motor Cortex. It would have been easy for him to send a command up there. He shrugged and shuffled to his feet.

'Sometimes,' he said, 'in order to have the momentum to go up a hill you have to go down a little first.'

That didn't mean much to me but Maxwell nodded as if it was a profound insight. I was starting to feel quite mellow and really didn't care who had caused the bang on the head. Alfred was an unlikely terrorist and I guessed that Maxwell wouldn't be spreading this revelation far and wide.

'Give us a song, Fola,' I shouted.

Fola sang her favourite: *Nobody Knows the Trouble I've Seen,* and then led us as in a rendition of *Heavenly Aeroplane.* She sang the verses and then we all joined in with the chorus

> *All you thirsty of every tribe*
> *Get your tickets for an aeroplane ride;*
> *Jesus our Saviour is coming to reign*
> *And take you up to glory in His aeroplane.*

Leaf produced a recorder from his waistcoat pocket and we clapped along as Fola and Jessie began dancing hand in hand.

'So what if...' Maxwell asked me quietly, 'what if Jessica had died? D'you think you and Alfred would have had a ticket for the Heavenly Aeroplane?'

I laughed, it seemed so unlikely.

'You'd better ask him. I guess Marcia and the Major seemed to think so. But maybe we were in the wrong place, maybe we should have been with Hathor, by her fire.'

'Shh a minute!' said Grace, 'you should all hear this...'

Leaf stopped playing and we looked up at the RTM. Jessica was back at home, sitting on the comfy sofa. She was speaking on the phone.

'Who's she talking to?' I asked.

'It's Giulia, she rang her about five minutes ago,' said Grace.

'It was just kind of weird and scary. Not sure if I'd have really done it. But I got close to it. Then there was this stuff from when I was a kid. You know,… stuff with my mum. Couldn't stop crying. This dosser bloke took pity on me…'

Giulia wasn't saying much, just making sympathetic noises. The call went on for a while and ended with Giulia telling Jessica to come around to her place after work the next day.

Leaf started playing again and Felicity pulled Maxwell to his feet. Jessie went up to Alfred.

'Will you dance with me and Fola?' she said.

Alfred stood up, flinging his arms out wide, and began doing a kind of Greek dance slowly in time with the music. We all joined in, dancing in circles, weaving in and out, not touching but staying in harmony with one another, as if we had known the steps since Hathor's day. And so we continued, well after the Early Night and into Dream Time, moving as one person, round and round until morning.

14

It is early spring and Jessica is at the corner shop checkout. Christopher is loading the items into a bag. They plan to cook at home tonight; a packet of penne, some mushrooms, a lettuce, tomatoes, a bottle of Chianti...

'Squashed-fly biscuits,' says Christopher, holding up the packet. 'Not had these for ages.'

'Garibaldi,' she says the word slowly, enjoying the Italianate syllables. 'Don't know why I chose those.'

'Ga-ri-baldi,' he repeats, 'well anyway, good choice.'

He links his arm in hers as they make their way back to the flat. The buds on the chestnut by the church are beginning to burst open; a bright vivid green.

Beautiful, she thinks. Very beautiful indeed.

Acknowledgements

Not Waving but Drowning Page 4. Poem title from Stevie Smith: A Selection 1983.

Heavenly Aeroplane Pages 30, 59, 85 & 238. Reprinted from Ozark Folksongs, Volume IV: Religious Songs and other Items, collected and edited by Vance Randolph, by permission of the University of Missouri Press.

Fall Leaves Fall Page 60. By Emily Bronte

To die: to sleep; etc. Page 62. From *Hamlet*, Act 3, Scene 1 by William Shakespeare.

Should auld acquaintance be forgot Page 85. From 'Auld Lang Syne' by Robert Burns.

Swing low, sweet chariot Page 89. African-American traditional song.

Keep your hand on the plough, hold on Page 93. From *Hold On*, African-American traditional song.

Nobody knows the trouble I've seen Page 93. African-American traditional song.

The leaves unhooked themselves from trees Page 130. From 'A Thunderstorm' by Emily Dickinson. *Emily Dickinson Selected Poems*. Dover Edition 1990.

Thanks:

For the hours spent giving thoughtful feedback on earlier drafts of The Department of Certainty: Rose Drew, Greg Michaelson, Debbie Bath,

Emma Cameron, Jane Cook, Giulia Edwards, Ashley Stokes, Lin White and Hannah Corbett.

For encouragement and advice along the way: John Munro, Lewis Phillips, Richard Moyse Fenning, Rosie Pannett, Lucy Roberts, Jill Fricker, Patricia Cunningham, Simon Rice-Oxley, Catherine Smith and Kim Lasky.

Note:

The author makes it clear that while working for a Local Authority she has never been asked to falsify data, nor is she aware of anyone else who has been asked to do this.

Other novels, novellas and short story collections available from
Stairwell Books

A Fistful of Ashes	Katy Turton
Widdershins	L.A.Robbins
100 Summers	Ali Sparkes
Skull Days	PJ Quinn
The Broke Hotel	Clayton Lister
Equinox	Ruth Aylett, Greg Michaelson
Not the Work of an Ordinary Boy	Victoria L. Humphreys
Black Harry	Mark P. Henderson
Eboracvm: Carved in Stone	Graham Clews
Down to Earth	Andrew Crowther
The Iron Brooch	Yvonne Hendrie
The Electric	Tim Murgatroyd
The Pirate Queen	Charlie Hill
Djoser and the Gods	Michael J. Lowis
Needleham	Terry Simpson
The Keepers	Pauline Kirk
Shadows of Fathers	Simon Cullerton
Blackbird's Song	Katy Turton
Eboracvm the Fortress	Graham Clews
The Warder	Susie Williamson
Life Lessons by Libby	Libby and Laura Engel-Sahr
Waters of Time	Pauline Kirk
The Water Bailiff's Daughter	Yvonne Hendrie
O Man of Clay	Eliza Mood
Eboracvm: the Village	Graham Clews
Sammy Blue Eyes	Frank Beill
Virginia	Alan Smith
Poetic Justice	PJ Quinn
The Go-To Guy	Neal Hardin
Abernathy	Claire Patel-Campbell
Tyrants Rex	Clint Wastling
How to be a Man	Alan Smith
Border 7	Pauline Kirk
Homelands	Shaunna Harper
The Geology of Desire	Clint Wastling
Close Disharmony	PJ Quinn
Poison Pen	PJ Quinn

For further information please contact rose@stairwellbooks.com

www.stairwellbooks.co.uk
@stairwellbooks

Milton Keynes UK
Ingram Content Group UK Ltd.
UKHW020612310824
447656UK00001B/19

9 781913 432973